D0734977

Also by Alan Burt Akers

TRANSIT TO SCORPIO
THE SUNS OF SCORPIO

Alan Burt Akers

Warrior of Scorpio

Illustrated by Tim Kirk

Futura Publications Limited
An Orbit Book

An Orbit Book

First published in Great Britain in 1975
by Futura Publications Limited
49 Poland Street
London W1A 2LG
Copyright © Daw Books Inc. 1973

DEDICATION: For Elsie Wollheim

This book is sold subject to the condition
that it shall not, by way of trade or
otherwise, be lent, re-sold, hired out or
otherwise circulated without the publisher's
prior consent in any form of binding or
cover other than that in which it is
published and without a similar condition
including this condition being imposed on the
subsequent purchaser.

ISBN 0 8600 78310
Printed in Great Britain by
C. Nicholls & Company Ltd.
The Philips Park Press
Manchester.

Contents

	A Brief Note on the Tapes from Africa	7
1	Pawn of the Star Lords	11
2	Seg Segutorio	22
3	I dive back into the Eye of the World	30
4	Rashoons command our course	38
5	The fight aboard the swifter	48
6	Delia of Delphond and I swim together	58
7	Thelda cuts hair and Seg cuts a bow-stave	65
8	Through the Stratemsk	76
9	Into the Hostile Territories	82
10	Great beasts of the air	92
11	Assassins in the corthdrome	106
12	The Queen of Pain	119
13	I go swinging at the tower of Umgar Stro	129
14	"It is my Dray! My Dray Prescot you covet!"	142
15	Seg, Thelda, and I stand before Queen Lilah	150
16	The army of Hiclantung marches out	156
17	Of downfall and of bondage	166
18	On my own two feet, then	176

List of Illustrations

"The winged hordes of Umgar Stro assaulted us from above."   ii

"I could see them pelting around the stable buildings, shrilling war cries."   15

"One after another the flaming missiles of destruction plunged down onto the decks."   33

"Delia was lolling back with the steering oar and laughing at me silently."   66

"The flying armada came on with cloud-driven swiftness."   102

"As I moved in, I could see how much alike they were, fierce, belligerent, habitual masters of the sky." 135

A BRIEF NOTE ON
THE TAPES FROM AFRICA

Although this is the third volume chronicling the strange and fascinating story of Dray Prescot, the editing has been so arranged that each book can be read as a separate and individual volume.

After publication of the first two volumes * of the adventures of that remarkable man, Dray Prescot, on the planet Kregen beneath the Suns of Scorpio some four hundred light-years away, I was completely unsure of the reception they would be accorded. So far Prescot's story has been given to us in the form of cassettes he cut on Dan Fraser's tape recorder in that epidemic-stricken village in a famine area of West Africa. Having been afforded the privilege of editing the Tapes from Africa, I have kept the promise Fraser made to Dray Prescot, and I have already written of the profound impression that calm sure voice makes upon me, and of how I feel uplifted as that voice quickens as the fire of memory burns brighter in remembered images of passion and action and headlong adventure.

The response has been surprisingly profuse and laudatory and there has been no opportunity for me to make adequate reply. We feel, in truth, that it is to Dray Prescot himself that we must look for that reply. The value of this account of life on Kregen is incalculable and the absence of certain of the cassettes containing portions of the story is a tragic loss. To my urgent inquiries, my friend Geoffrey Dean, to whom Dan Fraser had entrusted the Tapes from Africa and from whom I had received the cassettes in Washington, replied with sad and shocking news.

Dray Prescot had unexectedly appeared in the famine area in West Africa and had been assisted by and then in

---

* TRANSIT TO SCORPIO: DAW Books, Inc.
  THE SUNS OF SCORPIO: DAW Books, Inc.

turn had assisted the young field worker Dan Fraser. Now, Geoffrey told me, Dan Fraser was dead. He had died, mockingly, cruelly, wastefully, unnecessarily, in a stupid automobile accident.

With the death of Dan Fraser we lose the only direct link we had with Prescot. For Fraser was the only one of us ever to have seen Prescot in the flesh. Dan described him as being a man a little above middling height, with straight brown hair, and brown eyes that hold a light of incisive intelligence and a strange dominating quality that goes with the abrasive honesty of the man. His shoulders made Dan's eyes pop. And now Dan Fraser is dead and the whereabouts of the missing cassettes may never be known.

We must, it is clear, be thankful for what we do have. Of the transcribed material I have deleted as little as is necessary, and have edited lightly; but a few items remain to be mentioned. The first is the pronunciation of the word Kregen. Prescot rolls this out as though an acute accent rides the first "e"—Kraygen—with a hard "g." Despite his long sojourn on Kregen he often refers to things as an Earthman would—for instance he will say "sunshine" when, as Kregen orbits the binary Antares, he means "suns-shine." "Sunshine," however, trips more easily from the tongue.

Clearly, since Dray Prescot cut these tapes in the 1970's, he must be possessed of much more information now about Kregen than he was at the times of which he speaks. The whole planet could have changed in character and the most powerful of impressions remains that if it has done so then Prescot himself will have had a large hand in that change. But those long-ago days were as new to Prescot then as they are to us now, and without artifice he recalls those stirring times as he felt and experienced them. But, nevertheless, there are two levels of story unfolding and we must be mindful of that as we read. I have sought the advice of a distinguished author of long experience whose help has been invaluable, and, good friend that he is, whose sage counsel will one day receive the acknowledgment that is its due. We agree that in speaking of his life, some scenes and impressions have remained more vividly with Dray Prescot; it is as though when he speaks into the microphone he is living through these episodes again.

Dray Prescot, born in 1775, presents an enigmatic picture of himself. Through his immersion in the pool of baptism of the River Zelph he is assured of a thousand years of life, as is his beloved, Delia of the Blue Mountains, for whose sake he was first hurled back to Earth by the Savanti.

I feel it is clear he has thought long and carefully just what a millennium of life will mean and has come to adjust to and accept that fate. Returned to Kregen by the Star Lords—of whom he has given us no information—as a kind of interstellar troubleshooter, he rapidly rose to the position of Zorcander among his Clansmen of Felschraung in Segesthes, and then became the Lord of Strombor of the enclave city of Zenicce. At that point the Star Lords, apparently having no further use for him, returned him once more to Earth.

Some time elapsed before he was recalled to Kregen beneath Antares to find himself on the continent of Turismond, thousands of miles away from Segesthes, and up to his neck in problems. He witnessed the horrors perpetrated by the overlords of Magdag, escaped their slavery, became a corsair captain of a swifter—a Kregen galley—on the inner sea, the Eye of the World. We here lose portions of his story through the lamented absence of those missing cassettes, but we do know he was accepted into the mystic and military order of chivalry, the Krozairs of Zy, becoming Pur Dray. Returned to Magdag he organized the slaves and led a revolt which in the full tide of success was placed in jeopardy by the intervention of the Star Lords.

At the head of his slave phalanx he was surrounded by the lambent blue radiance that, together with the occasional appearance of a gigantic scorpion, accompanies a transition. In this case he was threatened with another ignominious return to Earth. However, once before he had managed by the exertion of a willpower we can only marvel at to negate the immediate effects and to remain on Kregen. So, now, he exerted all his willpower to remain on Kregen.

This volume, *Warrior of Scorpio*, takes up his adventures from that point and in the process almost exhausts the cassettes in our possession, leaving only a very few to see publication.

Unless Dray Prescot is able in some way to reveal some of his story, and this of course assumes he can in some way be afforded the opportunity of seeing the volumes already in print, this incredible saga of brilliant action and high adventure, of chilling cruelty and superlative courage, will come to an end.

Geoffrey Dean called me on the transatlantic phone to tell me of the tragic death of Dan Fraser.

"I am firmly convinced Dray Prescot is determined to have his story told," Geoffrey said over the line. "If it is humanly possibly—or superhumanly, given the intervention of the Star Lords—I believe, Alan, he will find a way of continuing to reach us and of carrying on with his story."

Even if the story does end here—and somehow I believe Geoffrey is right in his assessment and I await the confirmation that will come with a fresh communication from Dray Prescot—still I am convinced that on Kregen four hundred light-years away Dray Prescot, Pur Dray, Lord of Strombor, Kov of Delphond, Krozair of Zy, will continue his own living story.

Alan Burt Akers

Chapter One

Pawn of the Star Lords

"I will stay on Kregen!"

In my nostrils stank the odors of blood and sweat, oiled leather, dust, and my ears rang with the sounds of combat as swords clashed and clanged and pikes pierced mail and crossbow bolts punched into armored men. I could smell and hear, but I could see only an all-encompassing blueness lambent about me, and my gripping fist closed on emptiness where I should be grasping the hilt of my long sword.

"I will not go back to Earth!"

Everything was blue now, roaring and twisting in my head, in my eyes and ears, tumbling me head over heels into a blue nothingness.

"I will stay on Kregen beneath the suns of Scorpio! I will!"

I, Dray Prescot of Earth, screamed it out in my agony and despair. "I will stay on Kregen!"

A wind riffled my hair and I knew that old vosk-skull helmet with its panache of yellow paint had vanished with my long sword.

I was lying flat on my back. The noise of combat flowed away, dwindling. The screams of dying men and wounded sectrixes, the grunt and harshly indrawn breaths of men convulsed with the passions of battle, the clangor and scrape of weapons, all died. And the blue brilliance of light about me wavered and I sensed the inward struggle as obscure forms moved and merged past the edges of my vision. Against my back pressed hard earth—but was it the dirt of Kregen or of Earth?

That last battle against the overlords of Magdag had been violent and emotional and transforming, but any taint of battle-lust or battle-fever in me had been banished at a stroke by the unexpected intervention of the Star Lords. I have, I confess, sometimes been overwhelmed by the lust

11

of battle, not often, and have little time for those who prate of that red curtain that falls before their eyes and to whose existence they point as an excuse for actions of the most barbarous and savage kind. Oh, yes, the scarlet curtain before the eyes exists, but it is capable of manipulation by those whose humanity has not been destroyed.

You who listen to these tapes spinning through their little cassettes will know how often I have succumbed, to my shame, to that red-roaring tide of exultant conflict.

So it was that as I sat up on that hard-packed ground the blood-lust of battle had cleared from my mind. But the fever of instant action still gripped my body. As I sat up, then, expecting I knew not what, a vast odiferous mass of squelchy straw laid me flat down on my back again.

Dung and straw smothered me. Spitting out a mouthful of vile-tasting straw I sat up, blinking, trying to see, vaguely making out a barn door black in the light as the blueness faded, and—smack down again I went as another heaping forkful of straw-laced manure slapped me across the face. I spat. I blinked. I cursed. With a roar of fury generated as much by indignation and a sense of the ludicrous as much by anger I leaped to my feet.

This time I could dodge the flying forkful of dungy straw.

Thoroughly annoyed, I started for the barn door. As I expected, I was completely naked. The Star Lords had snatched me from Magdag; where they had deposited me I did not know—but I had urgent problems before finding out, problems to do with people who threw dungy straw into my face.

A voice shouted something I didn't recognize, but even in the midst of intending to deal with dung-hurlers I took comfort from the conviction that the language was not of Earth. It had that ring peculiar to the languages of Kregen, and I felt a surge of thanksgiving.

A man stepped out of the barn door.

My vision cleared and I saw this man bathed in the mingled streaming light of the twin suns of Antares. Then, without doubt, I knew the Star Lords had not snatched me from Kregen altogether and hurled me contemptuously back to Earth. Contemptuously, for I knew that in some way I had failed them, that I had not accomplished what they had brought me to Kregen and sent me to Magdag to do.

Staring at this man who stared back at me I was conscious only of a great and all-engulfing thankfulness. I was still on the same world as my Delia! I was not sundered from the only woman for me in two worlds by four hundred light-years of empty space. Somewhere in Vallia on this planet of Kregen my Delia of the Blue Mountains, my Delia of Delphond, lived and breathed and laughed and, I hoped and prayed, did not despair of me.

This man carried a pitchfork to which wisps of greasy straw still clung. He stood tall and lean, with the most infernal mocking smile taking in my nakedness and the dungy straw clinging to my skin and broomsticking my hair—and then he saw my face. He lost his smile and the pitchfork came up in quick automatic response. He possessed a mane of intensely black hair. His eyes twinkled brightly blue upon me. There was about him an air of recklessness and of action-before-thought-of-consequences, and I judged he had not been slave for very long.

My thought of Delia had halted me—in the glory of knowing I was still treading the same ground as my princess—so that this man was spared time enough to speak.

"Llahal!" he said, in the universal nonfamiliar greeting of Kregen. Had we been friends he would have said: "Lahal." He went on without waiting for my reply or for the making of pappattu. "You look a sight, dom!" And then he laughed. It was a light laugh, all mockery of myself gone from it and filled only with a delight in the circumstances. Any man who cannot laugh at himself is truly dead. But, as I think you will know, I, Dray Prescot, do not, for others and out loud, laugh easily.

I started for him again with the intention of wrapping the pitchfork around his neck and then deciding what to do with the tines.

He skipped aside, still laughing.

His laughter changed to puzzlement.

"You must be one of the new slaves, dom. I am Seg Segutorio. If you've been sent to help me you'd better get started before we're both in trouble and tasting ol' snake."

The tines of the pitchfork looked exceedingly sharp. This man, this slave, handled the implement as a warrior handles a spear. Now he had recovered from the first shock of seeing that expression on my face I have heard many men call the look of the devil; he balanced easily with the farmyard weapon covering me, confident in his own prowess. About to disabuse him of that idea, I checked.

We stood in a farmyard, with low buildings surrounding this stable area, with the rustic odors of dung and straw, urine and dust, heavy on the air. Over all the glorious rays of the twin suns of Scorpio streamed down in an opaline mingling of colors. Only moments before I had been leading the slave phalanx of my old vosk-skulls into headlong conflict with the mailed overlords of Magdag. Now, once more, I heard the shouts of men in furious strife and the screams of wounded, the shrilling of sectrixes, and the clamorous clangor of sword on sword.

A dog ran whining across the farmyard, his tail tucked down in between his legs.

Following him, a bedraggled band of slaves ran and fell and picked themselves up to stagger on. They were a mixed bunch of humans and half-humans, all wearing the gray slave breechclout, and their screams and crying panic made my hand reach out for a weapon. On Kregen a man without a ready weapon to hand is a man with a foot in the grave.

Flames shot up beyond the stable buildings and I guessed the great house itself would be burning. A rout of bloodied men-at-arms stumbled after the slaves, their mail coats ripped, their helmets dented and awry, some lost altogether. There were men and Rapas and Chuliks among the mercenary men-at-arms. Some had flung away their weapons in order to run faster.

"A raid!" Seg Segutorio hitched up the pitchfork. I didn't like the look on his face. "Those Froyvil-forgotten rasts of sorzarts!"

Now I could see them pelting around the stable buildings, squat on scaled legs, bedecked with gaudy strings of clanking bronze and copper ornaments, befeathered, cockscombed of helmeted head, fierce and predatory and shrilling war cries that struck absolute horror into the fleeing people of the peaceful farm. They wielded cut-down long swords and throwing spears not unlike narrow assegais, and they presented a sight calculated to overawe peasant opposition in the twinkling of the first blade. The few mercenary guards maintained by the farm had been powerless to halt this raid.

Although I had heard of these sorzarts, I had not previously encountered them. They inhabited a cluster of islands toward the northeastern end of the inner sea and were the subject of endless speculation among the other peoples of the Eye of the World as to who would instigate the great crusade against them and who would follow the Banners and when; but while the bitter enmity between the green north and the red south persisted the sorzarts were left unmolested. Their faces were vaguely lizard-like in their wide cheeks and virtual absence of forehead, but their eyes were quite unreptile-like, being dull and deeply set.

Everything, as is usual in moments of crisis, happened at

KIRK

"I could see them pelting around the stable build-ings, shrilling war cries."

breakneck speed and by the time Seg had leveled his pitchfork and broken into a run the sorzarts had mostly vanished beyond the opposite stable building. A woman clutching a child to her bosom ran into view, saw the last three
sorzarts, swerved in her run, saw Seg Segutorio, and
screamed at him. Her bared legs beneath the lavender gown
covered the ground rapidly, but it was clear to us that the
sorzarts would cut her off and catch her before she could
reach us.

"Help me!" Even in her terror and despair the words
cracked with the snap of habitual command. "Seg! Help
me!"

"The mistress." Seg bounded forward afresh. "She bought
me ten days ago and I have no love for her—but—but she
is a woman."

That was an irrational thought in a culture possessed of
many types of beast-humans and human-beasts encountered
daily in ordinary social intercourse.

Now I knew why the Star Lords had condescended to
keep me here on Kregen and why they had not flung me
through the interstellar gulfs back to the Earth of my birth.
They had found another task for my hands. As usual, they
had dumped me down naked and defenseless in the midst
of a situation of extreme peril. I knew that away in Magdag my slaves, wearing their old yellow-painted vosk-skulls
and wielding the weapons I had created and taught them to
use, were fighting with savage intent against the might of
the overlords and, most probably now I had gone, losing.
But I had been snatched from them and in return for not
being banished to Earth had been presented with this crisis
to resolve.

I scooped up a heaping double-armful of odiferous manure-
fouled straw and sprinted after Seg. I passed him with ease
and then I was beyond the woman and her child and facing the three sorzarts. They looked mean and ferocious and
they held their weapons with the skill of long experience.

The nearest flicked his cut-down long sword at me and I
angled my run so that he obscured the view of the second,
who lifted his assegai in frustration, balked of his cast. I
checked, lifted on my toes, and hurled my dung-straw full
in the face of the first sorzart. He ducked lithely enough
and avoided the straw. But his movement slowed him and
then I was up to him. His back broke with a soggy snap
and I had his sword and snatched it aloft to parry the
assegai cast. The shaft rang against the blade. I lunged forward. The sword felt good in my fist. Longer than the short

sword as used by my Clansmen, this brand balanced oddly; but it served its purpose and as I withdrew the blade befouled with the sorzart's blood there was time to meet the challenge of the third. He hesitated.

"Hail" I said.

He eyed me warily from those deep-set eyes. Abruptly, like a striking lizard, with a bunching of muscles and a jangling of bronze and copper disks, he hurled his assegai. I brushed it aside. Seg saved me the final thrust, for, as I waited for the sorzart to draw his sword, the pitchfork flew past my ear and buried its two center tines deeply into the scaly neck.

"Why did you hesitate?" demanded Seg, panting. "You know these sorzarts are the most treacherous of beasts."

I wiped the blade on the sorzart's brown apron.

"I have killed a man before he has drawn to defend himself," I told Seg. "And, sink me, no doubt will do so again, Zair forgive me, if it is necessary. In this case it was not."

He looked at me oddly. Reckless and wild, as I was to find him, his ideas of warfare were also extremely practical.

The unpleasant sounds of raiding half-men reached us from beyond the stable block and the wind drew coils of greasy smoke from the burning house about our faces. The woman caught her breath. I had looked at her once, and then gone about my business. There has been more than enough in my life of seeing screaming women clutching their infants to them—the tears soaking into their dresses, their faces distraught, running blindly from rapacious reavers of all kinds —for me ever to treat such scenes lightly. People prate of the values of human life, and of how nothing outside the context of human activity is of worth, and on Kregen, willy-nilly, the existence of half-human, half-beast peoples must figure into that context, and yet I wonder how often such academic postulators have been presented with situations in which their actions must match their words. Of course I was not insensitive to this woman's naked bloody feet, the tears on her cheeks, the infant mess around her child's mouth and nose, his inflamed eyes and his crying blubbering. But raiders of the stamp of the sorzarts know well the weakness of men unmanned by women's sufferings.

I said: "We must leave here. Now. Come."

Without bothering to await their reply I stripped a length of brown cloth from a dead sorzart—the cleanest length— and wrapped it around my waist, pulled the end through between my legs, and tucked it in to form a breechclout. I balanced all three of the cut-down long swords and selected the one I felt the best. The belt and scabbard were neatly stitched from the skins of the little green and brown lizards called Tikos and as Seg picked up a sword and an assegai I thrust the sword I had chosen into the scabbard, took the third up together with the three assegais remaining. I ignored the helmets. This took but little time and during it the woman stood first on one leg and then on the other, hoisting her child up on her hip and shushing it, and staring at me with an uncertainty I had no time to bother over just then. She would know well enough I was not one of her slaves.

We set off in a line directly away from the burning house.

I felt completely confident that this woman and her infant were the people I had been sent here by the Star Lords to succor. Just why I should be so sure I did not know. My natural instincts sometimes coalesce with a darker and rarer judgment. I had saved Gahan Gannius and Valima there on the edge of the Grand Canal when, for the third time, I had found myself on Kregen. They had given me no thanks but had taken themselves off. Now I assumed they must play some part in the complicated games with destiny played over the years by the Star Lords—with assistance and interference from the Savanti. That these thoughts were true and just how the world of Kregen was influenced by my own interference, you shall hear.

We spoke little. I was concerned to find a riding mount for the woman. The stables were empty—the men out on an expedition and leaving the estate vulnerable to just this kind of sudden raid—and the quicker we found a sectrix, one of the six-legged riding animals of the inner sea littoral, or a calsany, or even an ass, the better. When Seg asked my name I had no hesitation in choosing my own among the plethora of names I already possessed—a quantity of nomenclature I found, to be honest, more amusing than otherwise.

"I am Dray Prescot," I said. And then: "Of Strombor." The name meant nothing to them.

It was unlikely that they would know of Strombor as a place, for until I had resurrected that enclave in Zenicce with the gift of Great Aunt Shusha—who was not *my* great aunt, I must remember—the name of Strombor had been obscured for a hundred and fifty years by the house Esztercari. But since they had not heard the name of Pur Dray, Lord of Strombor, Krozair of Zy, renowned corsair upon the Eye of the World, it surely indicated the cut-off nature of their life. I had convinced myself that I must still be within the sphere of occupation around the inner sea, as witness the sorzarts, and so I was not unduly alarmed. Had I been so minded I might have chuckled at the haughty reception such ignorance of their noble names and deeds would have received from some of the swifter captains and Krozairs and Brethren of my acquaintance.

"This is the Lady Pulvia na Upalion," said Seg Segutorio, and despite the situation and his clear detestation of his slave status, some respect was evident in his words.

I looked at the woman. Nothing about her impressed me so much as the way her head came erect and her eyes widened to meet my regard. She was in no sense beautiful, rather she was a sturdy, strong-limbed woman habitually in command, conscious of her position, and no doubt in normal times somewhat in despair over the hint of a moustache beginning to darken her upper lip. I reached out my hands.

"Give me the child."

Instinctively she clasped the infant closer to her breast where tears and mucus stained the lavender material. She wore a gold and ruby trinket upon a slender gold chain. I gestured impatiently to her naked feet. She looked into my face and I saw her eyes darken in shock. Then, silently, she let me take the boy from her. He was no great weight. In a little group we left the stables and at once were among the standing crops, tall green-stemmed bloin loaded with golden fruit in which we were hidden as though by a million tongueless cathedral bells.

From the rear black and oily smoke rose and spread to cast dark shadows from the mingled light of the twin suns of Scorpio.

Any thoughts I may have had that my task for the Star Lords was thus easily accomplished were speedily dispelled. With the three spare assegais tucked under my left arm which cradled the child, the second sword naked in my right fist, I brought up the rear, with Seg in the van.

The sorzarts must have landed from their raiding ships—for they habitually disliked voyaging with only a single ship—and marched inland to fall on this estate of Upalion, which I had already seen enough to know was composed of broad acres and rich land, heavy with crops. Upalion, some distance from the sea, had considered itself secure, as the weak mercenary force of men-at-arms testified.

Now the sorzarts burst into the wealth of golden bloin fruits, seeking our blood.

"You go on, Seg," I said, and handed him the child, pushing past the woman unceremoniously, "I will hold them."

"The mistress can take the child," said Seg. His eagerness to stand to die with me was surprising.

"Sink me!" I exclaimed, not angrily but exasperatedly amused. I can find amusement in strange situations. "She can barely walk, let alone run with the child. You must get her away, Seg, for the sweet sake of Zim-Zair. Do not argue!"

"By the veiled Froyvil—" began Seg, his black mane of hair wild among the golden fruits.

I cut him off, with a rolling Makki-Grodno oath.

"Go on!"

I own, then, that a deal of that unpleasant rasp must have sharpened my tones, a dominating, domineering almost, way of talking I assumed in automatic response to opposition and that came from many years walking the quarterdecks of King's Ships, of handling my Clansmen as Zorcander and Vovedeer, of reaving as a Krozair captain of a Sanurkazz swifter. Seg took a look at my face. He took the child.

"There are ruins of the sunset folk about a dwabur south," he said. That was all.

I felt I could get to know this volatile yet practical man.

Seg and the Lady Pulvia vanished among the golden bells.

The swords I now held had once been regular long swords. Now they had been cut down and sharpened with wedge-shaped points into a blade-length of some twenty-four inches. For a tiny nostalgic moment I thought of those superlative Savanti swords with which we had so lightheartedly gone from Aphrasöe the Swinging City clad in our Savanti hunting leathers in bloodless pursuit of the graint. Maybe these sorzarts knew more of swordsmanship than I guessed, more, even, than the Krozairs of Zy, although in my pride that seemed so remotely possible as to be unthinkable. Well, I would soon find out.

Harsh cries rose into the air and the golden bells of the bloin hanging from stems curving in such subtle beauty from their straight green stalks waved and twisted over our back path as agile scaled bodies thrust their way through.

A fighting-man's life is stitched together with vivid scarlet incidents patching the gray drabness of days and my experience had taught me that on Kregen the scarlet outweighed the gray. I thought of my Delia of the Blue Mountains, and prayed she would not despair of me away in her awe-inspiring Vallia.

Then, with weapons in my hands, I turned to face the dangers that had ensured my continuance on Kregen beneath Antares. It would need many swords to force me to flee from all that kept me on Kregen under the suns of Scorpio.

Chapter Two

Seg Segutorio

This was what life on Kregen was all about, this continuous challenge that set the blood pulsing through my veins, that brought all my alertness alive, that made me aware of myself as a man. Only moments before I had been fighting in the dust and sweat of my slave phalanx against the overlords of Magdag and then, because I had in some way unfathomable to me failed the Star Lords, I had been thrown into this new situation. Well—I thrust the second sword carefully down through the lizard-skin belt and hefted an assegai—well, the Star Lords or Savanti or scaled-skin sorzarts, all would meet my defiance distributed with an impartiality that held fast to one ideal only—I would win my way back to my Delia of the Blue Mountains. At that time the simplicity of this concept could hold no irony for me whatsoever.

The golden fruits waved and parted and the first lizard-man stepped through.

I waited.

He was followed by another and then a third. Still I waited. They had not seen me yet, concealed by the dark-green stems of the bloin, and I did not move. The first was very near now, so near I could see the way his scales grew smaller and smaller as they reached his neck and spread over his face in a kind of pseudo-skin in which his snout-nose and mouth protruded beneath those deep-set eyes. The mingled red and green light fell across the bronze and copper ornaments slung about him and sheened golden from the tall helmet with its arrogant bronze cock's comb. He held his assegai slanting over his shoulder in the ready-to-cast position.

I saved that one for my sword.

His three companions went down, shrilling, each with an

assegai through him, sprawling kicking among the brittle hard stems of the golden bloin.

The first sorzart's cast assegai sprang for my chest. My sword flicked free from the belt and knocked aside the flung assegai with a vibrating twang in that swift wrist-roll we Krozairs of Zy so often practiced against arrows. Then I was on him. This time my scruples about killing a man or half-man before he had time to draw could be put aside, with whatever of morality remained in this situation. Other sorzarts were following fast; three or four assegais whickered past. I lunged, withdrew, leaped back to avoid the next clump of assegais.

So far I had made no mistakes. I had not spoken; the full-scented odors of the golden bloin bells and the smell of blood and dust among the brittle green stems seemed to render out sounds, so that the dusty crackling of the stems as sorzarts sought my life came as through a golden afternoon haze. I did not know how many there were, but I did not intend to be chopped by their swords or struck by their assegais. I had no time, given what the Star Lords had brought me here to accomplish and that which I meant to accomplish for myself, to stay. In an instant I vanished from the lizard-men's sight among the silent golden bells of the bloin.

It would be useless just to scamper after Seg Segutorio and the Lady Pulvia. He would be hampered by her and the child and the sorzarts would catch up with them with results the Star Lords would disapprove of. So it was that those bold raiders of the inner sea were set on and bedeviled in their pursuit through the golden bloin and then—with more difficulty for myself—through orchards of gnarly-trunked samphron trees, whose juicy fruits with their glossy purple skins would soon be picked to be crushed into fragrant oil.

The second sword broke off short during one fierce interchange, but I came away with a replacement and with two more assegais that were almost immediately targeted off to good effect.

The blood that smothered my right arm was not mine. The two swords, I found, formed an interesting combination, rather like an overbalanced pair, a too-short long sword or broadsword for the right hand and a too-long main-gauche. The sorzarts probably shortened captured long swords because of the half-men's somewhat short stature, but they were nonetheless swift and sturdy fighters for all that.

Swords, of course, are objects of worth and price and not

easily come by in a culture without an extensive metallurgy, either of bronze or iron. The sorzarts' assegais—not the true assegai of Africa, I hasten to add, but an altogether slighter and narrower-bladed weapon—were their own natural weapon. Not all the lizard-men by any means possessed swords. Many of those swords I saw were easily identifiable as to previous ownership by their armory marks; weapons from Gantz and Zulfiria, from Sanurkazz and far Magdag.

The twin suns of Scorpio moved across the heavens and the streaming light settled more regretfully across the land. Soon darkness would fall with the temperate-zone twilight of not overlong duration. Somewhat to my astonishment the sorzarts kept up their pursuit. I no longer count the men or beast-men I have slain and so I do not know how many they lost in that long and agonized pursuit. Only when the twin suns at last sank beyond a distant ridge of mountains that ran down from the interior into the inner sea could I discern any reluctance on their part to continue.

Sharp trilling cries rose from one and then another. The last one I dispatched—without regret, for he had nicked me with his flung assegai and would have killed me without compunction had I allowed him to finish his sword-blow —fell headfirst into a little brook that meandered from the borders of the last orchard and trended away through open meadowland toward the sea. Purple shadows gathered and the water glimmered like cold steel. Thoughtfully, I wiped my blade on the sorzart's breechclout, picked up all his weapons, and walked on south. Soon the darkness was complete and I could gaze upward at the Kregen night sky and see those strange yet blessedly familiar constellations wheel above my head.

A comfort could be taken from the distant chips of light that fancifully formed animals and people and monsters, pinpricks of light that could form meaningful patterns only in a man's mind, his own rationality plucking from form an inchoate star-spattered infinity. I saw the stellar images, and I stumbled over a thorn bush and I cursed, and thereafter kept my eyes fixed on my path with only the occasional navigating glance aloft.

All the warmth of combat had passed from me. I did not shiver, for the night was mild, but inwardly I felt once again the essential futility of blind killing. How often—I remember musing as I trod southward to fulfill whatever of destiny the Star Lords would allow me—I had seen men who appeared actually to enjoy inflicting pain on others. These were the uniformed men of the bludgeon and the whip, who recruited their own warped desires into the punishment of the unfortunate. Did I enjoy the sensation as I cut a man down? Did I thrill to the jolt as my sword pierced a man's guts? God forgive me if I did—but I did not then and do not now. Perhaps my punishment is that in a situation in which it is kill or be killed I choose the easier path and kill to save my life and the lives of my loved ones.

Thus musing in a somber frame of mind—for I missed my Delia of the Blue Mountains beyond the mortal capacity to endure, or so I thought—I came to a rearing mass of toppled stone, twisted columns, broken arches, and collapsed domes all shining pinkly in the first of Kregen's nightly procession of moons.

The little stream broadened here and washed the worn steps of a landing jetty. Shadows jungle-hostile hung between truncated columns. I caught strange glimpses of pagan sculpture, serpentine forms that twined upon the surfaces of the blocks, hints of a demonology older than any current civilization thriving on this continent of Turismond.

The men of the sunrise had built their cities along the shores of the inner sea. Today, the shores lie mostly barren and untended except where the vicinity of a strong castle or fortified town or city affords some protection from corsair raids. I had raided the north shore myself, that shore of the green-sun deity Grodno; I had heard horrific tales of similar raids upon the red southern shore, dedicated to the sun Zim's deity, Zair. And the sorzarts raided both north and south and the eastern shore of Proconia—where I must now be—with the impartiality of the true unbeliever. I touched the hilt of one of my swords—for I remembered with affection the impressive armory of Hap Loder and my Clansmen of Felschraung—and went on.

"Stand and declare yourself—or you are a dead man!"

The voice sounded hard and confident and reckless. It was the voice of Seg Segutorio. I could not see him.

Undoubtedly, then, he was a warrior of skill.

"Dray Prescot," I said, and did not stop.

Seg and the Lady Pulvia waited beside the stone lip of a wide and shallow basin, shell-shaped, into which an arm of the stream poured continually, pinkly silver in the moons' light. Above them a chipped and defaced statue of a woman whose marble wings hung splintered from narrow shoulders cast a peaked shadow.

"You are safe, Dray?"

"Safe, Seg."

We had fallen into names thus easily, then.

"Thank the veiled Froyvil for that, then!"

"And you—the Lady Pulvia?"

She lifted her head from above her child as I asked, and gave me a blank, unseeing stare that told me that we would have to support her on whatever further voyage we must undertake. She bent her head and crooned softly to the child, who lay, his soft mouth stoppered by a plump thumb, fast asleep.

For a moment I could not recall when I had last slept. In all my bones that laxity of alert feeling told me that I was tired, deadly tired, but a sea officer of a King's Ship comes early to learn the knack of using his strength against long periods of wakefulness. I could go on for a space yet, but I considered the situation, knowing that sleep now would set store of strength by for later emergencies.

A movement in the purple shadows beneath the statue's splintered wings brought my sword out instantly, but Seg laughed and said: "Easy, Dray, you wild leem! That is Caphlander. A stylor, one of my lady's servants."

The man stepped into the moonlight. Tall, he walked with a stoop, and his sparse hair glinted in that wash of pink light. He wore a white robe bordered with a checkered design of red and green—a sight I must admit bewildered me for a moment with all the fierce clash of red and green still echoing in my skull—and his face reminded me somewhat of the ugly bird-head of a Rapa. There were significant differences, however, and his humanity seemed to me more pronounced than the remnant left to a Rapa. He was a Relt. Numbers of these usually gentle people when made slave pined near to death; others found reasons for living in serving their masters as librarians, stylors, accountants. His bright bird-like eyes studied us from a face held to one side, so that I knew his sight was affected in one of those eyes.

"Llahal!" he said, and then waited, stooping, subservient.

Brusquely, Seg said: "And?"

Caphlander the Relt wilted. "All burned," he said. "All dead. Such sights—"

"There's no going back, then. The Lord of Upalion having gone on his expedition will return to dust and ashes and corpses."

The impression I gained then, briefly and fleetingly, was that Seg was not overly dismayed at this catastrophe to his master, the man who owned him as slave. And—no wonder.

"Is there no safe place for this woman, Seg?"

He looked at her and sucked in his lower lip.

"The city—that is the only safe place. And we would never reach it on foot now. The sorzarts must be out in force."

"The day of our doom is here." Caphlander spoke with complete subjection and acceptance of his fate.

"I do not believe that my day of doom is to be brought by a bunch of lizard-faced scaled beast-men. There are other ways to cities than by walking," I told Caphlander and Seg.

"All the sectrixes were taken—"

I lifted my head and sniffed. On the night air, whose lush odors of nocturnal plant life told of many of those immense moon-drinking flowers twining among the ruins, the tangier smell I knew so well infiltrated like liquor at a funeral.

"The sea is not far. This city—"

"Happapat," said Seg.

"This Happapat—is it a port?"

"Yes."

"Then let's go."

We reached the coast. Seg carried the child and I carried his mother. She lay in my arms, a soft flaccid sexless bundle, a human being for whom my only concern had been dictated by the Star Lords—whoever they might be. We rested in a rock cave halfway up the cliff as the night passed.

With the gaining light, and refreshed by a few burs' sleep, we could plan again. I think, even then, Seg Segutorio had realized something other than mere concern over the safety of his mistress impelled me, for his people may be wild and reckless and filled with song, but they also possess that hard streak of practicality that has maintained their independence.

As the first sheening light of Zim spread in scarlet and golden radiance across the calm waters of the inner sea we looked out and down onto the ships of the sorzarts.

"Eleven of them." Seg spat. I did not waste good saliva. "They have to voyage in company, for they cannot face a Pattelonian swifter in fair fight."

On the curved beach the ships had been drawn up stern first. Ladders were lowered with the dawn and the anchor watch began their preparations to welcome back their comrades with loot and gold and prisoners. My hand tightened on the hilt of one of the swords. We could wait here until the sorzarts sailed away. . . .

Call me a fool. Call me a windbag full of braggadocio.

Call me prideful. I do not care. All I know is that while
my Delia sought me from her island home of Vallia by
rider and flier and I yearned above all things to hold her dear
form in my arms once more, I could not thus tamely
crouch hiding in a cave. On the hilt of the sword were
marked letters in the Kregish script: G.G.M. That meant
that a mercenary warrior employed by Gahan Gannius had
died some time in the past and his sword had been taken
as battle booty by the sorzarts. I wondered what had happened to Gahan Gannius, whom I had rescued on my last
return to Kregen, and if his manners and those of the girl
Valima had improved.

The plan must be nicely made and as nicely decided.

Those eleven ships down there on the beach beyond the
nearest crumbling wall of the Pattelonian fishing village were
not swifters nor were they broad ships. They were dromvilers. They had chosen to land directly at the fishing village—which are rare enough on the inner sea's coastline,
Zair knows—to secure safe berthings. The coast here fell
sheer into the sea. The people of the village, sentinels
against just such raids, had been outwitted on this occasion,
for a huddle of their fishing boats, the familiar muldavy with
her dipping lugsail of the inner sea, were still drawn up on
the beach by the wall. No one, then, had escaped.

But those ships of the sorzarts . . . I had heard of them,
of course, during my seasons as a Krozair raider on the
Eye of the World. But I had never before penetrated this
far east. The dromvilers were, to phrase it loosely, a com-
promise between a galley and a sailing ship, although they
were not galleasses. They were more like those classical ships
sometimes remarked on by ancient writers, or the oared
merchantmen of the Middle Ages used considerably in the
trade to the Holy Land, shipping pilgrims.

Broader than a swifter, narrower than a broad ship, they
carried single banks of twenty oars each crewed probably by
three or four oarsmen, and two masts. I felt reasonably
certain that the masts could carry topsails, and a grudging
respect grew in me for the sorzarts' sailing skills, for from
topsails can emerge all the panoply of sails, skysails and
stunsails and all.

A further sobering thought occurred to me. With that
number of oarsmen—something between one hundred and
twenty and one hundred and sixty, plus essential reserves—
the sorzarts could not be using slaves as oarsmen. A large
war swifter can carry a thousand slave oarsmen, and feed
and water and clean them after a fashion, by extraordinarily

careful management. But a merchantman exists to transport goods. There would be no room aboard the sorzarts' ships for slaves. The oarsmen, then, were free—that is, they were sorzarts capable of standing and fighting along with the soldiers of the crew. Maybe the sorzarts were not the savage barbarians the men of Grodno and Zair believed them.

"I am thirsty," said the Lady Pulvia, breaking the silence. "And my son is thirsty. Also, we are hungry."

I said: "So am I. I will bring you food and water as soon as it is possible."

"And when will that be?" said Caphlander. He held his hands together, the long thin fingers intertwined. The veins stood out with a greenish-blue twinge.

I ignored him.

Why should I destroy these sorzarts? A peculiar feeling toward them of respect had been growing in me. They were small men—half-men—yet they fought well. They had adopted topsails. They employed themselves as free men as oarsmen. But I saw the fallacy of this materialistic argument. The Vikings had been free men employed as oarsmen—yet I would have had no hesitation, given this situation, in utterly destroying every Viking longship I could. The child gave a whimpering cry, which swelled until against all his mother's shushings it broke into a torrent of sobs. The child was hungry and thirsty and he reacted as nature ordained he should.

Often I have been faced with a problem and reacted as I did because that was the way of my nature. That scorpion, that frog, they were impelled by forces stronger than themselves. Well, I have boasted that I can control my impulses, but I think that boast is on occasion an empty one.

I stood up.

"Caphlander. You will remain here. Do what you can for the Lady Puliva and her son. Seg, please come with me."

Without giving any of them a chance to reply or argue I went out of the rock cave and began to climb to the cliff top.

Chapter Three

I dive back into the Eye of the World

Seg Segutorio looked at the bow in his hand and his mobile lips drew down in a lopsided grimace. The bow spanned about twelve Earthly inches. He had made it with swift expertise from a branch of the thin willowy tuffa trees in whose shade we stood. The string he had as rapidly fashioned from plaited strips torn from the living bark. I looked down over the edge of the cliff, squinting a little against glare striking back off the sea from the twin suns of Antares.

Our preparations were complete. It only remained to kindle fire.

Any distaste as a sailorman I felt for the task I had set myself had to be quashed.

Seg let loose a great sigh and lifted the bow to me.

He shook his head. "Had I my own great bow I'd guarantee to pick off those sorzart rasts so fast they'd be pincushions before the first one hit the deck."

He surprised me. You must realize, you who listen to my story as these tapes rustle through your little machine, that despite Seg's black hair I had taken him to be a Proconian, who are, as I have said, mostly fair-headed. The remarks about his people I have made refer, of course, to his own true people; but they are remarks made from hindsight, a crime you must forgive a man who has lived as long as I have.

"Great bow?" I said.

He laughed. "Surely, even you—who are a stranger of strangers—must have heard of the longbows of Loh?"

"You are of Loh?"

Again he laughed. "Yes—and no!" That ancient look of blood pride suffused his face, an arrogant, proud expression so familiar in those who trace their ancestry back and back into the dawn of their culture. I can understand it; but in many ways I am glad I do not share it, for that kind of pride so often leads to the chinless wonders who have so

30

"One after another the flaming missiles of destruction plunged down onto the decks."

blighted life on our own Earth. But, with Seg Segutorio, as you shall hear, pride in race and ancestry burned with a steadier and truer flame.

"I am an Erthyr, of Erthyrdrin. . . ."

Of Erthyrdrin, that convulsed mass of mountains and valleys forming the long northern promontory of Loh, I had indeed heard. I had used longbowmen from Loh as a special sniper force in my slave army when we went against the overlords of Magdag, and some of them had had red hair, and some had not, and all had been superlative archers; but none had come from Erthyrdrin, although they had spoken of the place with some awe, some respect, and not a little bile.

Although tempted to contest a little in words with Seg over the relative values of my Clansmen's horn and steel compound reflex bows, I desisted. The wind was just right. The trees selected and bent and staked. The grasses gathered.

Now only the flame remained to be kindled.

"Go down to the Lady Puliva, Seg. Prepare them. You know the boat. If I am delayed—do not wait for me."

"But—"

"Go, now—"

He handed me the bow, his face glowering. "I see that at a more suitable opportunity, Dray Prescot, I shall have to teach you some respect for a warrior of Erthyrdrin."

"Willingly, my friend. I trust the good Zair will grant it—"

"Pagan gods!" he said, with a flash of cutting temper. "The mountaintops whereon the veiled Froyvil sends out his divine music from his golden and ivory harp would soon teach you the true values, my sad and unhappy friend."

"As to that," I said, taking the bow and squatting down to work, "I make no claims for Zair beyond those his followers make. And," I added, looking up suddenly, "they have been known to claim by the edge of the sword."

He made some kind of exasperated snort and hurried off down to the rock cave.

I shook my head over Seg Segutorio. From what I had heard of Erthyrdrin, that mountainous promontory of the continent of Loh thrusting up into the Cyphren Sea between eastern Turismond and Vallia, he was a good representative of his race. They were reputed reckless and wild, forever screeching crazy songs and thrumming on their harps; yet I knew of the strong streak of realism stabilizing their characters and lending always the calculated risk to the actions that other men called foolhardy.

So Seg was a longbowman. That could prove interesting.

The little bow whizzed rapidly back and forth twirling the drill of harder sturm-wood against its sturm-wood hole wherein chippings and dry grasses awaited the first ember. Gently and then with greater boldness I blew on the glow. You, who are so accustomed to flicking your finger for heat or light or a naked flame must remember that I had known flint and steel from childhood; perhaps I was a little quicker and defter at thus creating fire than a modern civilized man would be. It is of little consequence.

By the time I had a twisted torch well alight, the flames pale and writhing in the twin suns' rays, I figured that Seg must have reached the rock cave and gathered up our companions. He should be creeping cautiously down toward the beach now and, as I had judged him aright, taking every opportunity for cover the way provided. I walked across to the first bundle of grasses, wrapped and wadded around a flighting stone, where it lay poised on the forked-branch end of a sapling bent over and staked into the ground. Seg had sighted these rude catapults, and I had let him do that and had then merely checked them. He seemed to me to have done an excellent job. My ballistic knowledge had been gained at the breeches of twelve pounders and then all the way down to four pounders and up to thirty-two pounders, with one stint I looked back on with a grimace on the clumsy old forty-two pounders. In addition I had handled varters aboard swifters from Sanurkazz, and added to all this a natural eye for estimating distance and elevation and trajectory, and I knew myself, with all the necessary modesty required, to be a first-class shot. As I sliced through the first retaining fiber and released the first weighted bundle of flame I knew Seg Segutorio, also, to be a great marksman.

That first flaming missile arced into the suns-lit air, some smoke trailed from it, then it was a roaring mass of consuming flame arcing high and over and down onto the deck of a sorzart vessel.

I ran along the line of staked-down tuffa trees, their supple stems bent into graceful arches, and I seemed somehow to sense all their necessary springing effort as they flung themselves erect once more. It seemed to me all of their essential nature was pent up in those supple stems. One after another the spouting missiles of destruction plunged down onto the decks of the sorzarts' dromvilers. A pure pang of relief pierced me that the lizard-men would have no slaves chained to their dromvilers' benches. Already flames were licking malevolently at masts and rigging, shooting from oar ports; already the most dreaded foe of the seaman was consuming the wooden vessels and I knew, not without another pang, that nothing could be done now until the dromvilers burned down to the waterline—and their sterns were drawn up on the beach. . . .

This was a sight I need not stop to watch; this was a sight I did not care to stay to watch. It sickened me.

The necessity of the act alone could make me burn a ship. Halfway down toward the rock cave I halted and looked over the drop toward the beach. All eleven ships were blazing, although the one farthest away, which we had had to reach with a smaller incendiary missile, showed signs of resisting. Gangs of sorzarts were running like crazy people with buckets of seawater; others manned the pumps and streams of water jetted. I doubted they would hold back the flames. Once fire gets a hold aboard a wooden ship with her paint and tar and canvas and wood dried internally, there is practically no hope of extinguishing it.

At the cave I paused again, just to make sure they had gone. They had. On again and so down out of sight of the beach and around the last corner over the bluff above the fisher-folk's jetty wall.

Down there three figures struggled toward the boat we had chosen. The Lady Pulvia fell and Seg thrust the child at Caphlander and snatched up his mistress, slung her over his shoulder as he must have slung the bags of feed oats on her farm. They would reach the boat safely—and then I saw the group of sorzarts running from the heat and the smoke of their burning fleet.

I looked down.

It was a long way—a hundred and fifty feet in Terrestrial measurement. The sea looked blue and calm and serene. Shadows flitted across that surface as smoke clouds wafted by. The twin suns shone in all their resplendent glory. And, away in distant Vallia, my Delia of the Blue Mountains waited for me. . . .

You have probably read of experiments carried out to test from what distance a man can safely fall without a parachute. There are remarkable cases on record. Impact velocities of the order of a hundred feet per second have resulted in the survival of the person—in what state depending very much on the angle of impact or entry into the water. I knew nothing of that, then. All I knew was that I had to get down to the beach rather quickly. There were things to be done down there which if left undone would bring the wrath of the Star Lords down on my mortal head.

Without stopping further to cogitate I put my arms out and dived.

Even now I can remember the sensations.

Free-fall diving from aircraft is a modern sport.

I have practiced it and enjoyed it.

Then, when I dived off the cliff in Proconia above a Pattelonian fishing village, with the sorzarts running with naked swords, I just dived and let what fates held me in their hands take control.

Mind you, I did assume a diving position, and I entered the water straight. Confused images of that immense waterfall in the sacred River Aph billowed and echoed in my mind, and my whole body felt as though I had been compressed in some giant vise. Then I was cleaving through the water, down and down, seeing the daylight fade, feeling the growing resistance in the water, curving up, rising and rising until my head popped out and I could shake my hair and look back at the beach.

That first gulp of air tasted very sweet.

The Lady Pulvia, Caphlander, and the child were in the boat. Seg had just hurled an assegai and brought down the leader of the band of vengeful sorzarts. I started to swim.

When I scrambled out Seg accounted for four more and was crossing swords with the sixth.

I must admit I had been extraordinarily lucky since neither the Star Lords nor the Savanti had taken a hand to preserve a life they might consider of use to them. Certainly the risk had been entirely of entry. The almost vertical cliffs of this coast had told me the water would be steep-to right up to the rock, deep and commodious enough for me to avoid knocking my brains out on the bottom. The overhang of the bluff assisted also. I had merely to swim around the tiny spit of land to reach the beach and Seg and the others.

"Hai Jikai!" I yelled. I drew my sword and slogged into the lizard-men. Seg circled a sword, thrust, recovered, shouted: "What kept you?"

A joke, a reprimand, mere bravado—I do not know. I never asked. But I felt a warm glow of elation at the presence of this black-haired and reckless man from Erthyrdrin.

There was no time for nicety in that fight. We had to dispose of this band of sorzarts—there were about eight left—very rapidly before their comrades left off hurling ineffectual buckets of water over their burning ships and hastened to their assistance. No niceties—that meant hard, fierce, dirty fighting. Tricks I had learned boarding enemy ships of the line in the battle-smoke of Earth, tricks I had picked up with my Clansmen, even a few passes from those days as a bravo-fighter in Zenicce came in useful. All the miraculous-seeking swordplay given me by the disciplines of the Krozairs of Zy, of course, enabled me to stay ahead of my opponent, but some of the stunts I pulled would have turned a young college boy fencer of this Earth green.

Seg and I—we very quickly cleared the sorzarts away.

"The three boats on your side, Seg!" I yelled.

Without a word he did as I directed, and together we stove in the bottoms of the boats lying in this huddle. One boat, the largest, a fifty-footer, lay some distance off, toward where the bonfires of the dromvilers spouted flame and smoke.

I started for it, waving Seg back to the boat we had selected.

The Lady Pulvia na Upalion stood up in the bows of the boat. Very erect, she stood.

"Leave that boat!" she shouted. "They are coming! Look! Hurry back and push this boat into the sea! Hurry!"

A further group following the non-reappearance of those sent to investigate, no doubt, was indeed running from the burning ships along the beach toward us. Suns-light glinted on their bronze and copper ornaments, from their tall golden helmets, and winked back from their naked weapons.

I turned to the Lady Pulvia.

"Get out and help Seg and Caphlander push the boat out! Move yourself! Hurry!"

Then, before she could give vent to her outraged anger and surprise, I yelled at Seg: "Get the boat off, Seg! Make her help—and the Relt. I will swim out to you." Then I hared off toward the remaining boat and the swiftly advancing party of sorzarts. When they saw me they shrilled their horrid war cries—but mere yelling has not so far harmed me at that distance.

Reaching the fifty-footer I stove the bottom in with four quick blows—not without once more that pang of displeasure at myself for this destruction of property that gave livelihood to the poor fisher-folk—and glared out to sea to get the best line for my swim.

The boat had not moved. The Lady Pulvia still stood in the bows, gesticulating to the two—Seg and Caphlander—who were vainly attempting to thrust the boat's keel into the water.

I kept down the immediate icy welling of rage. That, if I so chose, would come later.

The boat felt thick and hard beneath my hands as I reached it. At any moment the sorzarts would be within assegai-casting range.

"All together!"

We heaved. The boat lurched, the keel screeched, it stuck —we all bent and thrust with desperate effort—and then the boat jerked and slid free into the water. I took Caphlander around the waist and fairly flung him up into the boat. Seg went in over the other side and I, after a last fierce thrust that sent the craft surging out into the tiny waves, leaped in after him.

At once I seized the oars Seg had readied and fell to. I rowed with a long swing and now all those horrific days of labor when I was an oar slave aboard the swifters of Magdag paid handsome dividends. The boat clove the water. Spray danced inboard. I bent and pulled, bent and pulled, and only incidentally was aware of Seg snatching an assegai from where it had plunged into the transom and, standing and balancing awkwardly, flinging it back into the throat of a sorzart prancing in fury on the beach.

A few more assegais plunged in alongside and then they were hissing into the water astern of us.

I steadied the rhythm of my stroke and glared with a most uncharitable wrath upon my Lady Pulvia na Upalion.

She saw that look, and her chin came up; then a deep flush spread over her cheeks and she lowered her eyes. She breathed unsteadily.

"The next time I give an order," I told her, knowing that infernal rasp was back in my voice, "you will obey instantly, do you understand?"

She made no reply.

"Do you understand, Lady Pulvia?" I repeated.

Caphlander started to burble something about being respectful to the mistress, but Seg shut him up. At last she raised her eyes. She had evidently made up her mind to be cutting, authoritative, contemptuous. But she saw my face and her resolution and no doubt her set speech faltered. She opened her mouth.

"Obey—understand," I said, not ceasing from rowing.

"Yes."

"Very well."

I rowed then in a simple long rhythm that sent the little boat out across the suns-lit waters of the Eye of the World.

Chapter Four

Rashoons command our course

I took no pleasure—on the contrary I experience no little shame—in thus browbeating a woman rightfully concerned over her child and attempting to uphold her own dignity and not give way to the fears that must have been clamoring to turn her into a sobbing ball of defenseless weakness. But there can be, as I know to my cost, only one captain aboard ship.

And—she was a slave-holder, and a representative of that class of authority most distasteful to me after my experiences in far-off Zenicce, and more lately in Magdag.

We sailed the muldavy with her dipping lug rig safely to the town, the port and arsenal and fortress of Happapat, and delivered the Lady Pulvia na Upalion into the hands of relations who cooed over her and the child and whisked her off to their palace.

When their guards—fair-haired Proconians clad in the iron ring mail of warriors all around the coasts of the inner sea, and armed with long swords that were not cut down—marched Seg and me off to the local barracoon, I felt no surprise whatsoever.

This kind of attitude on the part of slave-holders seemed inseparable from their nature, as abhorrent to Seg as to myself.

We wasted no time in breaking out, whooping, cracking a few skulls in the process, and with a couple of wineskins and a vosk thigh tastefully cooked and browned, we helter-skeltered off to the harbor. The fishing muldavy we had stolen in order to rescue the Lady Pulvia and her child and Caphlander lay still tied up where we had left her. In her, I knew, there was a full breaker of water. We tossed our meager belongings in and cut the painter—a gesture of defiance, that—and rowed out. We had the lugsail up and

were foaming off into the suns-set long before the guards
had pulled their scattered wits about them.

"And so, Dray Prescot," said Seg Segutorio, "what now?"

I stared with a glad affection at this volatile man with the
lean tanned face and those shrewd yet reckless eyes. He was
a good sword-companion, and for a moment I remembered
with a choked nostalgia all those other good companions I
had known. I am essentially a lonely man, a loner, one who
stands or falls on his own merits and I take ill to being be-
holden to anyone. This is a fault in me. I thought of Nath
and Zolta, my two oar comrades, those two rascals who
could not keep away from wine and women. And I remembered how Nath would lean back and quaff a full tank-
ard, and wipe his forearm across his shining lips, and belch,
and say: "Mother Zinzu the Blessed! I needed that!" and
how Zolta would already have the prettiest girl in the inn
perched laughing on his knee.

Sitting resting on the oars and looking at Seg Segutorio
with an awakening awareness—I cannot dwell on that, as you
will come to understand—I remembered Zorg of Felteraz, my
other oar brother, and I thought of Prince Varden Wanek, and
of Gloag, and of Hap Loder—and—and remember I was
still young at the time as age is measured on Kregen—I
wondered how it was that Seg Segutorio could sit on the opposite thwart and look back at me so cheerfully and say so
matter-of-factly: "Well, Dray Prescot, and what now?"

These memories of my comrades affected me, and I admit
to a tired, dejected, defeated feeling creeping over me then.
You would be forgiven if, from all I have so far said, you
jump to the conclusion that Kregen is essentially a man's
world. Despite the Princess Natema Cydones, and the Princess Susheeng, and other highborn ladies of enormous
power, including among their number the Lady Pulvia na
Upalion whom we had just rescued and delivered safely to
her kinfolk, you might well think that Kregen is dominated
by the male principle where brawn and muscle and fighting
ability count for everything.

You would, of course, be wrong.

Through this sudden gloom on my part for my old comrades I never for a single instant forgot my twin destiny on
Kregen beneath the suns of Scorpio.

Whatever plans the Star Lords had mapped out for me as
a troubleshooter, I held to my own purposes. First, I would
find my beloved Delia of the Blue Mountains. And, when that
had been accomplished, I would travel this world of Kregen
to find my way back to' Aphrasöe, the City of the Savanti,

the Swinging City, for there I believed paradise awaited me.
In all these simple and primitive emotions and ambitions
I could still find joy that I did not seek vengeance.

We sailed out into the waters of the inner sea, and Seg
appeared perfectly satisfied to allow me the conn and to run
the muldavy. As he said, with a laugh: "We Erthyr are a
mountain people. The sea is not a second home to us."

The night breathed gently about us. The sea ran with
a calmness that cradled the little boat. The stars glittered
above our heads. The wind blew a mere zephyr.

I looked at the stars. I knew them well. I had studied
them night after night from the deck of my swifter as we
sailed in unexpected nocturnal raids against the overlords
of Magdag, or any of the green cities of the northern
shore. I had often shocked my crew by this nighttime sailing; their ideas were those of daytime sailing only and a safe
beach at night.

I steered to the west.

It was necessary that I return to Magdag as soon as possible.
From thence, before the rebellion, I had sent the Vallian
Vomanus back to his home island with a message for Delia.
He would return—that I knew with fair certainty—and if
he landed at Magdag now, his life would be snuffed out in an
instant as a friend of the arch-criminal Pur Dray of Strombor,
Krozair, arch-fiend and deadly foe to Magdag.

We steadied on our course west and the wind gusted up
suddenly and heeled the muldavy so that water creamed in
over the lee gunwale until I let her pay off a trifle. I frowned.
The wind veered and strengthened. Now the stars were
being blotted out in great clumps at a time as clouds
gathered. A brilliant zigzag of fire split the heavens. The
thunder, when it reached us, rolled and reverberated around
our ears. Rain started to slice into the sea in an abrupt and
deafening uproar. In moments we were soaked, our hair
tangled about our ears. Seg started to bale. The wind blew
directly from the west.

I knew.

This storm not only confirmed my fears that the Star
Lords would not allow me to return to Magdag, it also
strengthened my suspicion that after my summary ejection
from the fight as my slave phalanx in their old yellow-
painted vosk-helmets raged on to tear the mailed overlords of
Magdag to pieces the battle had swung against us. Perhaps I
had overstepped my authority when I had really and truly
organized the slaves and workers of the warrens so that
they could actually win the fight against the overlords? Per-

haps the Star Lords did not want the overlords of Magdag crushed and banished? It could be their plans called for whatever I had done to slumber a while, to gather subterranean strength, to smolder until at some time in the Star Lords' plans for Kregen that spirit I had kindled with the help of the Prophet could burst out in renewed fury. I did not know.

What I did know was that I could not reach Magdag.

Very well, then. Gradually a kind of structure of devices for coping with the Star Lords—if this was truly their work and not the mortal but nonetheless superhuman work of the Savanti—was being wrought out in my mind. I had successfully appealed and been granted reprieve the last time, in that I had been permitted to stay on Kregen, in a dissimilar fashion to the way in which I had been reprieved at Akhram. The idea began to grow that provided I did not actively contest the dictates of the Star Lords—The Everoinye—I might go about my own business on Kregen beneath Antares.

Yes—very well, then. I put the steering oar up and we surged away on the starboard tack. I would go to Pattelonia. Vomanus would be there if I was lucky, and I could stop him from going on to Magdag. Then—then we would take over the Hostile Territories to Port Tavetus from whence we could sail direct for Vallia.

And then—Delia!

Immediately our bows swung to the eastward with the necessary touch of southerly in the heading for Pattelonia; the wind eased off and the rain ceased. Amid a last grumbling of thunder I heard the harsh croaking shriek as of a giant bird. I looked up. In the darkness I could not see the Gdoinye—but I knew without shadow of a doubt that the gorgeous scarlet and golden raptor of the Star Lords had swung over us in its wide hunting circles.

"In the name of the veiled Froyvil himself!" said Seg. He looked about. "What was that?"

"A seabird," I said, "caught in the gale. It seems, friend Seg, we must sail to Pattelonia—rather the chief city on the eastern coast of Proconia than any other, yes?—and we will reach it safely, never fear. You asked me what now—this is your answer. What do you say?"

"Pattelonia." Seg spat the name. "That may be the chief city, but the fighting-men disgust me."

"Oh?"

He swagged up a wineskin and stoppered his mouth to the spout very expertly, as the boat surged along, considering he considered himself no sailor. When he had gulped and

wiped his mouth and said, "By Blessed Mother Zinzu, that
fires up the cockles of my heart!"—and what a pang of Nath
there was in that for me!—he went on to say: "I hired out as
mercenary to Pattelonia in one of their infernal wars, you
know?"

I nodded. "I know."

His story was commonplace, ugly, and painful. Men of Loh
could usually find employment as mercenaries without
trouble, for their prowess as archers was renowned throughout
the known lands of Kregen. Seg had entered the inner sea by
the western end, through the Grand Canal past the Dam of
Days. I reflected that he had seen that colossal construction;
I had not. I forebore to mention that to him; it would
arouse too many questions. His fighting career had been of
the normal routine and monotonous kind associated with mercenary fighting; when the Pattelonians had been defeated by
a combined force of a number of the Proconian cities assisted by Magdag, he had been captured and sold as slave.

"So Pattelonia fell," I said.

"Mayhap. I did hear that Sanurkazz was coming to our
assistance, but I tripped into that damned thorn-hole and was
scooped up by a diabolical overlord before it did me any
good."

I made suitable sympathetic noises.

"There are friends in Pattelonia, Seg, although I have never
been there. We will be returning to Vallia." This was a lie.
I could never return to Vallia for I had never been there
in the first place; but as I had told Kov Tharu of Vindelka,
I thought of Vallia for all its frightening reputation as home
simply because my Delia lived there.

"Vallia?" Seg drank more wine, his shape a dark expres-
sive blot beneath the starlight. "I took passage aboard a ship
of Pandahem. The Vallian was too dear. But I know Vallia—
they maintain a great fortress depot on the northernmost tip
of Erthyrdrin. Many times have my people gone down
against them."

"You don't like Vallians?"

He laughed. "That was in the past. Since Walfarg broke
apart like a rotten samphron the Vallians have been markedly
more friendly toward us, and now we tolerate their fortress
depot and it has grown into a sizable city, and we do business with them, for they are essentially a nation of traders."

Walfarg was a name I had heard here and there, a mighty
empire of the past which had broken apart. It had originated
in Walfarg itself, a country of Loh, and some of the stories of
Loh hung about its faded glories. There are many countries

in the continents and islands of Kregen; only Vallia, as far as I know, boasts that it is a single land mass under one government.

And that boast was to cost it dear, as you shall hear.

"So you are for Pattelonia, then?"

"A pity, Dray Prescot, your friends could not await you at a point nearer the Dam of Days. From Pattelonia we have —oh, I am not sure of the distance, five hundred dwaburs, is it?—to cover before we even reach the outer ocean. Then we must sail south past skeleton coasts to Donengil and thus swing around up the Zim-Stream and so to the Cyphren Sea —and there, before us, lies Erthyrdrin!"

For the moment I was content to let Seg believe this.

He said, with a sharpness to his voice, "You are not a Vallian?"

Vallians, I knew from the example of the glorious hair of my Delia, were often brown-haired, as I am. I had successfully passed as Kov Drak in Magdag, acting the part of a Vallian duke. But I did not wish to lie unnecessarily to Seg Segutorio.

"I am Dray Prescot of Strombor," I said.

"So you have told me. But—Strombor. Where might that be?"

Of course—what was now the enclave of Strombor would have been Esztercari for all Seg's life. A fierce joy welled up in me as I thought of my Clansmen riding across the Great Plains of Segesthes, of the way with good friends' help we had taken what was to become my enclave fortress of Strombor within the city of Zenicce.

"Strombor, Seg, is in Zenicce—"

"Ah! A Segesthan—well, even that I wonder about, for I call you a stranger of strangers, and I know what I know."

"What do you know, Seg?"

But he would not answer. That fey quality associated with mountain folk must have alerted his senses; but I was doubtful that he could guess I came from a planet distant from Kregen by four hundred light-years.

He swung away from that as the muldavy creamed through the night sea and the stars once more reappeared above. The twin second moons of Kregen, the two that revolve one about the other as they orbit the planet, sailed above the horizon and in their wash of pinkish light, strengthened by the presence of two more of Kregen's seven moons, I saw Seg watching me with an enclosed and contained look on his lean face. He brushed a hand through his black hair.

"Very well, Dray Prescot, of Strombor, I will go with you to

Pattelonia." He chuckled. "For all that the army in which I served lost the fight, the Proeonians still owe me my fair hire, and they shall pay me."

"Good, Seg," was all I considered necessary to say.

"And I refuse by all the shattered targes in Mount Hlabro to return to slavery."

We slept on and off during the night and when the twin suns rose to burn away a few patches of mist, there, broad on our larboard beam, lay one of the many islands that dot the inner sea. I steered to pass it with plenty of sea room, for islands are notorious as the lair of pirates and corsairs— I had used them enough times myself—when Seg noticed what I had seen and mentally filed as part of the habitual stock-taking of a sea officer the moment he reaches the deck.

He pointed aft where a low black and purple cloud like a massive bruise again the gleaming sky whirled onward.

"A rashoon!"

At the moment I was more concerned with the identity of the swifter shooting out from the lee of the island. She was large, that I could tell—and then as flags broke from her mast and flagpoles I saw their color. My lips compressed.

Every flag was green!

"A Magdag swifter," I said to Seg. "Hold on—we are going into some fancy evolutions now—"

And then the rashoon enveloped us and we fought the lug down until I could control the muldavy in the screeching wind. The seas piled and knotted about us. We went sweeping on, and the swifter was left floundering. Even then I noted the seamanlike way in which her skipper brought her around and scuttled back with all his double-banks of oars stamping the sea in neat parallel lines, back into the shelter of the island. We were sent weltering past and out to sea. When the rashoon had blown itself out and we could get back to an even keel and rehoist the lugsail and take stock, I found Seg with an expression on his face which, allied to the green tinge around his jaws, gave me an odd feeling of compassion and unholy glee.

I offered him a thick juicy slice from the vosk thigh.

He refused.

It pains me now, in recollection, to think how badly I treated Seg Segutorio then as we hauled up for Pattelonia across the Eye of the World.

We called in at various islands on the way to water and to acquire fresh provisions, mostly fruit and vegetables, for we avoided the habitations of men and half-men. Seg told me much of his home in Erthyrdrin—which I shall relate when it becomes necessary—but one fact he told me made me think on.

"Arrow heads?" he said one day as we burbled across the sea with the limpid sky above. "You won't find an Erthyr archer using steel in an arrow head. By Froyvil, Dray! Steel is hard to come by in my country."

"So what do you use, bronze?"

He laughed. "Not a chance. It's a pretty metal, is bronze, and I have an affection for it. But we use flint, Dray, good honest Erthyrin flint. Why, we kids could flint-knap as pretty a point as you could wish to see when we were three years old! And, mark you, flint will pierce solid lenk better than almost anything. Perhaps your steel is better, but not bronze, certainly not copper, or bone or horn, or even iron."

I stored that away in my mind, thinking of the sleeting rain of arrows my Clansmen could put down. But then, the city of Zenicce controlled what was in effect a vast metallurgical industry, with immense iron deposits nearby with woodlands to furnish charcoal. The same was true of both Magdag and Sanurkazz here on the inner sea.

In talking into this little cassette tape recorder in these heartrending surroundings of famine and despair I have sometimes found it difficult to give a coherent account of Kregen. The planet is real, it is a living, breathing, fully-functioning world of real living people, both men and women and beast-men and beast-women besides all the monsters you could desire. Things happen there as they do on Earth, because necessity impels men to invent and to go on developing these inventions. There could be no long crisp loaves of Kregan bread without cornfields opening to the twin suns, with back-breaking labor to plow and plant and hoe and harvest, with mills to grind and bakers to bake. No man who values life can take anything that life offers for granted—even the air he breathes must be tended and cared for, otherwise the pollution that so worries you here on Earth will poison the uncaring hosts.

So Seg and I talked as we sailed toward Pattelonia, the chief city of Proconia, and the city to which I had been posted as a swifter captain of the forces of Sanurkazz before I had taken off in that abortive journey to Vallia that had terminated back in Magdag, hereditary foe of Sanurkazz. Whoever ruled now in Pattelonia ruled by right of sword, whether red or green or Proconian. Navigation was simple; the suns and the stars kept me on course over seas I have never traversed before, and soon I calculated we must be approaching waters in which more traffic must be expected.

By this time Seg could take a trick at- the steering oar and he it was who was conning the muldavy when another of those inconsiderate rashoons whirled down upon us in a whining torrent of wind and a lumping roaring sea.

At once I leaped to the dipping lug and rattled the yard down, leaving a mere peak to give us steerage way. White water began to sluice inboard and I took up the baler and started in on flinging it back from whence it had come. We steadied up and I could look back at Seg Segutorio. He clung onto the steering oar with a most ferocious expression on his face. He fought the waves with the same elemental force as he would expend in hunting among his beloved mountains of Erthyrdrin. He fought a new element with a courage and a high heart that warmed me.

Smiling and laughing do not come easily to me, except in some ludicrous or dangerous situations, as you know; but now I looked on Seg Segutorio and my lips widened in a mocking smile, an ironic grimace to which he responded with a savage wrench on the steering oar and a rolling string of blasphemies that burst about my head as the rashoon was bursting.

We rolled and rocked and I baled, and Seg hung onto his oar and kept our head up and steered us through. Again I look back in sorrow at the way I treated poor Seg Segutorio. He was a man to delight the heart.

When we came through it, Seg heaved in a tremendous breath, blew it out, glared at me, and then ignored me altogether. I did not laugh; now I am sorry I did not, for he expected it.

Following the wild moments of the tempest in the inner sea—the rashoons varied as to name and nature—we glided on over a sea that fell calm with only a long heaving swell.

The broad ship lay low in the water, wrecked by the rashoon, her masts gone by the board and her people running about her decks in panic. Then we saw the cause of that alarm.

Circling in toward the broad ship—a merchantman Seg told me by her devices as being from Pattelonia—the long narrow wicked shape of a swifter cleft the water in absolute and arrogant knowledge of her own power. As we watched, the swifter broke her colors. All her flags were green.

A swifter from Magdag! Attacking a broad ship from Pattelonia. From that I deduced that Sanurkazz had succeeded in retaking the city, and I felt a bound of delight.

Now if I have not made it clear that Seg Segutorio was reckless to the extreme, despite that streak of practicality, then I have not drawn the man aright. He stared at the green-bedecked swifter and his nostrils tightened up. He turned the steering oar so that our head bore on the two vessels.

"What, Seg, and you're going to attack a Magdaggian swifter on your own?"

He looked at me as if he had not heard.

"She's a big one, Seg. A hundred-and-fiftyswifter. I'd judge, by her lines, she's a seven-six-six."

The faint zephyr of wind bore us on.

"We don't even have a knife, let alone a sword, Seg."

Our prow rustled through the water.

Oh, how I regret baiting Seg Segutorio!

Perhaps, just perhaps, then, when I was young, I had not forgotten that forkful of dungy straw smacking me full in the face.

"They're from Magdag," Seg said. "They made me slave."

We bore on over the sea and now the sound of shrieks and screams reached us, the ugly sound of metal on metal. I was a Krozair of Zy, dedicated to combating the false green Grodno—no other course occurred to me.

Chapter Five

The fight aboard the swifter

"It's the oldest, hoariest trick there is, Seg," I said as we slid through the calm water toward the Pattelonian broad ship and the Magdag swifter. "But it's all we have to work with. It's worked in the past and no doubt it will work again in the future. All we're concerned with now is that it works for us this time."

"How many men, Dray?" was all Seg Segutorio said.

"The swifter's a seven-six-six, one hundred and fifty. That means she has three banks of oars each side, twenty-five oars a bank. The upper deck oars are crewed by seven men each, the two lower banks by six men to an oar. That's about a thousand men or more, given spare oarsmen carried below."

"And all slave?"

"All slave."

"You seem to know about these things, Dray."

"I know."

"And the warriors?"

"That varies. Depends on the purpose for which the swifter has been put into commission. I'd guess, again, that there won't be less than a couple of hundred. If they're on a big one, there will be a lot more." I thought of my days as a slave aboard swifters from Magdag. "They crowd the men, Seg. They keep them chained to the oars and they feed them water and onions and slop and cheese and they douse them out with seawater twice a day and they fling them overboard when they're exhausted and all the strength has gone from them and they're lashed to death."

"We're approaching nicely," said Segutorio. He laughed. "All I regret is—I do not have my own longbow with me, my bow I made myself from the sacred Yerthyr tree that grew up on Kak Kakutorio's land. He near caught me, the day

48

I cut my stave. I was twelve, then. I built that bow for use when I'd gained my full stature—and when I did she balanced out just right. Kak's tree was almost black, so dark and secret green it was. He near caught me—"

Seg checked himself. I saw the way his shoulders hunched. That streak of practical common sense had thrust hard at his reckless spirit and he could apprehend clearly just what we were getting into. He was driven by hatred for the green deity worshipers and by a habitual recklessness. I was impelled by my vows, my own dark memories—and because I was a Krozair of Zy.

Being privileged to be a member of the Order of Korzairs of Zy means a very great deal to me. That they are a small group of dedicated men tucked away in an inland sea on a planet four hundred light-years away, bound up with their fanatical adherence to a mythical red deity and in absolute opposition to an equally mythical green deity, has no bearing on their inner strengths, their gallantry, their selflessness, their mysticism—which contains profundities beyond profundities—their remarkable disciplines of the sword, their essential courageous integrity. These are qualities found only in a debased coinage on the Earth you inhabit today, it sometimes seems.

Seg Segutorio hated slavery and slave-holders—as did I. Yet only when I had been the captain of a Sanurkazzian swifter and a Krozair had I, too, employed slaves. They had rowed for me in conditions little better than those of my own misery when I had pulled for Magdag. This surely must mark the power of the Order of Krozairs of Zy over me. When I had attempted to free my slaves and had adopted free oarsmen I and my crew had been so close to a horrific and murderous end as to cause nightmares.*

So, thus thinking, I waited as the muldavy closed the final gap between us and the swifter's stern. Everyone aboard had their attention occupied by the dying moments of the struggle to take possession of the broad ship. I had thought she was sinking; no doubt the swifter captain considered he could plunder her and take her people prisoners before she sank. Now the high upflung curve of the stern rose from the water before us.

The swell slopped us up and down. I stood up in the bows. The swifter was large and her apostis, the rectangular rowing

---

* A further reference to the missing cassettes' information we do not have, as related in *The Suns of Scorpio*.　A.B.A.

frame, extended well out from the smooth curves of her hull.
Her oarsmen, arranged *alla scaloccio,* still held to their
looms as the blades were all, every one, in perfect alignment.
Every now and again the drum-deldar would give a signal
double-beat of his bass and tenor drums and precisely together all the oars of either the larboard or starboard banks
would dip and give a short jabbing thrust to keep the swifter
lined up against the broad ship, beak extended and jutting
over her beam.

I looked up the arrogantly upflung stern and put aside
instinctive thoughts of equally arrogantly upflung tails of
scorpions.

Among the elaborate scrollwork and what we would call
gingerbread I found easy handholds. As my bare feet gripped
and heaved me up so Seg followed. We were both unarmed. I wore simply the same strip of brown cloth taken
from the sorzart, and Seg wore his gray slave breechclout.
Carefully, now, I put a hand on the deck below the rail. One
of the steering oars extended past my back. I lifted myself
gently. I looked.

The steering-deldar lay on his oar, ready with curling
movements to keep the head of the swifter against the
broadship in time with his companion on the other side and
the occasional thrusts from the oars. The drum-deldar would
be sitting with his drumsticks poised, and the oar-master
would be sitting in his little tabernacle below the break of the
quarterdeck. An officer—very resplendent in green silk and
gold lace—strode about looking pleased with himself. I
cursed his black Magdaggian heart.

As carefully I lowered myself.

Seg was looking at me. His face was wrinkled up, his
whole expression one of absolute distaste.

"They stink," he said.

"Yes."

Swifters are built on lines laid down by naval architects
of varying talents. I recognized the lines of this example and
I knew my way about her as slave or captain. We made an
entry into the aft lower cabin—what would on an Earthly
seventy-four be called the gun room—and found the space
deserted of life. Beyond the doors opening onto the lower
or thalamite bank of oars lay the manpower I needed. This
galley was of the cataphract variety so that her upper thra-
nite banks of rowers were protected by a fenced bulwark.
At the time I was still undecided, as I was undecided between
the long keel and the short keel theories, whether the open

un-bulwarked style, the aphract with its free passage of air, was better than the cataphract which did at least offer some protection from arrows. However that might be, that extra protection afforded us an extra level of concealment as we went about our work.

First out of the double-folding doors I saw the nearest whip-deldar and before he could so much as turn I held him in a grip from which he slumped lifeless to the gangway.

The slaves stared up with lackluster eyes. Their heads were bushy mops, clear indication that the swifter had been at sea for some time, for the heads of oar slaves when they clear the mole at Magdag are shaved as smooth as a shot trimmed for a twenty-four pounder bowchaser.

Seg started for the other whip-deldar at a dead run.

Down here in the odors and the confinement the whip-deldars took turns at duty, or received thalamite duty as a punishment.

The fellow I had dropped carried a knife. It took me only a few moments to pick the lock of the great chain to which all the other chains were attached.

The nearest slave looked at me in a puzzled fashion. His back carried the marks of his trade. The one next to him also looked up, his jaw slack and mumbling over broken, decaying teeth behind thick slobbering lips. I experienced a moment of despair.

These slaves were completely broken. Would they rise, as they *must* rise, if we were to succeed?

There would be no question here of an immediate flinging off of the great chain, a gathering of their own chains into vengeful fists, and an immediate abandonment of the habits of slavery. They must see what could be done. But—the lower deck held the recalcitrants as a rule, the troublemakers, the extra-tough. Had I disastrously miscalculated?

Then from that twin channel of upturned faces, bearded, filthy, a man clambered up dragging his chains. He stared at me.

"Pur Dray!"

I did not recognize him. But he knew me. I sensed the change, then. I heard the word "Krozair!" and I hurriedly raised my hands.

"Be silent! Free yourselves now the great chain is loosed. Keep the oars at the level—you know. We will free our comrades above—and then—*silence!*"

Of course, they could not keep silent.

Once the traumatic bludgeon of release had shocked them,

once they suddenly realized that they need not be slaves again, there was no holding them.

Whip-marked naked bodies began to spill out into the central gangway with its slits of sky above and the long rows of naked legs of the oarsmen of the upper two banks. A whip-deldar looked over his narrow split-deck and yelled. I hurled the knife as I had hurled the woman's weapon of my Clansmen, the terchick, and he toppled over spouting blood from his mouth. I put my foot on his body and drew the knife from his throat. I rather cared for that economical use of a weapon.

The slaves were clambering up the supporting timbers of the upper banks, hauling themselves up over the inboard ends of the oar looms where they rested in the level position within the patterned rowing-frames. They were screeching and yelling and waving their chains. I knew few of them would think to release their comrades; their minds were now shocked into one desire only—to kill the overlords of Magdag. Mind you—that was a desire I then considered eminently worthy—Zair forgive me.

Like some grundal of the rocks I went up hand over hand, the bloody knife between my teeth. That, I admit, is one time when I grin.

The twisted and pulped body of a whip-deldar crunched underfoot as I leaped for the locks of the zygites' great chain. The knife point probed, there was a click clearly audible above the uproar, and then the zygites, prepared by the astonishing appearance of their fellows from below, were roaring and raging with chains in their fists.

A few arrows fleeted down and a slave shrieked and toppled back with a shaft through him. The crew had reacted swiftly.

I had not expected otherwise.

Only the overwhelming manpower of the slaves could win the swifter for us.

It is difficult to conceive of the uproar and violence of those moments. In an exceedingly long and narrow space, a mere slot walled in by timbers and chains, naked hairy men howled and struggled to reach the light. Up we went and with us went Seg Segutorio, brandishing a whip with which he took the ankles from under a whip-deldar and so brought him screeching down into the merciless talons of the slaves.

On the upper deck with its central gangway and gratings to either side over the lower banks the slaves were raging like a sea breaking against cliffs. The task of reaching the locks of the thranites' great chain would be difficult. Already soldiers of Magdag in their iron-linked hauberts were running back from the bows. Arrows were flickering through the air. I took off in a long run toward the oar-master and his tabernacle. The drum-deldar let out a single long scream and went scuttling aft. Up there the officer I had seen drew his long sword.

I wanted that sword.

Still—the locks must come first. Then Seg was with me. His whip flicked the oar-master into a gibbering panic. I bent to the first lock and an arrow feathered into the deck at my side. The officer ran toward us, leaned over, shouting. His face, browned by wind and sun, looked in the last stages of apoplectic fury.

I clicked the lock, stood up, let fly the knife.

The officer gurgled, slumped, toppled down.

I caught the long sword as it spun through the air, taking its bone grip—which I dislike—leanly into my fist. It would have been a fine catch at first slip.

"Forward!" shouted Seg. "The rasts are waiting for us!"

Indeed, the battle to take the broad ship was over. Now the swifter's crew and soldiers were turning about to face the frenzied slaves. We had begun with the lowest bank so as to avoid detection. Now that all the slaves were free nothing stopped us from hurling ourselves into the fight.

"Grab a sword first, Seg!" I yelled.

"Had I my bow—" he yelled back.

I sprinted forward along the gangway, hurdling various bodies, until I could thrust through the back of the press. Hundreds of slaves were crowding forward, waving their chains, humming them about their heads in deadly arcs. But many were going down as the swifter archers shot with flat trajectories, rapidly and professionally.

The struggle for me to reach the front ranks was severe; but in a few moments I pushed aside the body of a slave who, swinging his chains, had been thrust through the belly by a long sword. I stepped out, the long sword held in the fighting grip of the Korzairs of Zy.

Blades crossed. An arrow brushed through my hair. I kept on the move. The long sword was a fine weapon despite its bone grip and I felt it slog crushingly into the rib cage of the first Magdaggian, biting through the mesh. He fell away. There was another, whose face above the ventail I smashed in. More arrows were fleeting past—then I realized some were going the other way. An overlord before me abruptly threw his hands in the air, dropping his sword. An arrow stood out from his right eye.

Seg Segutorio had found himself a weapon he knew how to use and was in action.

Now the sheer mass of slaves told. Perhaps there were as many as three hundred men of Magdag aboard: overlords, overlords of the second class, soldiers, and crew. Of them all the captain of the swifter seemed alone to be alive as I reached the entrance ramp onto the lower beak. The scene was fantastic. The whole upperworks of the swifter were crowded with the naked bodies of slaves, all howling and screeching like—no, not like, they were—demented souls.

I knew what emotions they were experiencing.

The long extended beak of the swifter hung over the water-slopping deck of the merchantman. She had had two masts, their stumps now jagged tangles among the raffle of wreckage, so she was a fair-sized craft. Her forecastle—it was that, proper, and not a fo'c'sle—had been badly battered by the swifter's varters. These were mounted somewhat higher in the bows of the galley than I considered proper, and had been rigged to hurl stones, as was fit in the circumstances. The merchantman's sterncastle, an imposing edifice of two decks, was cluttered by the raffle fallen from the mainmast. Bodies lay everywhere.

The swifter captain glared up at me. He was a big man, his mail bulging, his long sword a weapon of exceptional size. Around him among the circle of slain slaves lay sprawled other men in mail and half-mail, mercenary marines carried by the merchantman.

"Hail!" he called up.

He waved his sword in a gesture that plainly said: "Come down here where I can chop you."

He knew that against all those enraged slaves he had no chance of survival.

He was of Magdag—yet he was a brave man. Even then, when I was young and bore a hatred for the green burning in my breast, I recognized a man's courage.

I leaped down to him.

With only a breechclout to cover my nakedness I fought at a disadvantage against his mail. But also, against his knowledge that he was doomed and his desperate determination to make a fight of it and die well, I could put my skill and my own determination, the red against the green.

Our blades crossed once, and I felt the strength in his arm.

The broad ship lurched beneath our feet as water gushed in.

"You will die, slave, and join your fellows here!"

I did not answer. Again the blades crossed and I swung on the disengage, but he was quick even on that cumbered deck and avoided my blow. He bore down on me, anxious to kill me and take as many as he could with him to the ice floes of Sicce.

A slave shouted from the deck, high and exultant.

"Jikai! Chop him, Pur Dray, my Lord of Strombor, Krozair!"

The swifter captain's blade faltered. He drew back. On his face grew such a look of fury and despair as sickened me to see.

"You—" he choked. "You are the Lord of Strombor— Krozair!"

Without bothering to reply—for I felt the broad ship's sluggish wallowing movements and knew she would go down any instant—I leaped forward. And now our blades clanged and rang with that ferocious screech of steel blade on steel blade. He was good and he was strong but I was in a hurry now and in a quick passage of murderous blows he fell.

Someone shouted: "The ship's going!"

And amid the tumultuous shouts of the freed slaves as they saw the hated Magdag overlord dead at their feet I leaped nimbly up onto the swifter's beak. A florid but sea-bitten man rushed forward, his slashed blue finery proclaiming him the captain of the merchantman.

Seg was there and with the help of slaves who seemed to carry some authority among their fellows a space was cleared. The merchant skipper grasped my left hand, babbling his thanks. His ship had gone, but his life was safe. Overside now the broad ship wallowed deeper, and thrashing around her and waiting for their grisly harvest the chanks with their twin stiff upright fins, the sharks of the inner sea, patrolled hungrily.

"May Ta'temsk shine upon you, my Lord of Strombor!" He let my hand go as I began to strip away the bloodied brown rag from my loins. "We fought as well as we could, but the rashoon dismasted us. My crew fought like demons, as you can see—even my passengers fought—ah, how they fought—"

"Passengers?" I had found a length of red cloth wound about the body of a dead man—evidently one of the passengers the merchant skipper was speaking of—and I wrapped it around my waist and drew the end up between my legs and tucked it in. The brave scarlet color cheered me.

"Yes—a strange lot. The man fought like men possessed. Look, Pur Dray—there is one now, dying, and yet still he thinks he fights."

Hauled out of the way beneath a varter a man lay dying. What the skipper said was true, for he kept opening his arms wide and closing them again in the rapier and main-gauche drill known as the "flower" although his right hand was empty. He wore long black boots and a snug-waisted brown coat which flared wide over his hips and up to his shoulders. He wore no hat, but I could guess what sort of hat he would own. In his left hand he carried a bejeweled main-gauche with which he kept up his laborious flow of passages at arms.

I knelt by his side.

"You were with Vomanus?" I said. I spoke as gently as I might, but my words cracked harsh and impatiently for all that.

"Vallians," said the merchant skipper. "A strange lot."

"Sterncastle," gasped the dying man. Blood dribbled from his mouth. I looked up at the broad ship's captain.

"Alas, my Lord of Strombor. The men of Vallia were insistent that every care should be taken of the passengers and so on my orders they were shut up in the sterncastle, for safe-keeping. But the fall of the mainmast, and the ferocity of the attack—we could not get them out. I fear they are doomed."

I was puzzled. Granted that Vomanus had shipped aboard this vessel now sinking into a chank-infested sea, I couldn't understand my not seeing him. He would never be shut up in a safe place when there was a fight brewing.

The Vallian was young, handsome, with a long brown moustache and neatly trimmed beard. He tried to speak, spat blood, tried again, managed to blurt out: "They must be saved!"

"There is no saving them now," said the captain, with a grim nod at the decks of his ship about to submerge beneath the water and the twin fins of the chanks circling nearer. "My old ship is taking them to their grave, may Ta'temsk smile on them."

The dying Vallian opened his eyes and there was reason in them. He had stopped his ghastly phantom swordplay. I took the dagger from him, gently, respectfully. Blood gushed from his mouth as he burst into an impassioned and mortal shout.

"You must save her! She is trapped, drowning, doomed—you must! The Princess Majestrix of Vallia! Princess—"

The blood choked him. I felt—I thought—I—

Delia! My Delia! *Delia!*

Chapter Six

Delia of Delphond and I swim together

I have no memory until I stood before the doors to the broad ship's aftercastle with its hideous tangle of wreckage blocking them off, tearing at them with my bare hands, the dagger naked in my clenched teeth.

It was all a long time ago and four hundred light-years distant, a drama played out on a distant sea beneath the lurid fires of the twin suns of Antares; and yet—and yet!

Water slopped about my thighs, pouring in an ever-thickening flood over the gunwales. I heaved timber aside, used the keen dagger edge to slash through water-soaked ropes. I reached the door and now I became aware of the yells and shouts from the swifter.

"It is too late!" "Come back!" "You will be drowned!" and— "My Lord—the chanks!"

I ignored the jabbering.

A stubborn balk impeded me and I put my shoulders to it—those shoulders that had been the despair of my ever-sewing mother—and heaved up until the blood seemed to compress all my brains and threatened to burst from my eyes and nostrils. My muscles rippled and bunched and I heaved—how I heaved!

With an abrupt screech the balk slid aside and I lurched forward into the doors. I used that lurch—there was no time to draw back—and smashed solidly into them. I heard metal snap. Water roiled around my waist now and I felt the ship wallowing and lurching like a drunk staggering from The Fleeced Ponsho in Sanurkazz.

I kicked the doors in and a frenzied woman was in my arms, all dark hair about my face like damp laundry, and softness against my naked chest, and a screaming mouth and fiercely clawing fingers.

A voice yelled in my ear.

"Pass her back!"

58

"Here, Seg."

I knew it was him, and there was no time for my gratitude. He was no seaman, he could probably swim with a dog-crawl; he was risking more than I here, on the deck of this sinking ship.

I plunged into the cabin.

The whole ship shuddered and the ominous roar of thousands of gallons of water suddenly victorious pouring into her told me she was gone. Water smashed me forward and I swirled around in the sudden green gloom.

With the dagger between my teeth again I held my breath. And then—

Delia! My Delia of the Blue Mountains, my Delia of Delphond was once more in my arms and I held her dear form to me in that water-choked cabin of a sinking ship. I felt her waist as lissome and as lithe as I remembered, and I swung around and struck out for the door. Timber and cordage and canvas floated like octopuses with groping tendrils, seeking to ensnare us and drag us back. But we pushed through the door and the gloom decreased. Light struck down from above. I kicked with a savage exultant fierceness and we rose upward.

I could see the whole extent of the deck of the broad ship with only a few bubbles bursting from her shattered hatches and all the miserable aftermath of the battle. And, among those twisted shapes of corpses, hunting like ghouls, the long sinuous shapes of the chanks nosed in from all sides.

We broke surface.

The swifter's proembolion had nudged off the sinking merchantman. She moved now some distance away. Nearer to us swam the little muldavy in which Seg and I had escaped from Happapat. We had to reach that before the chanks reached us.

I looked down.

Too late. . . . The chank was already here, was nosing up with that characteristic shark-like belly roll to expose all his corpse-white underbelly. I thrust Delia away from me, took the dagger into my right hand.

"Swim for the boat, Delia! *Swim!*"

The breath I drew in scorched my lungs. I dived. The chank saw me coming and half rolled. I went with him. I would not grasp his pseudo-scaled skin for those scales would lacerate my own human flesh like rasps.

As he rolled so I rolled with him and flicked aside so that his gape-jawed attack sliced water. As he went past I thrust the dagger in as hard and as fast as I could. Blood poured out to roil in a thick cloud-like mass in the water. He went on and slowly began to roll, his tail seesawing. A quick look around showed me no more ominous shapes immediately in my vicinity and I kicked hard after Delia.

The water was limpid clear, with the surface, the exotic silver sky, all rippled and chiaroscuro-shot with color.

I caught Delia around the waist and heaved her up into the muldavy.

I had to be sure.

I ducked down and, sure enough, another chank was circling in. He would razor off my legs before I could scramble into the boat. As I went under again I headed straight for him. He moved aside, those immense jaws gaping, then straightened and headed for me, trying to roll sideways at me. Chanks only need to roll over to seize their prey when it is above them on the surface. Otherwise they are quite capable of gulping a man down from any position.

I went with him, then scissored my legs in a franctic explosion of energy, scythed around his thrusting snout, and buried the dagger six times into his belly. Blood streamed out like a wake. He went on, turning slowly, and I glared up against the radiance. The curved wedge-shape of the muldavy's bottom showed like a balloon against that silver sky, water-rippled. I shot up stiff-legged, burst from the water, hooked an arm over the gunwale, and hauled. I could feel the expected snap of gigantic chank jaws and expected to pull a legless torso aboard.

When my feet hit the bottom boards the jolt came as a reassuring bolt. I was light-headed, for I would not have attempted to leave the water had I anticipated the chank could return to the attack before I could clear the surface.

The muldavy bounced.

The chank—or another—had returned and was trying to overset us.

I saw Delia standing up, lithe and lovely in a blue short skirt and tunic, hefting the water breaker up over her head. She tensed and then, *whoosh*—down went the water breaker over the side to bash the chank on the snout. With a flick of his tail he took himself off.

She stood there above me, gazing down, her water-soaked garments shining and clinging, and she smiled—she smiled!

"Dray!"

We were in each other's arms, then, and if the muldavy had rolled over spilling us into the chank-swarming sea I do not believe we would have noticed.

When we returned to a semblance of sanity a hail reached

us and I saw the swifter turning and moving gently down on us, twenty or thirty oars clumsily splashing. Seg shouted again.

"You are all right?"

I waved and shouted something.

"Thank the veiled Froyvil for that, then!"

"Thelda!" Delia said suddenly, her sweet face changing expression to one of concerned alarm.

"If that is the buxom hell-cat who near scratched my eyes out back there in the cabin," I said, "friend Seg took her off me. Thank the Black Chunkrah," I added, lapsing into a blasphemy of my Clansmen.

"I am glad," Delia said. "For Thelda means well." And she laughed in that old thrilling spine-tingling way. How incomparable a woman is my Delia of the Blue Mountains!

The muldavy was hoisted aboard the swifter. Thelda rushed to Delia and gathered her in her arms, cooing and sighing and sobbing. Thelda's hair, already drying in the sunlight, was a darker, deeper brown than Delia's without those glorious auburn highlights. She tended to plumpness—I would not go so far as to say fatness—and she bubbled with eagerness. She was all over Delia. Her ripe red lips smiled easily. I saw Seg giving her his undivided attention, and sighed, for I foresaw only problems for him there. In that, as you will hear, I sadly underestimated the whole truth.

Somewhat on the stocky side was Thelda, but she was built magnificently, with thick ankles somewhat detracting from her attempts at languorous beauty when she remembered to forget her eagerness. I cannot be too cruel to Thelda, for Delia clearly suffered her with a good heart.

The first order was obtained. With so many men aboard unchained I had thoughts of mass rape; but the knowledge that I was Pur Dray, the Lord of Strombor, a famed and feared Krozair of Zy, corsair of the Eye of the World, had impressed the ex-slaves. Very willingly they agreed to return to their oar benches, this time as free men, and pull fo Sanurkazz. I took hands with many of them, and was not surprised to feel that secret sign of the Krozair from many of them. Also there were men of The Red Brethren of Lizz, and others from the Krozairs of Zamu—famous fighting Orders of Chivalry dedicated to Zair. But none, as I had known even before I was one, as strict, as famous, as notorious where it mattered as the Krozairs of Zy.

One of the ex-slaves who had given me the secret sign, a man of superlative musculature, as must any man possess if he is to survive at the oar, a massive black beard and a head of that curly black Sanurkazzian hair, gripped my hand and said: "You do not recognize me, Pur Dray?"

I studied him closely. Seg was taking care of the girls as I sorted out the swifter. I shook my head, then halted that instinctive negative.

"By Zim-Zair! Pur Mazak! Pur Mazak, Lord of Frentozz!" We clasped hands again.

"We shared a raid against Goforeng, you and I, Pur Dray. You with your *Zorg* and I with my *Heart of Zair*. You recall?"

"Can I forget! We took—what was it?—twelve broad ships and dispatched three large swifters into the bargain! Great days, Pur Mazak."

"Aye, great days."

"Well. They will come again for you." I had made a decision. We must pull for Sanurkazz. Now I had Delia with me again we might spend a little time on the inner sea, for there were things still to be done there.

But as soon as we settled down on our course, south with a heading of west in it, that damnable gale got up, the sea rose, lightnings and thunders raged and roared. I shouted to the helm-deldars—men from the slave benches who had been rudder-deldars before their capture—to ease off and head east. As miraculously as it had arisen, the gale, which was not a rashoon, died away.

"Pattelonia," I said to Delia, and I saw her face light up. Arrangements were speedily made.

Clearly, the Star Lords wanted me out of the inner sea. Well, that suited me well enough. I felt sincere regret that I would not again see—for how long I knew not—my two oar comrades and rascals, Nath and Zolta, or Pur Zenkiren, or dear Mayfwy—I had wanted muchly for Delia and Mayfwy to meet, for I could not express adequately the thanks I owed Mayfwy, widow of my oar comrade and friend Pur Zorg.

As for Delia, she had loyally agreed to accompany me to Sanurkazz, but there was no denying her joy that we were to go directly to Pattelonia and from thence to Vallia. There was no problem over who would command the swifter we had captured—her name was *Sword of Genodras*—and I clasped hands again with Pur Mazak and entrusted him with the ship.

"She is a fine vessel, even if the apostis is a trifle bulky for my taste," I said. "I would be inclined to pack a few more benches in along the upper deck—but that is of another time." Mazak looked at me with the calm firm gaze of a true brother in Zy, and I knew the prize was in good hands. I gave him instructions that should the king, Zo, allow, *Sword of Genodras* should be bought into the service under the aegis of Felteraz, for I owed Mayfwy much. "At any rate," I said. "My shares go to the Lady Mayfwy of Felteraz. You will speak with my agent, Shallan, who is as honest a rogue as any agent can ever be. And now, Zair go with you, Pur Mazak."

"Remberee!" The shouts came across the water as the swifter gathered way. Delia, Thelda, Seg, and I watched from the muldavy which had been hoisted over the side and fully provisioned and watered. "Remberee!" and "Remberee!"

From the mass of booty and other materials in the aft cabins I had selected a number of fine Sanurkazzian long swords. Also I had fine silks from Pandahem, and leather of Sanurkazz, cloaks woven from the finest curly ponsho wool from Wloclef and, to prove how villainous a character I am, there was also a strong leather purse bulging with silver and golden oars of Magdag, as well as the varied currency of the southern shore. Seg had also helped himself, and in particular had taken a full score of the small bows. He grumbled about them, their puniness, with which I fully agreed. Nonetheless, I felt safer—if I may admit to such a feeling, for Delia was now in my safekeeping—with the archer from Erthyrdrin aboard.

As we hoisted the dipping lug and set sail for Pattelonia, I was able to hear Delia's story. Characteristically, she remained silent about the parts I could guess had given her the most problems.

Vomanus, whom I had sent with a reassuring message to Vallia, had told his princess and then had been sent off on some errand or other by Delia's father, the emperor. Instead of Vomanus returning with an airboat for me, he was traveling in the opposite direction, toward Segesthes, and nothing was done about me. I fully understood about that, for I knew a little of the fierce opposition aroused in Vallian political circles by the Princess Majestrix's decision to marry an unknown near-barbarian Clansman, for all he styled himself the Lord of Strombor. So—Delia had immediately set about flying herself. With a few trusted companions of her personal guard, and with her lady companion, Thelda, she took off. There had been no trouble at Pattelonia after the long flight across the fearsome mountain ranges collectively entitled The Stratemsk that walled off the inner sea from eastern Turismond. The broad ship had been sailing, and Delia had taken passage, intending to transfer subsequently and so find her way to Magdag. I shuddered to think what would have happened had she arrived at that wicked city and fallen into the hands of the Princess Susheeng, or those of her evil brother, Glycas; for I was growing more and more convinced as I pondered the matter that the Star Lords had ensured my old vosk-skulls would not overcome in their revolt.

A keen sorrow for her slain guards made Delia need the comfort I could give her in my rough way.

"But, Dray—you are safe! I sometimes feel what a monster I am when I consider that I really cannot regret anyone's death if it helps you—my poor lads died in vain, but you are alive!"

She was no monster. I knew without a trace of remorse that I would wade through seas of blood if necessary so that not one hair of my Delia's head should be harmed. Kregen is a world of violence and ugliness as well as a wonderful world of vivid life and beauty and love.

Condemn me as you will. I know where my loyalties lie.

Thelda made a great fuss of me. She fussed and fussed, until I felt stultified, and poor Seg, who was getting absolutely nowhere with the buxom girl, glowered and took himself off to the foresheets to fiddle with his little bows.

Delia laughed and joyed in my discomfort, whereat I longed to take her in my arms and show her just who it was I required attentions from. As it was, we made a somewhat strange little party sailing across the eastern end of the Eye of the World to the Proconian shore and the city of Pattelonia.

We reached the island city without incident and I felt a great leap of joy as I saw the multitudes of red flags floating above the ramparts and the towers and the long seawalls. So Sanurkazz still held the city—we sailed in feeling in very much of a holiday mood.

Chapter Seven

Thelda cuts hair and
Seg cuts a bow-stave

Thelda it was who insisted on trimming my shaggy mop of hair, my long fierce moustache and my beard before we entered harbor. My hair was normally worn quite straight and almost to my shoulders. My moustache is of that kind that juts most arrogantly upward—sometimes I despair of its unruly nature—and my beard of that trimmed and pointed kind associated with cavaliers, lace, and rapiers. As a sea officer of wooden ships on Earth in the last days of the eighteenth century I had of course been clean-shaven; very often I reverted to shaving, but I had vowed never to return to wearing the queue.

The custom of growing a great long mass of hair so that it may be twisted up and worn as padding and protection beneath a helmet is a survival of primitive times in the evolution of ever-more sophisticated armor. I prefer a properly padded helmet—or basinet, sallet or, perhaps a favorite with me, a burgonet—and neatly trimmed hair.

All the time Thelda whickered the long dagger about my head and clumps of my brown hair tumbled onto the bottom boards, Seg sat glowering on a thwart. Fighting-men require haircuts as do other people. Merely to rely on a band around the head can be fatal in battle when a shrewd stroke can split the band to release a mop of thick uncut hair to shroud the face and obscure vision; you may wake up in some celestial barbershop in the sky with the blood still oozing from the wound your foeman's steel snickered in when you were brushing the hair from your eyes.

Delia caught my eye. She was lolling back with the steering oar tucked neatly into its notch and held in her small capable hands. She was laughing at me without moving a muscle of her gorgeous face! She was thoroughly enjoying my discomfiture as I sat shifting on the thwart, muttering and mumbling, wincing as the dagger sliced perilously close past my ear. I

"Delia was lolling back with the steering oar and laughing at me silently."

glared back at her and made a face whereat she burst into a peal of laughter that would have turned them all out of heaven to listen.

"It was sweet of Thelda to think of your hair, was it not, Dray Prescot?"

"Huh," I said, and then added, quickly: "Of course. Yes. Thank you, Thelda."

She lowered her eyes and a flush stained her cheeks.

I had to finish this somehow.

"And now it is Seg's turn—"

But Seg said: "I am happy as I am, shaggy as a thyrrix."

Delia chuckled with delight. She had seen me before when I myself was as disreputable as any mountain thyrrix, that grundal-nimble animal of the mountains of Seg's home, and I knew so long as I was all in one piece that was enough; she would take me as I was.

"For the man who wants to marry the Princess Majestrix," said Thelda, her habitual pushing eagerness evident, "you must take more pride in your appearance, Dray Prescot."

The mole drew closer as we approached and I could see the usual waterfront activity. The pharos here stood a good hundred feet less in height than the one at Sanurkazz. Nonetheless the smoke that curled from its summit by day and the light by night could be seen well out to sea. Whoever was in command here then, whether Proconian or Sanurkazzian, must feel confident. The overlords of Magdag must have been pushed back, they and their Proconian allies defeated, at least temporarily. Interference in an internecine war is never pleasant; and in the usual way Sanurkazz left Proconia strictly alone in the interminable feuds they waged; but once the green of Genodras had made its loathsome appearance the red of Zair must reply.

When we touched the jetty I was first out of the boat.

This was habitual; this was a mistake—I heard Thelda gasp and then I had turned and leaning down seized Delia under the armpits and swung her high into the air before setting her feet on the stones.

"There!" I said, to cover my lapse. "I may not look the part as the future consort to the Princess Majestrix of Vallia, but I do know how to help a lady from a boat."

Delia knew, of course, and she laughed back at me, and leaned close so that all her intoxicating scent wafted into my nostrils, dizzying me, and whispered close to my ear: "Poor Thelda—you mustn't mind her, dear heart—she means well."

We made the necessary calls on the port authorities, and were cleared for entry, for the peoples of the inner sea are more than somewhat lax over quarantine regulations. And the ideas of customs and excise which they employ are either barbaric—if you are on the paying end—or remarkably mild —if you are trying to build the seawalls of your city. We were rapidly able to walk up to the hostelry from which Delia, Thelda, and her young men had started off. Everywhere mixed up with the Pattelonian soldiery were the armed and armored men of Sanurkazz, fraternizing with them, laughing, arms draped over shoulders, engaging in friendly drinking bouts at the taverns, chasing wenches in the customary tactful way of the men from the southern shore. Evidently, a battle had recently been successfully fought and won.

A messenger arrived at the hostelry as I was downing a blackjack of Chremson wine—a vintage I had found as much to my taste as the superlative Zond wine so favored by Nath.

The messenger brought news that came as a staggering surprise and a most joyful reunion.

Four sectrixes had been provided, richly harnessed, and the messenger led us up through the terraced avenues of the city, wending past palace and villa, workshop and store, until we reached the lofty eminence of the governor's palace. Away on a neighboring hill, distinct in the limpid air, the palace of the Pattelonion ruler showed a multitude of Proconian flags. Where we stood the air seemed filled with the red banners of Zair.

From this height we could see around the curve of the island to the mainland side and there harsh black scars in the blocks of white houses showed where the city had burned. The struggle to take and retake Pattelonia had been severe, I could see easily enough. Also from here we could see the naval harbor with its placid waters disturbed by the passage of swifters, in and out. The long galleys lay ranked alongside the jetties and the columns of men carrying stores out to them wended like armies of warrior ants from the African jungles.

I recognized some of the swifters down there. But I could not wait now to count them and to check their condition and to remember. I heard a firm tread on the flagstones, and swung around, my hand outstretched in greeting.

"Lahal, Pur Dray!"

"Lahal, Pur Zenkiren!"

Our hands met and clasped in the firm grip of friendship and brotherhood in Zy.

He looked just the same, Zenkiren of Sanurkazz, tall and limber, with that bronzed fearless face, that fiercely up-brushed black moustache below his carved beak of a nose, that shining mass of curled black hair. On his white tunic above the apron the coruscating device of the hubless spoke wheel within the circle, embroidered in silks of blue and orange and yellow, blazed into my eyes. He smiled with warm affection upon me and I leaped in my heart to see him again, and although I did not smile the pressure of my hand told him of my joy in seeing him. He knew me—or that me who had fought as a Krozair and a swifter captain on the Eye of the World—did Pur Zenkiren, Krozair of Zy, admiral in the king's fleet, Grand Archbold elect of the Krozairs of Zy.

Introductions were made, and I noticed the courtly way in which Zenkiren treated my Delia. He did not miss our own heightened emotions, so that when I asked him of Mayfwy he replied she was well, that her son and daughter prospered, that she remained still a widow, not remarried, and that she missed seeing me. Nath and Zolta I heard, to my disappointment, had gone a-roving aboard a swifter into the western end of the inner sea. I would not achieve this joyful reunion with those two rogues here, then.

Seg, who I felt with an uncomfortable start of guilt, must have been feeling a little left out in all this handshaking and greetings, said: "Mayhap you will see them on your way through the Grand Canal and past the Dam of Days."

I looked at him, bemused for a moment. Then Delia nudged me and I managed to reply something and went on to tell Zenkiren of all that had happened to me since we had said "Remberee" in Sanurkazz. We went into the palace and were served wine and we helped ourselves to a heaping pile of palines from a silver dish. Time passed most pleasantly. I urged Zenkiren that now was the time to strike at Magdag. He agreed, and immediately sent off messages to the king, Zo, in Sanurkazz.

"My duty lies here, Dray, to help our Pattelonian allies against their foes and the devils from Magdag. I urge you, Pur Dray, now you have found your Delia of the Blue Mountains, to remain here. There is much to be done. We are pushing them back. Our army has gained success after success. Soon the call we all long for will go out, and all the men of Zair will rise and go up against the evil of Grodno."

"Greatly would I desire to do that, Zenkiren. But—"

The twin suns were slipping into the sea, far away across the western horizon. I persuaded Zenkiren to order a fleet liburna out. As we stood on the poop—she had no quarter-deck—and watched the single banks of oars, three men to an oar, pulling in that metronomic rhythm inseparable from the ideal of the swifter, I waited with apprehension.

That apprehension was for what I hoped would not occur.
But it did.

The wind roared, the sea got up, the thunders and the
lightnings cracked and fizzled about us. We turned for the
harbor and the gale dropped.

"I do not care to inquire too closely into these things,"
said Zenkiren, with a gravity habitual to him in weighty
affairs. "No doubt Pur Zazz could fathom the meaning. But I
take your point. You are fated to travel east—away over The
Stratemsk, over the Hostile Territories. I wish you well,
Brother, for the way is difficult, Zair knows."

"Pur Zazz has told me of many marvels and wonders in the
Hostile Territories. I am happy to know the Grand Archbold
still lives."

"Zair has him in his keeping, Dray. I pray he will live until
my work here is accomplished."

I knew what he meant.

"When you are Grand Archbold, Zenkiren, and the call
comes for all the Krozairs of Zy to answer—I will not fail."

He inclined his head in acknowledgment. But he was a sad
man that I could not go with him on this last expedition
against the forces of Magdag arrayed against us in the eastern
end of the Eye of the World.

I believe that Delia took an opportunity to speak privately
to Zenkiren, and can guess at some of the many questions she
asked about my life on the inner sea, and that she asked about
Mayfwy, too; I am glad that when we two spoke of these
things together we could be absolutely frank with each other.
Mayfwy, the widow of my friend Zorg of Felteraz, was a
wonderful person and a glorious girl; but there can only ever
be one woman in my life—my Delia, my Delia of Delphond!

Still and all, I gave Zenkiren the charge of making sure
that my agent Shallan got the best price for the prize swifter
Sword of Genodras and that all my shares should be paid to
Mayfwy.

"After all, young Zorg will be growing up soon, and he
must command the finest swifter that can be provided," I
said. My old oar comrade Zorg—I would not let his widow
or his son or daughter suffer if any way lay open to me to
prevent it. I knew my two rascals, Nath and Zolta, felt
exactly the same way.

During the short time we spent at Pattelonia, in a sense
getting our wind for the next stage of our journey to Vallia,
Seg kept much to himself. He was still trying his best to win
some sign of recognition from Thelda, but she persisted in

her fussing smothering of me, much to my annoyance and Delia's hidden and mocking amusement.

Seg came in one day bearing a monstrous stave of wood of so dark a green as to appear black. He flicked it about, speaking slightingly of it, but he was pleased.

"This is not true Yerthyr wood," he said. "The Yerthyr tree is deadly poisonous to the weak animals hereabouts, and the people do not like to grow it. In Erthyrdrin our nimble thyrrixes are able to digest the wood and bark and the leaves in their second stomach."

"So?"

"This stave will make a passable bow-stave after I have dealt with it." He ran his thumb along it, feeling. "But had I my own longbow—ah, then, Dray Prescot, you would see!"

A commotion broke out at the door, for we had by Zenkiren's kind invitation removed from the hostelry and quartered ourselves in commodious suites in the governor's palace. A Sanurkazzian guard—a young lad in a new hauberk and with a shiny new long sword, a parting present from his father—jumped back as a voluble, gesticulating, furiously angry Proconian popped in. Orange and green sunshine lay in slanting stripes on the patio outside the doors, and exotic blooms depended on vines from the white walls.

"Vandals! Pirates! Thieves!" the Proconian spluttered. He was plump, flabby, with ringed hands and a nose which wine had coarsened into a knob, and he wore no sword. His robes were twisted about him in the fury of his movements.

"I am sorry, Pur Dray," said the guard. "He insisted—and short of cutting him down there was no way of stopping him. . . ."

"It is all right, Fazmarl," I said, turning away from Seg and his bow-stave. "Let the gentleman in."

The gentleman shook a fist under my nose, saw Seg and let out a screech. "There he is, the plunderer, the reaver, the barbarian! He holds my property, Pur Dray—and he has destroyed the finest tree in the women's quarters—"

"Oh-ho!" I said. I looked at Seg. He gripped the stave with the clutch of a man sliding over the side of an airboat.

"I did but cut the best stave suited to a bow."

The little man danced and spluttered and shook his fist.

"Only! And ripped it out of the heart—the very heart—of the tree that gives shade to my favorite wife—"

The Proconians believed in the quaint habit of marrying three wives. They were a punishment-loving race.

"Is the tree mortally wounded, sir?"

"Mortally! It has suffered a wound from which nothing can save it. My tree—my favorite wife's favorite tree!"

"Then, if nothing can be done to save the tree, I think it best to uproot it and plant another."

He gobbled over that, and wiped his forehead, and found a chair and collapsed into it. I nodded at Seg and that reckless man had sense enough to fill to brimming a silver-chased goblet with noble Chremson wine and hurry it across. The Proconian wiped his lips and gulped the wine, and gasped and palpitated, a hand to his heart, and gulped some more.

"Very good," he said, looking at the wine afresh. "Booty from Chremson, I take it?"

I inclined my head, but the word booty had inflamed him anew. "Plunderers, reavers—that is all you red-raiders from Sanurkazz are! You tear down my best tree, leave it in shattered fragments across my tessellated pavement so that my second wife barks her pretty shin and removes at least a palm of skin—"

"Come, sir," I said, putting the merest fraction of that rasp into my voice. "You have not yet favored me with your name. I do not know it was your tree. You could be fabricating the entire story to gain my sympathy—and my wine!"

He staggered upright with the assistance of the chair back. He tried to speak and his fat lips popped and blew and his cheeks turned purple and his eyes stood out. Then: "By the fair hair of the Primate Proc himself! I am Uppippoo of Lower Pattelonia! I am respected in this city, with wide lands on the mainland beyond Perithia, owner of ten broad ships, and with three of the most delectable wives a man could boast—and now they have kicked me out because their shaded garden has been ruined!"

Seg couldn't hold himself in and spilled wine trying to stop from bursting a gut laughing. I remained severe.

"Very well, Uppippoo of Lower Pattelonia. I would not wish a man to suffer, particularly from three wives. Rest assured, I shall make complete restitution." A thought occurred to me. "Can another tree be procured?"

A kind of frenzy possessed Uppippoo. "You imbecile! Those trees take a hundred years to grow!"

That was half a lifetime or so on Kregen.

"In that case, my friend here, who comes from Erthyrdrin, will be returning to his country shortly. I know he will immediately take steps to have a fresh tree prepared and shipped out to you. There, sir, what can be fairer than that?"

Uppippoo merely goggled at us.

"In the meantime, if you would accept a little common

gold, which is nowhere as romantic as a tree, you could purchase a length of colorfully-striped awning, and thus protect your charming wives from the suns."

And I put down carefully onto a table a handful of gold scooped out of my waist-belt—for I had now, in the city, perforce to dress as a citizen with tunic, apron, and accouterments.

Uppippoo looked at the gold.

"An—awning?"

"Why—yes."

"An awning." He considered. "But a tree is alive, it looks beautiful, it soughs in the wind and its leaves create the most delightful patterns of shade and light upon my pavements—and the tesselae are renowned in Pattelonia, Pur Dray, renowned."

"Quite so. Take the gold. Buy an awning or buy a new tree of a different kind. But, Uppippoo, I would wish you to leave now. Do you understand me? The gold is fair payment, I think."

Uppippoo for the first time took care to look at me, instead of raging and roaring and blow-harding and glaring at Seg and the offending dismembered limb of his wife's tree. He saw my face. I was not conscious of any change in my countenance, but Uppippoo's snorts and ragings and breathy threats halted as though he had been gripped by the throat.

He backed a step. He bent his back, stealthily, reaching forward to take the gold from the table. He backed away. His protruding eyes were fixed on my face; his tongue kept licking his fat lips.

"Fazmarl!" I called. "The gentleman is leaving now."

The young guard showed the Proconian gentleman out.

He had not uttered a word since he'd had a fair sight of my ugly face.

Seg collapsed moaning onto a chair.

"As for you, Seg Segutorio, you should be ashamed of yourself. Cutting a stick from a tree—that's what kids do."

"Aye!" he roared joyously. "Just as I did when I cut my stave from Kak Kakutorio's tree! Hai—I could hurt myself laughing."

I must admit that I felt like allowing myself a laugh, also.

The incident of Seg's bow-stave and the shade tree of Uppippoo's wives convinced me that I had no need to worry so much about Seg Segutorio. He was still in form despite his conspicuous lack of success with Thelda.

Delia was anxious to leave, and now that I could not serve a useful part in the campaign I had nothing to tie me here. I told Seg, somewhat brutally, I fear, that he would have no time to put his new bow-stave into pickle. He chuckled with a grim sardonic humor that made me stare at him.

"You have a poor opinion of the bowmen of Erthyrdrin if you believe they are unable to fashion a bow-stave anywhere on this earth—aye, and pickle it, too. Put me thigh-deep in the mire of the Marshes of Malar with a stave and I'll fashion you a bow that can split the chunkrah's eye." He was as good as his word. He contrived a tall narrow tube of treated leather, well-stoppered, and into this with his precious stave he poured a concoction of his own—that stank to Zim itself —and shook it up and glared at me with a satisfied defiant stare on his face.

"By the time we are past the Dam of Days she'll be pickled—"

Even then I couldn't tell Seg just how we were traveling to Vallia, and there was no reason for this holding back. Delia knew exactly where the flier from Port Tavetus, on the eastern coast of Turismond beyond the Hostile Territories, had been hidden in the foothills which gloamed blue and orange and purple on the far mainland horizon. The people of Havilfar, where airboats are manufactured, did not care to have their products exposed on the inner sea. I gathered the airboats gave trouble, too, as I had before experienced. Thelda cooed over me and ignored Seg and so we passed the last days before we took off. Again it was time to say "Remberee" to Pur Zenkiren.

Everything that should be done was done. Our belongings were carefully packed into satchels and leather sacks, for Delia with a strict flier's wisdom wanted no sharp-edged packing crates aboard, and were stowed aboard the calsanys that would take them down to the jetty. I detected a strange look of sadness on the face of young Fazmarl as I bid him good-bye. I clapped him on the back—a somewhat awesome experience for so young a would-be warrior of Sanurkazz from a swifter captain and a Krozair—and felt I must be getting old and walked down with Zenkiren and Delia to the jetty. Thelda had gone with the baggage—riding a calsany— to superintend, although we all knew she didn't care over-much for walking. Seg marched behind with his revolting leather pipe of bow-stave-pickling over his shoulder.

At the jetty we all climbed down into the boat and this time we were not using our old stolen muldavy which I had made arrangements to have, when possible, returned to its owners with a suitable sum in gold to compensate for those we had smashed. We were using the admiral's barge, no

less, and twenty stalwart wights pulled lustily at the oars. As
we cleared the mole and the barge's head swung toward the
mainland, Seg looked back at me, sitting next to Delia. He
was puzzled.

"I do not see our ship, Dray. And, why are we heading for
the mainland?"

I realized he did not connect the storms that arose when
we steered west with our very act of heading on that course,
and I had not discussed that problem with him at all, as I had
merely hinted at it with Zenkiren. The mysticism of the
Krozairs of Zy armored Zenkiren against marvels of that kind.

But now the time had surely come when I must be honest
with Seg Segutorio and tell him of our means of travel.

I told him.

He gaped for a moment at me as the barge pulled through
the suns-lit water. Everyone was watching him.

"A flier," he said, at last, surprising me. "As to them, I
have seen them and I welcome the opportunity to fly in one.
But—"

"But, Seg?"

"The Stratemsk! The Hostile Territories! Man—do you
know what you're doing? They're murder."

Delia said: "We are going home to Vallia, and you, Seg,
to Erthyrdrin, if you wish. We would like you to be with us,
but if you do not come we understand." She added, mis-
chievously: "Anyway, that's the way Thelda and I got
here. . . ."

Chapter Eight

Through The Stratemsk

*"Ossa they would pile upon Olympos; and
upon Ossa, Pelion with its rustling forests, that
the very heavens might be scaled."*

This ambition of the Aloadai, Otos and Ephialtes, had always seemed to me a laudable goal, seeing that I myself had scrambled my way up through the hawsehole from the lower deck to the quarterdeck, and, since my startling arrival on Kregen beneath Antares, had fought my way to various arrogant-sounding posts and positions. But I had always thought of the tall twins' activities of ambition as rhetorical. The actual idea of mountains piled one atop another had always seemed to me figures of speech, devices of the imagination. I have seen the Himalaya—the other mountain ranges of the world are subsumed in the lofty and frightening grandeur of the Himalaya—and I had been suitably impressed and awed.

But The Stratemsk—Kabru piled on Nanda Devi upon Kangchenjunga upon Annapurna upon Nanga Parbat—with Chimborazo from the Andes thrown in as foothills—with K2 and Everest lofting beyond reason above— Yes, The Stratemsk, although not the loftiest or most extensive range of mountains on Kregen under the suns of Scorpio, are quite out of this world with the awe-inspiring terror and beauty of outraged nature flaunting her powers. The Stratemsk are big and wide and tall. They shatter reason. Snow mantles their upper slopes and pinnacles in an eternal and unbroken whiteness. The clouds hover around their feet. Savage and voracious animals haunt their lower ranges and gigantic birds and flying animals forever circle their valleys and passes with cruel talons and fangs seeking prey.

Above these mind-freezing precipices and crags and icy glaciers we flew, Delia, Seg, Thelda, and I, in our frail airboat through the cutting air.

We huddled close together warmly wrapped in flying silks and leathers, with immense furs wrapped about us.

The airboat was a mere shell of wood upon metal formers, shaped into the likeness of a petal and streamlined well enough with a windshield and leather thongs and wooden guard-rails. If it failed, as airboats notoriously failed, we were doomed. Below us lay certain death.

That death might come from cold and exposure. It might come from starvation or madness. It might come in the ravening jaws of some semimystical monster of the higher slopes where the tree line thinned and the screes stretched for miles before the snow line was reached in ice and penetrating cold.

Or—that death might come to us from the fangs and talons of any one of the many species of giant birds and animals who flew voraciously among the passes and valleys seeking what prey they might snatch. From their high aeries they could plummet down, their eyes sighted on a target so small at that distance only eyes superlatively endowed by nature could ever make out what manner of animal or beast it might be below them. We saw the ominous dots flying far off. I grasped my long sword hilt and determined that should anything or any monster attack us only my death would prevent me from protecting my Delia until none remained.

Coal-black impiters, corths, xi—the iridescent-scaled winged lizards of the humid jungle-valleys sunk in broad tracts within The Stratemsk—bisbis, zizils, the yellow eagles of Wyndhai, and many other monstrous flying beasts are to be found within the massive confines of The Stratemsk—or, to be practical about this matter, better not found.

For the first upward trending slopes before we rose high to seek the easiest of the passes opening out before us we flew over many crude encampments of the man-beasts who occupy the outer portions of The Stratemsk. There are many tribes, but they are referred to in general as crofermen, savage, untamed, cruel and suspicious, who delight in nothing so much as raiding down the outer slopes of The Stratemsk. It was their ponshos that the great winged beasts of the air would seize if given the chance. Life, indeed, was a hard and demanding existence within The Stratemsk.

So that with the sheer size and immensity of the mountains and the crofermen incessantly raiding and the monstrous winged beasts, The Stratemsk had provided a barrier between the Eye of the World and eastern Turismond that had endured for century after century.

And my Delia of the Blue Mountains had braved these

terrors and these dangers in order once more to clasp me in her arms!

No wonder the sailors of the outer oceans would sail all the weary way around by the Cyphren Sea past Donengil and up the skeleton coasts to enter the inner sea via the Dam of Days. For besides the dangers of The Stratemsk there lay ahead of us the unknown perils of the Hostile Territories.

We had safely negotiated the first passes and left the peaks on either hand and Delia had the control levers thrust full to maximum when she touched my arm and pointed.

"Look, Dray—"

The gorgeous scarlet and golden accipiter with those deadly talons extended flew above our heads, turning in lazy hunting circles. I knew it. Messenger or observer of the Star Lords, the Gdoinye croaked a harsh challenging call—either that, a challenge, or a farewell—and swung away. I did not think that any corth or zizil or other flying monster would seek to attack that blazing raptor of the Star Lords.

We waited out the flying time, eating and drinking sparingly as the dwaburs unreeled below us. The air remained thin and cold, for Delia would not dip down into the shrouded valleys for warmth for the iridescent shapes of the xi circled there, seeking their prey in the humid jungles beneath.

Gradually the high peaks passed away over our shoulders. Slowly the whole convulsed mass of The Stratemsk with its shining silver spears thrusting into dazzlement above dropped away behind us, but it would be days before those high peaks fell below the horizon. And slowly and gradually I came to thinking that we had successfuly surmounted—or threaded our way through—the first great obstacle.

And then the impiters struck.

They swooped in a wide-winged onslaught from a distant ledge, swirling about us in a monstrous beating of wings. They tried to pluck us from the sky. Massive talons extended like the claws of some Earthly power excavator. Raucous croakings of their fanged mouths from which the forked tongues emerged in a constant licking were designed to frighten us into frozen immobility. The airboat rocked. The impiters were wild and savage, but I protected Delia of Delphond and my wildness and savagery met and mastered theirs.

My long sword whirled, thick with blood. And Seg's arrows flew as fast as he could draw back the string and loose. In truth, he dispatched far more than did I, although I was forced to tackle those posing the greater threat as they sought to impale us with their whip-barbed tails or rend us with their claws or snatch us up in their gape-jaws.

Massive they were, the impiters, giants of the air, and yet they cavorted in the empty levels with the speed and agility of an Earthly falcon. My sword arm bunched with muscle and I struck and struck and still they came. Now the airboat faltered, it dipped, dropped, fell away.

"She won't respond!" shouted Delia.

Thelda was screaming away and impeding me in my work as she sought to throw herself into my arms. I knocked her back into the bottom of the airboat and yelled at Delia.

"Grab her, Delia! She'll have her head taken off if she sticks it out here!"

Arrows spurted from Seg's bow. My sword lopped and slashed. The impiters continued to attack as the airboat sank lower. There was no chance of my seeing where we were falling; every straining effort had to be bent on to picking the next flying beast, sensing his line of attack, guessing whether he would strike with his jaws or flick himself over to lash with that deadly barbed tail. I saw a tail strike into the wood of the rail, splintering it. The barbs did not hold; some muscular mechanism seemed to fold them in the instant the impiter knew it had missed its stroke. I hacked the tail off.

How long that insane aerial battle went on I do not know. Now my chest was crisscrossed by red welts where the barbed tails had struck, and blood—my blood—slicked down my belly and thighs. But I battled on. I could stand up and brace myself against the movement of the airboat. My long sea training gave me at least that advantage. But Seg, too, stuck to his task, loosing arrows as though from some fabled machine-crossbow of the ancient men of the sunrise.

Trees abruptly swooshed past and a branch almost accomplished what the impiters had failed to do. I ducked and just managed to get the long sword's swing to intersect neatly with an impiter's jaw. He screeched and spun away and then—suddenly, miraculously, enormously—we were surrounded by a vindictively smothering swarm of tiny pink and yellow bodies.

Tiny birds!

Thousands of them.

Tiny pink and yellow birds with shrill cheeping cries were hurling themselves at the massive impiters, were darting in to sink their long sharp beaks into tender spots, where wings met body, at the juncture of tail, into the glaring, bloodshot eyes. The impiters went mad.

I threw the long sword down—it had served me well but

all my arms-training could not prevent me from doing what
I had to do the quickest way I knew. I seized Delia and
thrust her hard under a heaping pile of silks and leathers.
I shouted.

"Seg! Cover yourself up—grab that idiot Thelda! Hurry!"

We cowered there, the four of us beneath silks and furs, as
we let a myriad tiny birds harass and torture the mighty
impiters into ignoble retreat. We could hear the sounds of
that strife clear across the broad valley into which we had
descended. The screechings and the shriekings persisted for
some time and then gradually faded and I was able to poke a
cautious head out from our cover to see the last of the flying
monsters circling aloft with heavy wingbeats as the tiny dots
of the little pink and yellow birds clustered thickly about.

Thelda was shaking all over and sobbing hysterically.

That was a normal reaction and I thought nothing of it.
Seg tried to comfort her, but she wiped her eyes and turned a
shoulder on him. Across that smooth skin lay a vivid weal.

"Well," said my Delia. "I shall always have a soft spot in
my heart for those little birds. What were they, anyway?"

No one knew their name; none of us had ever heard of
them. There is much to know of Kregen, and much that I tell
you now I picked up later—but to spoil the effect of those
thousands of little birds with their vindictive feud with the
impiters is something I cannot do. We were shaken, bruised,
cut—but alive.

After inspection, Delia pronounced the airboat as unusable.

Whether from a blow from the impiters or from an in-
herent failure we didn't know. What we did know was that
from here on in we must walk if we wished to reach Port
Tavetus.

All across the western skyline and extending out of sight
to north and south stretched the colossal mass of The
Stratemsk.

Before us lay a valley, and then open country with the
glint of rivers and the clumping of trees amid the grasses.

"We walk," I said.

Thelda had recovered and we had drunk and eaten. Now
she made a face. "I never did like walking. It's so unladylike."

Our preparations at the beginning were ambitious.

Thelda insisted on our bringing with us a mass of equipment she said was, "Absolutely vital."

I threw a handsome silver-mounted mirror into the grass.

"Sheer lumber, Thelda. If you want to preen—use a pool."

She started to argue and Delia started to try to persuade

her, but I just said, "If you want to bring all that junk you must carry it yourself."

That settled that.

We took long swords, bows and arrows, daggers and knives. We took sleeping equipment. We took what food I thought we would need before we got into our stride and could hunt what would be necessary. We took water bottles, large canteens of Sanurkazz leather, which is the best tanned and treated of the inner sea although perhaps not as fine, in the manner of tooling, as that of Magdag—Zair rot them!

On Delia's suggestion we buried all the treasures—the gold and jewels, the luxury trappings. If ever we passed this way again we might retrieve them, and if some unknown warrior stalking this way found the marker he would be suddenly rich, and good luck to him. As for footwear, we took every item we had, for although I prefer to walk barefooted, the others were mindful of the discomforts of the way—Seg must be used to hunting barefoot over his mountains of Erthyrdrin, and Delia, I knew from the time we had escaped from the roof-garden of the Princess Natema and had spent a wonderful time on the Plains of Segesthes, could cope adequately without shoes. No, it was a way of saying we thought Thelda would not keep up with us without shoes.

Poor Thelda!

Poor Seg!

He perfectly resigned himself to carrying her, if needs be.

I must admit that I had not a care in the world. We had landed safely. We had arms and food, we were fit, and we had a continent to explore. Vallia would be there when we got there. I was in no hurry to reach that mysterious, potent, terrible island empire and face the emperor-father of the girl I wanted to marry. The future would take care of itself; only the here and now mattered—for was not Delia of the Blue Mountains, my Delia of Delphond, walking so lightly and freely at my side?

Chapter Nine

Into the Hostile Territories

Delia sang.

As we marched along Delia sang.

My chest itched.

As soon as Thelda had recovered herself and seen the weals crisscrossing my chest she had cooed and pursed up her fat lips and gone off to pick some brilliantly-mauve wild flowers which she bashed and mixed into a paste. Delia had wondered across and bent down and looked closely at the flowers and at Thelda's intensely absorbed face as she pounded and stirred, and had smiled slantingly at me, and gone off, humming.

Now Thelda had splattered the mauve paste all over my fiery chest, saying: "This will do you the world of good, Dray! It's an old Vallian remedy and wonderfully efficacious. Why, these little vilmy flowers will have your poor dear chest healed in no time!" The confounded paste was irritating and fretting me like a hive of bees fastened to my chest.

And Delia marched on at the head of our little caravan and sang.

She sang wonderfully. Gay, rollicking airs that sped our feet over the grass, sad little laments that made me, for one, think back on all the great times and powerful men I had known who were now no more, silly little catch-phrase songs in which we all joined—Thelda with a self-important air of consciousness of the effect she was creating, Seg with a most powerful and musical tenor that truly delighted me, and me with my own wild and savage bellowings that always made Thelda jump and Delia sing on superbly.

But that damn chest itched until I could stand it no more.

"May the Black Chunkrah take it!" I yelled. I ripped the whole sticky mauve plastery mass off and flung it into the grass and jumped on it. "My chest's on fire!"

"Really, Dray!" sighed Thelda, sorely tried by my ingratitude. "You must persevere. You must give it time to work its healing magic."

"Healing magic nothing!" I shouted at her. "You try it! You stick it on your own imposing chest and see what it feels like!"

"Dray Prescot!"

"We-ell—"

The tinkling of a stream a short distance off by a line of salitas trees gave me the excuse not to exhibit further my sullen disgrace. I ran across and dived in and if all the monsters from the fabulous book called the *Legends of Spitz and His Enchanted Sword* that had been popular at the time I'd spent in Zenicce had started for me with gnashing jaws and talons I'd have scrubbed that confounded chest of mine clean first. Since Delia and I had taken that baptism by immersion in the sacred pool on the River Zelph in distant Aphrasöe— distant! No one knew where Aphrasöe, the City of the Savanti, was located!—we seemed to have picked up the valuable attribute of not only remaining healthy and with a promised life span of a thousand years but also of recovering with remarkable rapidity from wounds. We never seemed to get sick.

I rejoined them and I heard Delia, in a musing kind of voice, talking about a little blue flower she had picked.

"How pretty it is, Seg! See the petals, and the stamens, and the curious little silverish shape on each petal, like a heart—"

Thelda said "Oh!" and put a hand to her mouth.

"You are not well, Thelda?" inquired Seg, most anxiously.

"Oh! How silly— Oh, Dray, what you must think of me!"

"Now I've got rid of that debased paste from my chest I don't think anything," I said. I saw Delia's face, all glowing and glorious and I knew Something Was Up—

"Oh, Dray!" wailed Thelda. "What I picked was not vilmy at all! It didn't have the silver heart—I forgot! It was fallimy, that we use to scour cisterns clean—and I put it on your chest! Oh, Dray!"

I looked at her.

She put her hands over her face and started to sob, so I had to yell at her: "You silly girl—it doesn't matter! I'm not mortally wounded—oh, for the sweet sake of Zim-Zair, stop that infernal racket!"

"Say—say you—will forgive—me! I'm so—so stupid!"

"Now, now, Thelda!" said Delia, rather more sharply than I expected.

Seg tried to put his arm around the lady companion's shoulders, but somehow she eluded him and the next moment she was up against my abused chest and snuggling up to me, crying: "I am such a silly girl, dear Dray! What you must think of me—but—"

"Thelda!"

Delia hefted her pack and nodded at Seg.

"It's time we marched!"

I couldn't have agreed more. I managed to tuck Thelda somewhere around my left hip bone—she clung on—and started off after the other two.

Oh, how my Delia had joyed in all that! She was no white-skinned flaccid lump of lard who would lie back motionlessly. She was lithe and vibrant, a sprite, alive, full of mockery and yet absolutely dedicated and honest and fearless in our love. We had met and loved and we formed the perfect whole, meeting on all levels, profound and ethereal—no, there is no woman in two worlds like my Delia of the Blue Mountains.

The country closed in soon after that into a series of knobby rounded hills through which we followed the bank of the stream. Thick vegetation choked the hills but we found animal tracks beside the river and made good progress, always on the alert for the makers of these trails. Insects tended to be a nuisance, but Delia found a herb of pale and delicate green which, when she had crushed it and made a clear syrupy liquid seemed to my eyes a better proposition than poor Thelda's thick mauve paste. With this smeared over our faces and bodies the insects left us severely alone; I quite liked the scent of it.

Once more the country opened out and now we could see distant mountains—mere knobs on the ground compared with The Stratemsk; but nonetheless for that mountains through which we must find a way, walking. Numerous species of wild deer roamed the plains and I sighed for a fleet zorca between my knees. As it was Seg did some crafty stalking and with a single arrow provided us with our supper. We selected carefully-chosen campsites, for the horrific stories of the Hostile Territories, although so far nowhere borne out in what we had encountered, still rang in our minds. And so we proceeded across the land toward the far-off mountains. Twice we saw smoke rising from distant elevations in the plain, but these places we avoided.

Who—or what—lived here we did not know and had no desire to make their acquaintance.

An earnest of the wisdom of that decision came on a morning when the twin suns of Scorpio flamed into the sky and threw slanting sunshine gloriously through fluffed and meandering clouds above. We broke camp and strapped up and set off. The trail we were following dipped through a defile and so, naturally, we detoured that, clambering over scrubby hillsides and around thorn-ivy bushes. Ambushes are no places to take the girl one loves.

"Look—" said Seg in a low voice.

Ahead of us, in a crevice in the hillside that trended down to the defile below, something glittered. We approached with the silent tread of the hunter—Seg's learned in his mountains of Erthyrdrin and mine with my Clansmen in Segesthes.

Two dead bodies lay there. They were not men. Neither, for that matter, were they members of any of the races of half-men of Kregen with which I was at that time acquainted, Fristle, Och, Rapa, Chulik, Sorzart, or other—and my companions had never met these people before. Of medium height, they possessed two legs and two arms. Their faces reminded me of the hunting dogs of some of the clans that roamed the Great Plains of Segesthes, but there was a considerable admixture of the leem there, too. I was struck by the vast forward-thrusting lower jaw and the dewlaps that hung down. Mind you, the bodies were decomposing and the flies—they get everywhere—were busy. The girls moved back, out of range of the stink, but Seg and I were professionals and we knew what we had to find out.

Weapons first: Short thrusting swords like the short swords of my Clansmen. Long and slender lances with many-barbed tips. Tomahawk-like axes. Knives. Metal: From the mixture of steel and bronze, we judged these people to be in much the same area of development as the people of the inner sea where steel would be used if it could be come by, and bronze if not. Armor: Practically nonexistent, consisting of leather arm-guards, a leather cap, and a leather breastplate with strips of some pretty hard substance stitched into it. Seg thought this was a bone or a horn of some kind. Clothes: Minimal, breechclouts as worn all over Kregen, with a padding vest beneath the breastplate. No shoes or sandals. Accouterments: The usual leather belts and pouches.

Then we both looked at what had killed these beast-men. From the face of each one protruded a long arrow. An exceptionally long arrow. Working carefully with his knife Seg got the arrows out. He gave a grunt and lifted the points for my inspection. They were not the steel piles I would have expected.

"Flint," Seg said. His tanned face screwed up. "Seems I have relations around here."

He did a few quick flip-overs of his outstretched fingers, measuring the shaft, and then he whistled.

"They're from a master-bow." I knew that the esoterica of toxophily dominated much of Seg's life. Various grades of bow each had its name, every part, every action, every function, had its name and its ranking. The necessity of this was obvious. Seg, during our time together, had taught me much of the longbow, as I had swapped details with him of the compound bow of my Clansmen and the crossbow I had introduced to my old vosk-skulls. He had built himself a number of longbows, none, of course, from Yerthyr wood, and we had shot together in friendly rivalry. As was to be expected, at first he had outshot me by a margin. Then, as I got the hang of the longbow and mastered the transition from the compound reflex bow with which I was thoroughly familiar, as I have mentioned, I gave him a run for his money. They say you must start to train a longbowman by beginning with his grandfather. Once the society exists, however, and a man like myself with a lot of time to devote to the practice of arms is dropped into it, with the necessary requirements of an archer already existing, a great bowman may be made of him—as I had demonstrated on the Plains of Segesthes.

"You recognize the flight, Seg?"

He shook his head. "An expected master-set." He mentioned the technical jargon for the way the feathers were cut and set, the angle of the cock-feather, the twining and slotting. "Whoever loosed these knew his business."

"Whoever he was, he was ambushed and dealt with it."

"But good."

"These beast-men have no missile weapons. They must have flung them—"

"Much good it did them—nothing," said Seg Segutorio, "can stand against the longbow of Loh."

We marched on. All we took were the two arrows. The other weapons would merely weigh us down, although I regretted leaving them.

As we walked through this land, wary and always alert, we were able to talk. I believe you must have realized that having Delia with me had released my tensions, had loosened me up so that more than once I was astonished to find myself in the midst of a rib-straining laugh. A genuine laugh, at a joke, a witty remark, a funny situation. So we talked and joked and sang as we walked on toward the east coast of Turismond and Port Tavetus from whence we would ship to Vallia.

Thelda wore out the first pair of shoes and then the second. She persisted in her bright eager chattering and her pushing concern over me, but with Delia walking so lithely at my side I could put up with far worse than a boring woman. Seg and I grew closer together, too, as we joined in hunting for our sustenance. I remember those days as we walked steadily eastward away from The Stratemsk across the eastern plains of Turismond with a warm affectionate nostalgia. My search for Delia had been accomplished; we were together again. Vallia could wait, and as for Aphrasöe, to which Swinging City I fully intended to return some day, that was of the distant future. Everything was of the present. The journey itself was the adventure, the joy, the laughter, the zest.

Seg told me of Erthyrdrin, that country of his, that convulsed mass of mountains and valleys occupying the northern tip of Loh and peopled by a highly individualistic kind of person. The valleys resounded with song and the mountain peaks with the music of the harp. There were cliff-top strongholds everywhere, mere single towers of stone, some of them. Others had grown into battlemented fortresses of four or five towers linked by walls, and all were fiercely independent and devoted to protecting their crops and their flocks from neighboring raiders. Many of the young men hired out as mercenaries, for their longbows which had been developed over the centuries as hunting weapons proved mighty and invincible in battle. The Yerthyr trees were revered on the score of the quality of bow-staves they could produce; but it was considered a man's prerogative to cut his stave from the best tree he could find, wherever he could find it. The Yerthyr trees contained a deadly poison that killed any animal who ate of its leaves, and only, according to Seg, were the thyrrixes protected by virtue of their second stomach.

"We men of Erthyrdrin were the backbone of the armies of Walfarg. I doubt not but the bowman whose handiwork we witnessed came in the long ago from Erthyrdrin. Walfarg was a mighty country—it still is—but in its great days it ruled an empire over all Loh, and Pandahem to the east and south, and Kothmir and Lashenda, and over the eastern portions of Turismond. Only The Stratemsk halted the onward flow of the empire of Loh to the west."

"So all these so-called Hostile Territories were once a part of the empire of Loh?"

"Yes. I hold nothing in my heart for Loh as a country. They failed because they failed. Then the raiding barbarians from northern Turismond moved in, fiercer and ever more

fierce. What are now the Hostile Territories became walled
off to the east by barbarous tribes of men and half-men and
nowadays only a scattering of cities and trading posts on
the eastern seaboard remain open to the men of the outer
ocean." He gestured about him. "As for what goes on in the
Hostile Territories now—who knows?"

Seg Segutorio would sing of the old days of Loh as well as
his own high-flavored culture. I do not care to render into
English the words of his songs. They roared and rattled and
boomed in my head—and I can sing them now—but they are
of Kregen.

They echoed with deep rolling sounds—"oi" and "oom"
and reverberating drumrolls and profound bassoon-like
resonances, with the splatter of hard syllables like hail against
taut canvas. One of his songs of which he was particularly
fond reminded me instantly of "Lord Randolph My Son"
and I believe the frontier and border cultures of both worlds
hold much in common.

We saw occasional hunting parties roaming the wide plains
but we invariably went to earth until they had passed. Strange
beasts riding strange beasts—how those words recalled another time and another place to me!—were of no concern
of ours now. Although I sensed a growing need in Delia for
us to push on. She wanted to get back to Vallia.

"I cannot contract a legal marriage outside Vallia, Dray. It
is all part of this silly business of my being the Princess
Majestrix—you know."

"I can wait, my Delia—just."

"We must soon be there." She glanced at me quizzically
as we threaded the aisles of a forest which appeared to bar
our approach and around which we had been unable to trek.
"If you have any—" and then she stopped, to start again:
"If you feel somewhat—" And again halted.

"I know little of Vallia, Delia. All I know is that I wish
our union to be one in which you will take pride. I know
your father is the emperor and I have heard of the puissance
of his island empire. Maybe—"

"Maybe nothing! You will be my husband and the Prince
Majister! Have faith, Dray. It will not be so great an ordeal."

"As to that," I said, somewhat offhandedly and a little
thoughtlessly, as I realized afterward, "We have to reach
there yet."

"We will, dear heart! We will!"

Whenever we saw flying specks in the sky we took cover
at once and instinctively, without stopping to think.

Through this forest we did not expect to find impiters or

corths and so we trod along with a firmer tread. As night dropped with the refulgent sinking of the twin suns spearing in topaz fire through the intertwined branches we sought a resting place and soon enough ran across a series of old caves sunken into an earth bank. Gnarled tree roots thrust forth, naked and shining. The leaves around looked untrodden, the dirt trails unmarked. Seg nodded. We set about gathering wood and preparing camp.

I felt a slight twinge of concern lest Delia consider I was chary of visiting her notorious home and of meeting that powerful man, her father the emperor. Well, it was something I would have to do if I wished to claim Delia before the world, and having said that, that was sufficient. Nothing would stop me from doing just that—nothing. . . .

Settling down for the night in our sleeping bags we had fashioned from the soft Sanurkazzian leather with plenty of luxurious silk for linings I lay back for a moment reflecting as I often do before sleep. I could well understand Delia's desire to return home. As for me, now, my home was on Kregen and with Delia. But, still and all, I had felt very much at home riding with my wild Clansmen, and I acknowledged the surge of barbaric pleasure that savage and free life could always invoke in me. Seg had mentioned the barbarians who had swarmed down out of north Turismond to ravage and destroy the remnants of the empire created by Walfarg. I wondered if they were more violent and more barbaric than I and my Clansmen could be. . . .

As I was sinking into sleep I heard a tiny scraping sound from the rear of the cave.

Before the sluggish reactions of a city dweller of Earth would have prised his eyelids open in yawning query I was up out of the sleeping bag and with my naked long sword in my fist facing at a crouch whatever menace lurked there in the cave.

Seg said: "What?"

He stood beside me, a sword in his hand.

Delia said: "Do not make a sound, Thelda," and I heard the squashy sound of a palm over fat red lips.

Again the noise reached us and then the whole back end of the cave fell outward. We had searched the place carefully before taking up our occupation; we had not expected this. Pink light from the moons of Kregen washed in with a reflective uncanny glow.

In that wash of pink radiance I could see the squat ovoid outline of something moving. I saw two squat legs bending to bring the bulk of the body into the cave, and I saw the array of tendril-like arms bunching from arched shoulders. The thing's head was hunched down and in the darkened silhouette was invisible to me. The thought occurred as such thoughts will that perhaps the thing had no head at all.

It kept emitting a wheezing hiss, rather more like a faulty deck pump than a snake but nerve-chilling for all that.

Seg shouted. "Hai!" and charged, his sword high.

He brought the sword down in a brutal butchering blow and a tendril uncurled and caught his forearm and snapped straight. The long sword poised immobile over the thing's bunched tendrils. Two more grasped Seg about the waist, lifted him, began to draw him forward into the pink-tinged shadows.

I did not yell but ran forward fleetly, my head bent to avoid the overhang, and sliced the two gripping tentacles away.

They fell to the floor and writhed away into cracks in the rocks like snakes.

The thing shrieked—whether of rage or pain I did not know—and Seg managed to get his sword-arm free.

"The point, Seg!"

As I yelled I ran in again and buried my own weapon up to the hilt into the thing's body. Everything had happened fast. I know now that these things are inimical to most living beings and the thing had been clearly bent on surprising us by its trick back-end to the cave. Quasi-intelligent, the morfangs, quick and treacherous and incredibly strong. As the beast lay on the ground we could all see in that streaming light from Kregen's moons the gaped mouth with its serrated rows of fangs, the tiny malicious eyes, the thin black lips, the slit nostrils where a nose should be. It hissed as it expired. We found out about these morfangs later on; what we did not know then was—they habitually hunted in groups.

From the dimmer radiance at the mouth of the cave where the overhang cast shade, figures moved with unhurried purpose. I leaped for the opening. A quick glance showed me six of the tendriled beasts. Thelda was heaving and moaning and Delia was holding her down. I had no time for Thelda now. My Delia was in mortal peril.

"Seg! Gather what we need. Grab the girls! Hurry!"

I checked the back exit to the cave where the surprise had come from. Quasi-intelligent, these things, but clever. We were supposed to run screaming from its sudden surprise appearance—run straight into the tendrils of its fellows waiting outside. The back, which opened into a small shaft filled with moons-light, was clear.

"Seg!" I said again, harsh and dominating. "Take the girls out the back way—hurry—"

He tried to argue and I beat him down with a snarl and a look.

Thelda was clutching herself and rocking and moaning. Seg hoisted her up beneath the armpits and half carried her. Delia took our gear and as she went out she cast a look back and stopped, ready to throw down the sleeping bags and the food and the medicines and jump to my assistance, a long jeweled dagger in her hand.

"For my sake, Delia! Go— Hide and then create a little noise—not much, enough to draw them off—you understand?"

"Yes, Dray—oh, my—"

I didn't give her time to finish but waved her off with a most ugly look. Then I turned to face the front opening of the cave.

Chapter Ten

Great beasts of the air

The noise from the cave had not been what these tendriled monsters expected. In a body they headed for the entrance to the cave.

Pink moonlight lay thickly on the leaves, on the spilled earth, limned the branches of the trees, weaved and twisted with purple shadows in the coiling and uncoiling tendrils.

I stood at the entrance. I could feel my feet thrusting at the earth, the dirt of Kregen four hundred light-years from the planet of my birth. I could feel my heart thumping with a regular anticipatory pulse, kept unpanicked by the disciplines so carefully and painfully learned from the Krozairs of Zy. I could feel the heft of the long sword in my fist, and the balance of it, and the beginning movements that would turn that bar of cold steel into a palely glimmering instrument of pallid destruction until the clean steel glitter fouled and slicked with blood.

As I stood there I must have presented a wild and terrible picture, with the defiance that would not be beaten down because the girl I loved was in peril, with my ugly face ricked into an expression I am sure would have prevented me from shaving had I seen it in a mirror, with my muscles limber and lithe and ready instantly to bunch and exert all the monstrous power of which—sometimes to my shame—they were capable.

These morfangs were quasi-intelligent, as I learned later; that they clearly were not fully-intelligent is obvious. Had they sense enough they would have run from me, shrieking.

But not unintelligent—as soon as they saw me they halted in their advance and their hissing increased. One bent, picked up a stone, and threw it. I struck it away with my sword as one makes an on-drive to mid-on. The ringing clang acted as a gong-like signal. The half dozen of them, hissing and screeching, leaped toward me and the lashing forest of tendrils writhed above my head seeking to trap me and draw me into the fanged crevices of their jaws.

And now I struck and struck again and the keen edge bit and sliced and any pity or sorrow I might have had for these voracious beasts burned away in the fire of action. Only the sword could have saved me. Their intent was quick and deadly and obvious. Those tendrils clustered in seeking, groping, twining bunches, with immense coiled power striving to drag me into the crag-like sharpnesses of their mouths. Unarmed, I know I would not have lasted five minutes.

As it was I was forced to hack and skip and jump and strike again as though I were some phantom woodsman fated to hack his way through an animate mobile forest. All the time they kept up their jangling-nerved hissing screeching; and, too, I became convinced that shrilling was of anger and fury and not of pain. For the severed tendrils looped up with muscular strength and writhed like the furious contents of an overturned snake basket. And, too—instead of writhing off into the woods as the severed tendrils had wriggled into crevices in the cave, these serpent-like tendrils writhed toward me. They crept over the ground and began to drag themselves up my legs. I could feel their clammy coils lapping about me, constricting my muscles, and as I stepped back and chopped them free so each new severed portion began instantly to coil sinuously toward me over the leaves and the dirt.

Only one way waited for me if I wished to escape.

With full force I brought the long sword down onto the head of the nearest creature. That head split and gushed ichor and brain and the sword sliced on past the coat-hanger-like shoulders with their five-a-side ranks of lashing tentacles, drove cleaving on down into the ovoid body. The thing fell backward and I had to exert tremendous strength to jerk the sword free.

In that instant of hesitation tendrils lapped my neck.

Instantly my left hand whipped the main-gauche across and the razor-edged steel—razor-edged because when I shaved I found this weapon a useful implement on my stubble—sliced down the bunched coils. It left a thin scarlet line on my own neck, too.

This could not go on.

Now two of the beasts were down and then a third staggered away on one leg. I breathed in with long deep breaths, timing them to the swing of the sword. The main-gauche went into the eye of an attacker on my left—too deeply, for I was

again hung up on the withdrawal and only barely managed
to fend the sword blade above my head, shearing tendrils.
More tentacles looped me from behind and I felt myself
toppling backward off balance.

"Hail" I yelled—a complete waste of breath and yet a
psychological reminder. I twisted as I fell and thrust the
sword up so that the beast in falling into me fell instead on
the sword with its pommel thrust hard into the ground.

Dragging myself clear I shook my head. Two left, if the
others were truly hors de combat, and a host of writhing
wriggling tentacle-remnants like a pit of snakes from hell;
long odds they were, yet.

Then I heard a shout—Seg's voice: "Hai!"

The remaining beasts hesitated. Quasi-intelligent they were,
knowing when to stop fighting as well as when to go on with
unintelligent viciousness to death. Had they been armed . . .

I shouted.

"Hai! Jikai!"

I leaped forward.

The sword blurred. Left, right, left, right. I struck now
with the impassioned zeal of a man who knows he must
finish it fast.

The two morfangs dropped and I dragged the smeared
sword back. Now, with the death of the last two, all the
free snake-like tendrils wriggled away into the moon-
drenched forest. I guessed then, and was later proved right,
that they would grow each into a new morfang beast-monster.

Moments later I had rejoined my comrades, guided by
their voices, able to reassure them. We began a night march
at once to clear the confines of this accursed forest.

There had been only six. They had given me more trouble
than twice their number of armed men. One of the reasons
lay in those coat-hanger shoulders, each with five whipping
tendrils. Even allowing a man two arms, which on Kregen is
usual although by no means universal, the count was as
though I had fought thirty men. I touched the hilt of the
sword. I had lived then, by the sword. The balance of the
thought lay leaden and ugly in my mind, and I did not
speak as we marched through the pink-shot moonlight of
the Kregen night.

After that we redoubled our vigilance and only through
extraordinary good fortune were we able to avoid similar
encounters. The tendril monsters roamed over a goodly-sized
portion of the land here and we found ourselves traveling in
constant apprehension. A considerable extent of badlands
worked its way in from the south as we trended east,

forcing us to carry on in a slanting angle to the east-north-east. Delia shook her head and remarked that she did not recall flying over this kind of country at all when she'd come in from Port Tavetus. Although the feeling was marginal, I had, with that sea officer's sense of navigational direction, felt we had veered to the north during our passage through The Stratemsk and the attack by the impiters had further driven us off course.

But I did not express my concern, thankful that we were still alive and still fit to travel. Thelda was hardening, and Delia positively glowed with the fresh air and exercise.

The climactic shadow of The Stratemsk lay to our rear now, the forests indicated that, and the badlands must be an effect of absence of soil or presence of minerals and poor soil and the millennia-long erosion. The mountains had been traversed and although we did not know their names we were conscious of their puniness in contrast to The Stratemsk; all the same, they were arduous on foot, and we near froze a couple of times. On the eastern side the whole country changed in character.

Now we were hard-pressed to avoid cultivated areas, to bypass towns and villages, to keep off the highroads that intersected at towns and posting stations and gave us clear indication that this land was populated.

We would scout with the minutest attention to every detail of the land that lay ahead. From whatever eminence we could climb we would plot our passage. Some of the towns we saw and avoided were nearer cities than towns. Many times we lay in hedgerows while cavalcades of armed men and trundling wagons rolled along paved roads. The roads were, indeed, objects of wonder. I was reminded of the old Inca or Roman roads, and I suspected that they were still in such good condition only through the skill of their builders, for the present inhabitants of this land looked hard and brutal and contemptuous of labor, lusting after silver and gold and the good things of life.

"They remind me of my own people in their hardness," said Seg. "These cities and towns must be constantly warring one with another."

"I agree," said Delia. "The roads link them, but between each city and its surrounding cultivation lies barrenness."

More than once we saw high-flying birds or winged beasts, and concealed ourselves, for we knew what to expect.

Now we began more fully to understand why all the continent lying between The Stratemsk and the eastern coast of Turismond had been dubbed the Hostile Territories. The true hostility came from men and not from nature or the animals of the wild.

I continued to feel concern over the northerly drift of our course; but in the nature of things with an infuriating obstinacy events conspired to force us more northerly still. I knew that Turismond extended in a bold out-thrust promontory into the Cyphren Sea and if we were traveling eastward we could march as much as five hundred unnecessary miles to the east with the sea away down to our south. But I was not prepared to risk an encounter with the inhabitants of these pinnacled cities, these battlemented fortresses, for I sensed from what we saw of them that they differed in kind from those peoples I had already met on Kregen.

More than once we bypassed cities inhabited by beast-men, half-men of races with which none of us was familiar, although given the strangeness of human nature I felt a comical sense of relief when the semi-humans of these cities turned out to be Ochs or Rapas, much though I distrusted the former and detested the latter—emotions which, I hasten to add, were germane to my continued existence at the time, whatever subsequent changes a long life and a great experience have brought.

None of us had the slightest hesitation in giving the widest of wide berths to the sprawling city filled with Chuliks upon which we almost stumbled as we came down out of a hill-cleft into a wide valley.

We crawled back up into the hills again and when I tried to lay off a course southerly we were halted by a river on the banks of which a string of guard-towers had been built. Perforce we struck northward once more.

The whole land was cut up into city-states. Antiquaries say there were ninety city-states of the ancient Minoan civilization in Crete. They must have been very small. Here the city-states sprawled over vast areas of land, or huddled around a natural fortress-holding on a hill within a valley. The state of savagery of the intervening areas can best be judged if I tell you that Seg and I had often to cope with sudden attacks from leem, those eight-legged demons, furred, feline, and vicious, whose fangs in their wedge-shaped heads can strike through lenk. And, too, we met graints, those wonderfully vital and obstinate animals I had met and battled outside Aphrasöe with the magical swords of the Savanti that did not kill but merely stunned. These, and other wild animals, were not in the usual way to be found anywhere close to settled human or half-human habitations.

"According to my calculations," Delia said to me as we

rested in a fold of gentle, grass-clad hills, eating the rich flesh of a deer-like animal Seg had brought down and the girls had cooked, "I figure we have something like two hundred dwaburs between The Stratemsk and Port Tavetus."

"Yes."

"We must have covered that by now—we've been walking for ages—".

"Yes, Delia. But we are north of our course—"

"Oh, yes, I know you have been concerned. . . ." She pondered. Then, briskly, she said, with that defiant tilt to her chin: "All right, then. The airboat carried us a good way, and we have marched a long way. We do not seem to be able to head south—so we must go on. I think we will find the next Vallian port city up the coast will be Ventrusa Thole. There are port cities of Pandahem, but I think we would be wise to avoid them."

Pandahem, I knew, was a great rival of Vallia's in the carrying trade and in business of the outer oceans. But there was a quiet animosity in Delia's tones that startled me.

"Do you hate them so much, then, my Delia?"

"Hate? No, not really. We both seek to enrich ourselves on the leavings of the empire of Loh. We both maintain settlements on the eastern coast of Turismond. We both try to extend our business contacts to the west—"

"And a fat lot of good that does!" broke in Thelda. She pushed up on an elbow. Thelda had lost weight on our journey and her figure had trimmed off into statuesque beauty that poor Seg found mightily disturbing. "By Vox!" she said, with some force. "I heartily wish all the devils from Pandahem a watery grave!"

"Quite still!" said Seg. His voice cracked. The green radiance of Genodras lay on his face and turned that lean tanned visage into a ghoul-skull newly-risen from the grave with the grave-mold crumbling upon it.

We all remained absolutely still.

Now I could hear the beat of many wings. From the sky that susurration floated down, ominous, breath-catching.

Shadows flitted across the grassy hills, twinned-shadows from the twin suns, at first in ones and twos, and then in clumpings until the whole sky darkened. We did not look up.

Delia still looked at me and I at her, and her face remained calm, her eyes bright and mocking on my face, and I yearned to take her in my arms. But we lay there rigid and unmoving.

And now I could hear a strange clinking from the sky, mixed with the massive gusting as enormous wings beat at the air.

The noise dwindled and the fleeting shadows drifted away again into twos and threes. Seg touched me on the arm, for he had been able to watch everything.

"Gone."

We looked and saw the host of flying beasts like a low cloud vanishing beyond the farther hills.

Seg's face remained grave and serious, despite Thelda's babblings of relief.

"What is it, Seg?" asked Delia.

"I have heard the tales—all men of Loh have heard the tales of our great empire that Walfarg forged on Turismond. The legends that creak with age and are hung with cobwebs. But—" He wiped a hand over his forehead and I saw the sweat slick there. "But I never thought to see them come to life!"

"What do you mean?"

"They were impiters. But—they carried men upon their backs!"

At once I remembered what Pur Zazz, the Grand Archbold of the Krozairs of Zy, had spoken to me when we had said Remberee. "I would welcome news, Pur Dray, of your adventures and the sights you encounter. Men say that beyond the mountains, in the Hostile Territories, there are whole tribes who fly on the backs of great beasts of the air."

And so there were.

Of course, when one considers that men on this Earth have tamed horses and camels and donkeys and ride them as a mere fact of everyday life, and on Kregen men and half-men ride zorcas and voves and sectrixes and yulankas and many more wonderful animals, and given that the impiters and corths we had seen were large enough to support a man's weight in the air, the wonder would be if there were not men flying birds and beasts, the miracle would be if men did not form aerial cavalries.

And so it was that I felt no surprise at Seg Segutorio's words.

"They did not see us," I said, "thanks to Seg's sharp eyes. But, by Zim-Zair, had we four of those flying beasts we could manage this journey to Port Tavetus or Ventrusa Thole with less damage to our feet."

Delia looked at me sharply. Her surprise was understandable; she knew how much this leisurely progress meant to me and then she smiled as the realization that I really did want to go to Vallia pleased her. And yet, she still felt doubts of the outcome, that I knew. Her father's reputation was a frightening reality.

"Aye!" said Seg, leaping up. "And we'd soon unravel the knot of how to fly the beasties. They must be well-trained."

"Assuredly," I said, "otherwise the riders would either fall off or hang upside down between the beasts' legs."

So saying, we gathered our belongings and took up our weapons and continued our journey.

Below us, in the valley, an army marched.

At once we sank down below the crest. We looked out and down onto infantry and cavalry and artillery—different types of varters and catapults—and I heard Seg whistle softly between his teeth.

"Tell me, Seg."

"It is as though I am Loh-borne again," he said. His eyes stared with a fey hunger on the marching host. "It is as though I am looking through the illuminated scrolls of my people—for I tell you, Dray Prescot, that army marching there is an army from the past!"

I said nothing, respecting the mood that had overtaken him. He had told me of the pictures in the illuminated scrolls of his people. They were artifacts common in lands where literacy was not high or widespread, and conveyed stories by many thousands of pictures stretching along scrolls that might be, when rolled up, as thick around as a chunkrah thigh. Many men dedicated their lives and the contents of their paint-pots to producing these items, and many of them were objects of great beauty in their own right, irrespective of the story they told.

Now Seg drew in a shuddery breath. "An army from the past, an army of Loh, marching in all the glory of the empire of Walfarg!"

In my time on Earth and on Kregen I have seen many armies on the march, and there are ways to assess the qualities and the strengths as well as the weaknesses of hosts of marching men. These men below me marched with a swing, in step and in ranks, their spears all slanted at identical angles. Cavalry rode picket. Artillery—strange-looking varters to me, used to the ballistae of the inner sea—all arranged in a neat symmetry. I studied the way in which the army marched, and came to certain conclusions. But it was Delia, watching with us that army of something like ten thousand men, who pointed out the most important observation of all.

"I feel like swearing just like Thelda!" said Delia, crossly. "For—do you see?—they are marching in exactly the same direction as the way we wish to go!"

And—as I said with a nice round Makki-Grodno oath—they were.

There was nothing for it but to wait out their progress and then follow along with the utmost caution, for as Seg and I observed, their scouts were very good.

"Although," I said, with a trace of dubiousness, "they seem a little too good."

"How come?"

"Well—they scout ahead, checking every knoll and defile, and they're spread to the flanks. But it seems to me, somehow, done by rote, as though each man has a drill book in his hand." The English word was: mechanical. "For instance— if I was commanding that army I would want to know if four desperadoes were lurking on a neighboring hill—there might be more."

Thelda looked alarmed for an instant, and then she laughed, and tapped me on the bicep, and said, "Oh, Dray! You mean—*us!*"

Very gravely, I said, "Yes, Thelda."

As we trailed them Seg relaxed his first incredulous disquiet and told us that the uniforms worn by the soldiers were those of three hundred years or so ago, and I was quite prepared to believe him, for in the main the uniforms of Kregen are colorful, practical affairs that change slowly. Although life and culture on Kregen varies widely from place to place, in general culture is outward-looking and thrusting forward, new lands opening up, new kingdoms raised, new empires being formed. Many new peoples were lifting their fortunes on the debris of the empire of Loh, and here in the Hostile Territories we had stumbled across an army constituted as Loh would have organized it.

"For a moment," said Seg, and his laugh did not sound genuine to me, "I thought they were an army of ghosts!"

The truth was that in the collapse of the old empire and the inrush of barbarian hordes, fragments of culture from Loh, Lohvian attitudes and customs, had survived. Clearly, this army belonged to a city-state that had retained its Lohvian character. I confess, now, that at that moment the idea cheered me. With a civilized people we might find shelter in this crazy patchwork of Hostile Territories and rest and relax.

Why then, do you ask, did I not run down and introduce myself to the army commander?

My friend—whoever you are listening to this tape—if you think that, you have not listened well to my tale of Kregen.

Since the eclipse of the green sun Genodras by the red sun Zim—an event that had entailed direful consequences for me in distant Magdag—the green sun preceded the red in sunrise and sunset. When we camped that night in the amber rays of Zim falling slanting across the land we could see the campfires of the army like a miniature flame-filled reflection of the stars above us.

In the morning the army formed up in a welter of heel-clicking and rigidly correct lines; there was much drilling about, parading, and wheeling past fluttering colors before they at last set off. My suspicions of the army spread out below me grew—and shattering confirmation came when that ominous low cloud dashed into sight above a crest a dwabur away.

We watched, fascinated.

The fight was not our concern and we wanted nothing of it. We sheltered in the lee of a crest and watched. We had drunk refreshingly from an upland lake, a little tarn, and we had palines to munch, and we did not wish to become embroiled in what was going on between the Lohvian army and the boiling mass of wing-beating animals and ferocious men. The flying aramada came on with cloud-driven swiftness and immediately began a long series of diving attacks on the men on the ground. These reacted with all the strict order of men obeying the rule book. And this was where I saw the weaknessess I had suspected revealed. Their dispositions for combating the aerial attack were excellent, but the manner in which they carried out their instructions left them shattered and confused.

The flying beasts were impiters, right enough, possibly the same group we had seen before, possibly another tribe. The men perched on their backs were too distant to discern properly, but I guessed they would possess some, at least, of the attributes of humanity along with their obvious bestiality.

"Look at them!" screamed Thelda, and Seg had to reach up a hand to drag her down, so carried away by excitement was she.

The flying beasts would swoop down and the men on their backs would loose arrows or fling javelins. Then they would zoom up again and reverse to swoop again. The Lohvians were shooting upward, and many flying beasts fell, but the army was split, segments were running wildly. The whole confused area before us became covered with hundreds of separate combats.

"No, no, no!" Seg was saying, over and over. His eyes betrayed his excitement. His hands kept gripping into fists and relaxing, gripping and relaxing. He held his longbow now, and I said, softly: "Seg?"

He looked at me with blank, drugged eyes. He breathed very quickly.

"The flying armada came on with cloud-driven swiftness."

"They are of Loh!"

"You are of Erthyrdrin, Seg. But, if you will it . . ."

I started to bend my longbow and Delia said: *"No!"*

"No, Dray! This is madness! Suicide!"

"Oh, Dray!" wailed Thelda.

Only one woman in two worlds could hope to sway me in any decision I make, right or wrong.

I, Dray Prescot, hesitated. . . .

And then a dark shadowed shape gusted above us and there were a dozen great winged beasts circling us and circling, too, the dazed little group of riders who had spurred their mounts at the hill in the hopes of riding beyond it to safety.

The riding beasts were nactrixes, cousins of the familiar sectrixes, with their six legs and their blunt heads; but they were deeper of chest and taller, with an altogether more hardy look about them. Their slatey-blue hides were covered with a more profuse coat of hair, which was trimmed and cropped.

The riders were officers, with sumptuous saddle gear and brocaded cloths, with as much finery about their mounts as about themselves. Some attempted to shoot their arrows aloft, but absolute concern over their own safety drove them on and the shafts flew wide of their marks.

Thelda screamed.

Seg cursed. He drew, let fly, and his shaft hurtled true to bury itself in the body of one of the aerial attackers.

Even as the screech rang out and the great body pitched from the sky my own shaft winged its way to its mark.

At once Seg and I were in action. All about us beat the massive pinions of the impiters, shining and heavy, feather-flurried in the wind of their smiting. We dodged and ducked and avoided the flung javelin and the loosed shaft. In return our own shafts plunged home in wing and belly, in breast and head. I saw three of the barbaric riders shriek and topple from their high saddles, to swing wildly from restraining straps as their mounts struggled to stay aloft.

"Your back, Dray!"

Delia's voice.

I swung about and ducked and saw the monstrous talons graze past my head. They swerved with the swaying of the impiter's body and closed about the head and shoulders of a man upon a nactrix and dragged him screaming upward. Seg loosed and a blast of air from a slashing wing deflected his shaft. I saw another swooping flying-monster, and the creature upon its back, vicious, with narrow-set eyes and square clamped mouth, whose hair floated freely aft of his blunt head in a waving mane, dyed all a brilliant indigo. I saw the maleficent glare in those close-set eyes and I dodged the flung javelin, seizing it as it spun past in the empty air, and reversing it and hurling it back so that its flint head smashed into the leem-skin pelt and copper and bronze ornaments on the man's chest. The impiter swerved away, but I saw its rider jerk and open that square mouth and cough a bright stream of his life's blood.

A nactrix trailing its intestines gallopped madly past. Its rider fell sprawling at my feet, and I bent and lifted him as an arrow feathered into the grass beside us. His young, pale face sheened with sweat; one eye was closed and swelling purple-black and his fiery-red hair clotted into a great wound across his scalp.

"Take your sword and fight them off!" I said, twisting him upright.

His eyes widened and the horrified look of absolute panic on his face creased away into the semblance of sanity amid an insane world. He drew his sword—a toothpick compared with the great long swords worn by Seg and myself—and put himself into something of the stance of a fighting-man.

Thelda was still screaming.

I saw Seg loose three arrows so fast that all were in flight together before all three smote their targets, and three more of the indigo-haired aerial attackers shrieked and slumped in their flying straps.

My own bow sang and another square-mouthed man astride his impiter sagged back, and, writhing horribly, slid down and under his mount's neck so that its wings smashed remorselessly into his body as it sought to struggle upward.

Around us the sward was splashed with blood, nactrixes lay dead, with the bodies of their riders; but the young man whom I had forcibly pushed back from the pit of madness waved his sword, his red hair bright under the morning suns, and shouted brave, silly, vain words of defiance.

Seg gasped and loosed again and an impiter in its flight went straight on, with extended wings, straight on into the ground with the arrow imbedded through its eye into its brain.

I started across to deal with the rider, who leaped free very nimbly, and drew a long and thin sword. His leem pelt glowed with the dyes lavished upon it, his bronze buckles and buttons burnished to a blazing brilliance blinded me in the brilliant suns-shine. Still with my longbow in my left determinedly, aware that he had only to fight me off to be saved by his companions. Over his shoulder I saw one of his comrades shake the reins of his flying beast, drive in his leather-wrapped legs and feet, and wheel that monstrous bulk toward me, and I prepared myself to face two enemies at once.

"Hail!" yelled my man on the ground, and charged.

Meeting his blade with a solid shock, I caught that sliver of fine steel, looped it around, and thrust and with the thrust went on with my lunge, doubling up and jerking the brand free from his belly, doubling up and rolling over on the ground. I felt the beat of immense wings and felt the cold downrush of air. Almost, I made it; but a raking talon smashed searingly down my side, knocking the breath from my lungs and sending gouts of racking pain through me.

I could understand and deal with pain. I staggered up, gasping for air, still clutching my sword, and turned to see Delia being whisked aloft in the cruel clutching talons of an impiter.

I shouted—something, I know not what—as I saw my Delia being whipped up. The attackers were retreating now, unwilling to lose more men to these merciless foemen below. Then, from somewhere, a blow sledged down on my head and I pitched forward into the bloodied grass.

I rolled over sluggishly. Then I could not move. I lay there, seeing Seg topple as a last flung javelin bounced from his leg. I lay there and watched that accursed impiter as it sailed away bearing my Delia fast-clenched in its claws. The thing upon its back waved its spear and screeched in a high mocking crow of victory and revenge.

My Delia was gone, snatched away by as vile and merciless a being as any I had seen. Lost and gone, my Delia of Delphond, lost and gone. . . . With the blackness that closed over me closed also complete and utter despair.

Chapter Eleven

Assassins in the corthdrome

The performance of *Sooten and Her Twelve Suitors* presented in the covered theater aroused intense enthusiasm from the audience, and although I quite admired this tragedy known almost over the entire Kregen world of culture, the action irritated me, the words seemed trite, the melodious phrases mere cant. The crack on my skull had healed with the customary rapidity of wounds inflicted on my carcass, a useful by-product of my immersion in the pool of baptism of the River Zelph that had given me the promise of a thousand years of life.

But of what use or goodness or value were a thousand years if my Delia of the Blue Mountains was not there to share them with me?

A kind of psychic numbness had overtaken me. Seg had been wounded, also, and was being nursed back to health and strength in this city of Hiclantung, which he appeared to regard in much the same way as a denizen of my own time living in a remote corner of Cornwall would regard a recreation of Chaucer's London. As for Thelda, I had to resort to lies and trickery to obtain some respite from her constant lamentations and protestations and tears. At this moment she was under the impression I was lying fast asleep in the apartments given over to our use in the villa of red brick and white stone situated on a southern declivity of the city just a comfortable ten murs' walk within the walls. Sooten, in her interminable trickeries of the clamoring suitors—something, I fear, of a Kregan Penelope—wearied me in my numb and dissociated mood. All savagery and wild anger had shriveled. Without Delia the whole universe meant nothing.

If you marvel that we, three friendless wanderers, had so fallen on our feet as to have a comfortable villa in the Loh style given over to our use, I can remember my feelings then.

The young man I had snapped into a semblance of sanity had, as was clearly evident from his trappings and hauteur, a high post in the army of Hiclantung. Young Hwang—for such was his name with the very necessary additions of many sonorous titles and ranks and indications of estate-holdings—was the nephew of the Queen of the city, and although we had made her acquaintance in the most formal of ways she yet remained a stranger to us. Yet, it was she who in gratitude had given orders that we were to be well-treated.

Seg had wrinkled up his nose about this Queen, but he refused to comment when Thelda chided him.

There is no real coincidence in this train of events. Any fighting-man knows that on an open battlefield if he renders some distinguished service to a man dressed in brilliant uniform or otherwise marked for a man of distinction, then the gratitude of the powerful can be expected—*ceteris paribus*—and he may expect to benefit from that action. We had saved the Queen's nephew. So we were rewarded.

I would gladly have consigned all the Queen's nephews in the whole of Kregen to the Ice Floes of Sicce to have my Delia back.

A hand touched my arm.

"You are bored with the entertainment, Dray Prescot?"

"I know the piece well, Hwang, and admire the dexterity of construction—after all, I am told there are fragments of this play extant on clay tablets dating from five thousand years ago. But no; it's not the play. I am at fault."

Hwang, despite his somewhat foppish manner and his desperate loss of identity on a battlefield, was nonetheless for that a fine young man from whom something better than average might be made given the lad was conceded a chance. Now he laughed and said: "I can show you more full-blooded sport if you wish."

I had declined this sort of offer before in Zenicce, and so I said, simply: "I thank you; but no. I will walk a while."

Outside the covered theater the largest moon of Kregen—the maiden with the many smiles—sailed clear of clouds. The whole city lay floating in pink moonlight. Presently the two second moons would rise, eternally orbiting each other, the twins, to add their luster to the scene. As we walked along in this tide of radiance dark figures detached themselves from shadowy alcoves and fell in to our rear. Young Hwang's bodyguard, provided by the Queen, an insurance that her line would continue, and an infernal nuisance to a man like myself who wanted to be alone.

Every house and building in Hiclantung possessed a roof

which stoppered the night air, every roof-garden had its sliding ceiling panels, and they were unfailingly closed each night. Over the roofs thin strong wires stretched, wires patiently drawn by hand and forged and hammered hour after hour. Metal spikes projected in serrated and ugly fans at every vantage point of cornice and ledge. All the architecture had been designed to offer no single vantage point unprotected. Tall and thin columnar towers rose everywhere, and at their summits they broadened like tulips into minor fortresses with pointed roofs—tulip-shaped, onion-shaped, domed and spired, but never flat. No canopies with gilt-spearheaded posts projected with their awnings, as were everywhere visible in the other cities I had visited. Nothing was provided that could offer a perch.

"The dancing girls at Shling-feraeo are exceptionally fine," said Hwang. I was well aware that he had not yet summed me up; he didn't yet know what to make of me. Had I cared what he thought or did not think of me I still would not have bothered to worry over his enlightenment.

"Thank you, Hwang. But dancing girls, no matter how fine, do not suit my mood this night."

Under that moon-glow Hwang's red hair gleamed a curious color, rich and thick and curled. He was a good-hearted young fellow, I thought, amazingly friendly given the circumstances of his upbringing. He would benefit from a season or two with Hap Loder and my Clansmen of Felschraung out on the Great Plains of Segesthes.

He it was who had filled in the background picture of this city, this anachronism, this civilized survivor in a wilderness of barbarity. When the great empire carved out by Walfarg had fallen through dissension at home in Loh, here, in eastern Turismond, the cities had drawn their own culture tightly about them and resisted to their best the invaders from the north, away past the northern outskirts of The Stratemsk. Some had fallen and were now mere shells, inhabited by leem and plains-wolves and risslaca. Others had survived as cities but were now the homes of barbarians, of beast-men and half-men. And yet—some, some had retained all their old Lohvian culture and civilization and went on their own paths as cities and city-states, islands of light amid a sea of darkness.

Of Loh, they now knew nothing.

Legends and fables, garbled histories, and the occasional venturesome traveler alone provided any link with their ancient homeland.

I could foresee that both Vallia and Pandahem, the new,

lusty, sprawlingly-vigorous powers establishing themselves on the eastern coast, would not find this country easy, their penetration a mere matter of barter and sword.

Hwang, to do him justice, tried to jolly me out of this mood of black depression.

"If not dancing girls, then come with me to the nactrix stables. I have had to buy fresh mounts—" He stopped talking, and coughed. I knew well enough why he was forced to buy fresh nactrixes.

"I thank you, Hwang—but—"

He halted me with an upraised hand. His bodyguard froze behind us in the shadows.

Living was an everyday precious affair for the Lohvians of Hiclantung; they valued continued existence, always struggling against the seas of barbarism beating upon their ancient walls. These robes we wore now, old but finely woven and superbly maintained, were a part of that tradition. Loh had withdrawn and there was no way home for these people through the Hostile Territories occupied by beast and barbarian—even had they wished to leave their own homes and hearths. So I was not as hard on young Hwang as I might have been. No other thoughts had much place in my skull at that time except agonized fears and mocking, now they were gone, memories of Delia of Delphond.

"Then," said Hwang with youthful force, "we will go to see the corths that rascal Nath is trying to sell me."

I perked up at once; then reality supervened. Nath is a common name on Kregen—already in my life at this time there had been Nath the Thief from Zenicce, and my old oar comrade Nath of Sanurkazz, and I was to meet more.

This Nath was a fat but jolly man with a stub-nose and liquid eyes and a kind of loosely-rolled turban that slanted down over one ear in which a whole pagoda-like construct swung dwarfing any normal earring. His robes were new, embroidered in the Lohvian way with serpentine risslaca and orchids twining with the moon-blooms, and his slippers—to my intense disappointment—were mere plain squat-ended herring-boxes. He should have worn slippers flaunting extraordinarily long and up-curled points.

"Lahal, Dray Prescot," he said, when what passed for pappattu had been made—I did not have to fight him or give him obi as was customary on other portions, equally civilized, of Kregen—and he rolled his girth around and resumed his seat on a pile of trappings, cushions, gear, and flying silks. Hwang was already inspecting the corths, all securely chained up by wing and leg to their perches, beneath the arched roof of the corthdrome.

"A couple are to my liking, Nath," he said, without any attempt at bargaining. They began to talk prices, and I wandered across to take a closer look at the representatives of the flying monsters who had menaced our flight through The Stratemsk.

The corth is a truer bird than the impiter, although not as large or fierce—I believe that only two other flying animals of Kregen better the impiter—and in general will carry no more than two passengers. These birds possessed the large round eyes, the sleek feathered heads, the deep chests and wide wings of faithful fliers, their legs short and sturdy and varying as to the amount of feather-covering in different species. Now they shifted from side to side and cocked their heads to stare at me first down one side of their beaks and then the other. In color they ranged through the spectrum, with patterns of variegated feathers lending a powerful beauty to their forms. Compared to the fanged and whiptailed impiters with their coal-black plumage, the corths were indeed beautiful.

On a question from me, Nath laughed so that his array of chins and stomachs shook. "Oh dear me, no! We would not allow our beautiful corths to perch on a bar outside our windows! Why—the barbarians would simply dive on them and kill them and then they would have the perch on which to land freely provided for them. We make it difficult for fliers to land in Hiclantung."

"I had noticed."

The corthdrome had been built at the summit of a high building on one of the hills of the city, on the southern declivity of which our villa lay. I thought of Seg, slowly recovering, of Thelda, keeping as she thought a vigilant nighttime watch over my sick bed. They were good comrades. When we quitted the place, to Nath the Corthman's wheezy: "Remberee, Dray Prescot!" and the chinkling of the fresh golden coin in his wallet, I was ready to turn in.

Hwang held me back. His face tautened. Looking down the long flight of stairs that led to the street, each section of twenty treads with a separate side wall looped for arrow-slits, I saw a body of armed men climbing the white stone that glimmered duskily pink and purple in the moons-light, for the twins were now wheeling across the sky after the maiden with many smiles.

Hwang suddenly laughed softly and I was aware of the

rapid putting away of the longbows in the hands of his body-guard.

The two parties met.

"You are abroad late, Hwang."

"Yes, Majestrix." Hwang inclined. They inclined in Zenicce, and I had never liked the custom, so, as before, I merely bowed. Queen Lilah of Hiclantung looked upon me, there in the fuzzy pink moonslight.

"It seems I have pierced two impiters with a single shaft. I came to haggle for corths from that fat corthman Nath, and now I find the pleasure of meeting you, Dray Prescot. I had planned a more formal meeting, for I fear I have not thanked you enough for saving the miserable skin of my foolish nephew."

Against that kind of polite nonsense, a plain sea officer and a fighting-man is usually out of his depth. I merely bowed again and said: "The pleasure is mine, I assure you."

How long the inanities would have gone I do not know. This Queen Lilah stood very tall, her dark eyes on a level with my own brown ones, and her red hair had been coiffed into a high pile resplendent with gems and strings of pearls. Her dark blue gown, thickly embroidered and stiff with bullion and gold and silver threads, gave no hint of her figure; but her face was very white, unlined, her eyes picked out with kohl and her mouth painted into a cupid's bow of allure. She gazed at me most intently as we spoke, and I gathered something of her power and her majesty, the immediate response she could always elicit, for that pallid face tinged with the pink radiance from the moons of Kregen and those darkly glittering eyes held a kind of hypnotic power, emphasized by the shadowing beneath her cheeks and the upslanted eyebrows, the widow's peak of red hair over her forehead.

A man with her, elegant in dark green robes—dark green! —and with a powerful bearded face and eloquent hands adorned with many rings on the carefully tended fingers, was speaking of the lack of news of the scouts sent out to track the destination of the flying tribe who had so sorely bested the Hiclantung army and carried off Delia.

"But in a day or two they will return," said this man, one Orpus, a councillor high in the Queen's confidence. "Then we will know what do do."

"I doubt not but they were employed by those rasts of Chersonang. Soon, now, our plans will be ready and then—" The Queen did not finish her words, and the inanities might have turned into some conversation more welcome to my ears, for Chersonang was a city-state of great power whose borders marched with those of Hiclantung and with whom, as was to be expected, there was constant friction, had it not been for the sudden and wholly unexpected slaughter caused by a shower of arrows that whistled down about our ears.

At the same instant a body of men in dark garments rushed upon us. The next second I was fighting for my life.

"Stand firm!" roared a Hikdar and went down screeching with a cloth-yard shaft in his breast. An arrow hissed by me and buried itself in the back of a bodyguard who had swung around to face the oncoming assassins. Hwang was yelling and tugging at the Queen's sleeve. I saw her face, pale and pinkly-illuminated in that streaming radiance, and she looked firm and powerful, and yet haggard and ill, all at the same time. And, too, I saw the harsh lines curving about that painted mouth and understood more of the burdens she carried and the absolute intolerance with which she carried out what she conceived of as her duty.

Then, to what must have appeared as the seal of our doom to those attacking us, a cloud of impiter-mounted men swooped from the sky and gusting in over the walled stairway fell upon us with all the impetuosity of a chunkrah charge.

If we were to come out of this alive not a moment could be lost. Hwang had still not budged the Queen, who stood, tall and straight in those heavy brocaded garments. Her bodyguard fell about her, and now it was clearly apparent that these night raiders had planned this assault to carry off the Queen.

"The Queen!" someone shouted.

"To the death!" screeched the defiant answers from the bodyguard.

Hwang's little sword flickered in and out very expertly. My own great long sword, suddenly clumsy in this civilized company, swept away three of the attackers, lopped heads and arms; but they pressed me back and soon Hwang and I were left isolated with the Queen at our backs, pressed against the stairway wall.

I felt cramped in, hemmed and penned. I had not used a rapier and main-gauche as a pair in a long time, the Jiktar and the Hikdar, and all the advantages of a long sword were being lost to me.

"We must break through and reach the corthdrome," I shouted at Hwang. If only Seg were here! I felled a man who lunged at me, skipping aside from his glittering point with accustomed unthinking skill. "You must force the Queen—"

"They will never take me alive."

Queen Lilah of Hiclantung held a dagger, jeweled and ornate, but needle-sharp for all that. I knew that dagger would plunge into her breast when the end came. Somehow, in my agony for my Delia I found a strange sense of outrage that another beautiful woman should die.

I leaped forward, whirling my sword in tremendous overhand circles, rather in the fashion of the Clansmen of Viktrik with the Danish ax, and cleared a space in which the ghastly slashed trunks and sliced heads of my opponents sank down bloodily. Moving now very rapidly, even for me, I scooped up Queen Lilah, hoisted her under my left arm, and with a great yell to Hwang to follow, bounded up the stairway.

Two, three, four of the dark-clad assassins I slew as I raced up the steps. I forced my breathing to fall into that old familiar regular rhythm. The only thing that would stop me now would be an arrow through the spine. Even then, such was my wrath, that I believe I would have reached the lofty doors of the corthdrome with a quiver-full of arrows feathering in my back.

Just as we reached those arched doorways a figure scuttled out and the doors began to close. In seconds they would slam in our faces. From below us on the wide stairway the beast yells lifted and the rapid patter of feet and the clink of steel eloquently told of what fate lay in store for us there.

I let rip with a furious, atavistic, enraged yell and bounded up the last flight, shoved my shoulder against those closing valves, and thrust vigorously.

A frightened squeak answered from within, and then we were through and Nath the Corthman and three or four of his stable slaves were pushing frantically at the doors again. Hwang pitched in to help them.

"Put me down, you great oaf!"

I had forgotten the Queen, bundled up under my arm. As I set her on her feet, she called out in her most imperial way: "The bar, you fools! Put the bar across! By Hlo-Hli—hurry!"

Nath the Corthman was dancing around and wringing his hands and sobbing. "My beautiful corths! These barbarian beasts will take them all, or slay them, my flying wonders of the sky!"

"Cease your babbling, cramph, or I will nick your ears!"

Nath bobbed and bowed before the Queen as we struggled to close the doors, our feet slipping on the tessellated paving, our muscles bulging, our breaths clogging in our throats.

Flint-headed spears thrust through the slit opening between the two valves. Arrows flew through. We could hear the

yelling outside, the whip-like crack of orders, and hear the
bestial grunting of the assassins as they sought to thrust the
doors wide and rush in upon us.

Behind us the corths, whose unease manifested itself in a
great whistling chirruping, had now begun to emit their
strange feathery-dusty odor. I glanced up. Long before we
could unchain a corth and open the ceiling valves, which
drew back in segments, the assassins would have completed
their work.

As we surged against the doors Queen Lilah stood back
from us, tall and regal, her embroidered robes falling in
sheer lines to her feet, her face as waxy white as a votive
candle, the dagger in her hand catching the light from
torches in their wall brackets and splintering strange and
disturbing colors over the scene.

"The defense wires had been removed from this stairway,"
she said. Her voice cracked as flat and hard as a falchion
blade. "There were men waiting in hiding. Oh, Orpus, unhappy man! If you have survived it were better had you not!"

If the high councillor had been a party to the plot then he
wouldn't hang around Hiclantung; if he had not been then
he would be lying on the stairway weltering in his own
blood.

The doors groaned as weights thrust unequally against
them. Their bronze hinges squealed. Slowly, the stable slaves
and Hwang and I were being thrust back. It was a mere
matter of moments before the murderers broke in.

All my natural instincts urged me to fling wide the doors
and with my sword in my fist to hurl myself upon these beast-
men.

Such a course—which is deplorable in itself—often seems
to me the most natural one in two worlds in circumstances
like those when I fought the assassins in the corthdrome of
Hiclantung. I can wait for an attacker to expose himself and
then counter-strike. I can charge headlong and carry the
fight to him. But now—such a course would mean the inevitable deaths of Hwang and Queen Lilah. I glanced back
at the torchlit interior of the corthdrome.

Beyond the ranked perches where the corths whistled and
shrilled and ruffled their feathers beneath the arched roof
a narrow stair ran winding around the interior wall. At its
summit a narrow door of lenk wood gave ingress to the
windlass room, where were situated the necessary drums and
levers and apparatus for opening the roof. I shouted at
Hwang.

"Hwang! Do not argue! Take the Queen up there—at once!"

Before Hwang could reply she had stamped her foot and rejected the suggestion in an icy manner of high hauteur.

"If you do not go, Lilah," I said, "I shall put you under my arm again, and this time I shall beat you."

"You would not dare!" Her eyes flamed at me. "I am the Queen!"

"Aye—and you'll be a dead Queen, by Zim-Zair, if you don't do as I say! Now—*go!*"

She looked at my face in the vivid light of the torches and I must have been wearing that old ugly look of demoniac power that transfigures my features into a devil's mask, for she shuddered and turned away.

"Go!"

With what I took to be either a curse or a sob she lifted the heavy brocaded hem of her robe and I saw her slippered feet twinkling as she ran across the floor between the perches and started on the lung-bursting climb. "After her, Hwang!"

"But you!"

"If I am to die, then this is as well a way to go as any other." I shooed him away and the doors squealed as they opened further. To the stable slaves in their gray slave breechclouts I said: "When I give you leave—run! Hide! These evil men do not desire to kill you!"

"Aye, master," they wailed, thrusting with their lean naked arms, the sweat running down their lined faces.

I stripped off the gorgeous Lohvian robes with their rich and encumbering embroidery. Against a long sword the cloth mass I bundled around my left arm would be useless, but these flying men used long and thin swords—not rapiers—and I could perhaps deflect them enough to strike back. From a natural nostalgia I had selected a brilliant scarlet loincloth and I own I felt a thrill of the old pride in the color nerve me—vain young words and feelings, to my shame!

Also, I kicked off the elegant sandals provided by my Lohvian hosts in Hiclantung. The long swords we had picked up here and there on our travels had not been the great long sword of the Krozairs—but Zenkiren had graciously given me a real Krozair long sword when we had parted in Pattelonia. Its handle was a full four fists' width in length, perfectly balanced for single-handed work, deadly when counterpoised by the left fist beneath the pommel with all that leverage that could be exerted. It was, perhaps, when wielded by a practiced and expert two-handed swordsman even faster than a single-hander—I knew this, yet I needed some protection for my left arm initially, and I could wield the sword two-handed even with the embroidered cloth bundled about my left arm.

"Now—go!"

With frightened shrieks the stable slaves scampered away from the doors and vanished into the shadows.

I poised, ready, and I felt the night breeze upon my naked chest and thighs, the floor hard and firm beneath my feet, the grip of the Krozair sword in my fist.

Yes—my Delia, my Delia of the Blue Mountains—if I was to die then this was the way I would go.

The doors smashed back.

Like an indigo tide the assassins poured in and I met them headlong, with a bestial roar that stopped them in their tracks. I was among them, smiting, thrusting, before they were aware, and they recoiled as though from some inhuman monster of legend.

"Hai!" I roared, leaping and slashing. "Hai, Jikai!"

We were too close-packed for them to bring the mighty Lohvian longbows into action. I swung the sword in economical strokes now, aiming for targets, smiting them to the ground. Twice I was able to wrest the thin sword from the grip of a surprised man, and, leaping forward, grasp him about the throat with my left hand and, after throttling him, hurl him back among his fellows.

How long I might have gone on thus I do not know. Not forever, that is certain. But then I heard a high-pitched, cracking voice from the interior of the corthdrome.

"*Dray!*"

And I knew Hwang and the Queen had reached the door to the windlass room.

For an exit I surged into the nearest man, hoisted him over my head, flung him horizontally into the men jostling to get in through the doors over the bloodied bodies of their comrades. Swiftly, then, for I did not relish this part, I turned and ran. I, Dray Prescot, Lord of Strombor, turned and ran. But I ran with a set purpose. I reached the foot of the stairs before they had recovered and I went up in gigantic leaping strides that must surely have confused those men of Kregen who had never witnessed an Earthman's muscles exerting their full power against the fractionally weaker gravity of their planet. Halfway up I judged to be the moment of danger, and a yell from Hwang from above confirmed that.

I swung about, the Krozair sword lifted, and I beat away

the arrows as we used to do in those strict and demanding disciplines on the island of Zy in the Eye of the World.

Up again, and a turn, and more arrows to be dodged or beaten away with sword or robes, and up yet again.

Now the indigo-haired men were at the foot of the stairs and were racing up, their swords slivers of steely glitter in the torchlight. They wanted the Queen; they would dare anything for that end.

At the top I struck sideways an arrow that would have found Hwang, and then we were through the small lenk door.

I slammed it and barred it. I breathed deeply and easily, aware of the sweat shining on my chest and thighs, runneling down between the ridged muscles. Blood dripped thickly from my sword and gobbets and gouts of it matted the hair on my chest.

"You—" stammered Queen Lilah of Hiclantung.

A new and stronger roaring began outside the barred door and the first few blows upon its stout lenk wood were the only ones. We could hear, distantly, the shouting of men and the clash of steel.

"The guards!" exclaimed Hwang. His face radiated a fresh and sudden confidence. "We are saved!"

I grunted.

I put my hand to the bar.

Queen Lilah stood, and I could see the heaving tumult of her bosom thrusting now against the concealing stiff brocade. "Dray—" she began, then, again: "Dray Prescot?"

I looked at her, eyes on a level with eyes.

"You have witnessed what few have ever seen," I told her, unaware then of the irony of it. "You have seen Dray Prescot run from his foes. Now I go back to settle with them."

Of course—that evil and fascinating blood fever was upon me then.

I lifted the bar.

She put a small white hand on my arm.

"No, Dray Prescot. There is no need. The guards will deal with those rasts of assassins. But—I would not wish you wounded now, perhaps killed."

"You would have me skulk behind a locked door?"

She shook her head angrily, her dark eyes filled with a reflected torchlight that made of them a dazzlement and a glory.

"I would have you live, Dray Prescot—and do not forget, I am the Queen! My word is law! You would do well not to cross me, Dray Prescot—stranger!"

"I agree—and I would do even better to obey my own wishes!"

And I lifted the bar and opened the door and ran down the stairs.

Chapter Twelve

The Queen of Pain

"Oh, Dray Prescot!" said Thelda. "I just don't know what I'm going to do with you!"

We stood in the sunny morning room of the villa and Thelda regarded me with her head on one side, her ripe red lips pursed up and her hands on her hips. She wore a scarlet —because she thought that would please me—breechclout and a simple silvery-tissue blouse that was as near as made no difference to being transparent. Her dark brown hair had been meticulously coiffed by one of the house slaves we had been obligated to accept—we had no powers to free them, as Seg and I would have instantly done—and the lush coils sparkled with gems and pearls. Her fingernails and toenails had been lacquered a pleasant scarlet. Her face received such care and attention as it had surely never known since leaving Vallia. She did look alluring and lovely and voluptuous, no question of it, now that her fat had been worked off and the natural firm and Junoesque lines of her figure could be seen. She stood with her legs braced, her hands on her hips, and she regarded me as a risslaca regards a rabbit.

"You, Dray Prescot, recovering from a terrible wound, go slallyfanting about the city at the dead of night—getting into fights—rescuing the Queen—oh, Dray—look out for her! She is a deep and devious one. I know, for Seg has told me of the notorious Queens of Loh—"

"I know," I said. "I have heard. They call her the Queen of Pain. But only when she cannot overhear them."

"They were terrible—the Queens of Loh! The things they did turned my stomach over when Seg merely hinted at them. And this one is right in the line. I wouldn't like to inquire into just how many husbands—husbands! That's a laugh!— how many poor silly believing men she's toyed with and discarded and had tortured to death. . . ."

"Thelda! It's you who are slallyfanting, not me."

"But surely you can see why I am so worried about you, Dray!"

"No. And, anyway since the Walfarg empire crumpled Loh has left only some of its culture behind here—why, the women don't wear veils, as they do in their mysterious walled gardens of Loh."

"You have been to Loh, Dray?"

"No. But I have heard of it—"

She was standing straight and firm, but now she seemed to melt and flow, the tenseness leaving her thighs and calves, her shoulders, and she bent and flowed and moved against me so that she pressed into my chest. I was wearing a plain white loincloth, having come straight from the bath, with my hair still wet, and I could feel the warmth of her through the silver tissue. Quite evidently she expected me to put my arms about her as she put hers about me, tilting her head to gaze up at me, her lips half parted, moist and clinging in that way that can madden almost any man of sensibility. I kept my arms away from her.

"Oh, you fond, silly, silly man! Don't you know why I worry so over you, so that my heart seems to burst right out of my bosom?" She unclasped one hand and grasped my fingers. "Feel my heart, Dray, and you will know how passionately it beats—"

I had had enough of this. I simply didn't let my arm bend in, and I said, gently: "I think Seg is up and about. His wound mends well—"

She flounced away, her lips plainly wanting to rick into a snarl and yet forced by a will I was coming to recognize to curve into a fetching pout.

"It is no good thinking of Delia, Dray—"

"What?"

She wouldn't be checked now.

"Why—didn't you see? I thought you knew—"

I was at her side and I gripped her by the shoulders, crumpling the silver tissue, dragging her half upward so that she staggered up onto her toes. I glared down on her upturned face where now that silly pouting look vanished to be replaced by a sudden startlement.

"Knew what, Thelda?"

She gasped as my fingers drug into her shoulders.

"Dray—you're hurting—"

I let her down, but I still held her hard.

"Tell me!"

"Delia—the Princess Majestrix—the impiter dropped her,

Dray—I thought you knew! It dropped her into a pond—you know, one of the little tarns that you find all over the uplands—and I screamed—why did you think I was screaming, Dray, for myself?" She wriggled and licked her lips. "I knew Delia was dead, and I was screaming in fear for you, Dray!"

I let her drop so that she went down in a flurry of silver tissue with the brave scarlet breechclout sprawling in an ungainly back-slide, and turned away, and Seg said: "I did not see Delia fall from the impiter! By the veiled Froyvil—she cannot be dead! It would not be allowed!"

He came into the room with most of his old reckless air still about him; his limp had almost gone. He was better, he was the old Seg again, with the reckless laugh and the damn-you-to-hell manner.

"No," I said, my voice a croak. "No—it would be unthinkable—it could not be allowed. My Delia, she is not dead—" I swung to Thelda, who raised herself on her arms, the silver tissue bulging and crumpling with the force of her breathing. "What tarn was it, Thelda? I will go to this pond and see for myself!"

Nothing would stop me.

When Hwang pointed out the dangers, that travel between cities anywhere in this land was beset with peril, that the winged host might still be in the vicinity, that wild beasts would rend me, I brushed all that tomfoolery aside. I donned my scarlet breechclout, buckled on my long sword, and I found a blanket roll, and some odd items of food. I took my new longbow in my hand, slung the quiver over my shoulders, mounted a borrowed nactrix, and I was off.

As I had expected Seg soon spurred up to ride at my side.

By the time we had ridden back over that ground and found the site of the battle—massacre, really—where the bones lay white and bleaching under the suns of Scorpio, Hwang and a regiment of his own calvary were hard on our heels. I had heard from the Queen's nephew something of the reasons for that disastrous battle in the valley; that the men cherished their traditions and fought in disciplined bodies held together by rules sacrosanct with age. That the treacherous councillor Forpacheng—and not Orpus whom the Queen had suspected and who had miraculously escaped the ambush on the stairway—had led the troops into the valley, and had then let them be cut to pieces. That the discipline had broken under Forpacheng's malicious and contradictory orders. Now, Hwang had said, a new army was being forged from the remnants and new recruits, and they would not repeat the mistakes of the past.

The pool lay black and ominous beneath the suns.

I dived. I dived and swam beneath the water until my lungs burned and all the suns of the universe flamed before my eyes; I did not find my Delia.

Memories of that time blur. I remember men talking to me and urging me not to continue; and of myself taking deep agonizing breaths and cleaving the dark water of the tarn and swimming, swimming, swimming, and always that nightmarish expectancy that my groping hands would close on the obscenely bloated, water-logged, half eaten body of my Delia of Delphond.

Exhaustion had no place in my scheme of things.

I would search every single square inch of the bottom of the pool, and every cubic inch of its water; and if I did not find my Delia, then I would begin all over again. I did not want to find her there, God knows; but I did not want to leave the task unfinished and be haunted for the rest of my days.

Perhaps, in the end, I was only saved from insanity by the arrival of Orpus and more soldiers. They seemed to my dulled senses smart enough, Zair knows. With them rode a man whose hair was dyed a deep indigo.

I reared up and from somewhere my long sword was in my fist and I started for this man with the indigo hair and I heard Seg shout and his hand gripped my arm.

"No, no, Dray! He is of Hiclantung—his hair is dyed because he has been scouting—"

"A spy," I said stupidly.

"Yes, yes—and listen! He believes he has found where Delia is held captive!"

When I had somewhat recovered my senses and the news had been expounded, my next step was obvious.

The name I now focused on with an intensity of purpose at once hateful and vengeful and obsessional was—Umgar Stro.

The spy, one Naghan, a common name on Kregen, had been clever; clearly he was a courageous and resourceful man. Charged with the task of discovering who had instigated the nighttime attack upon the Queen he had begun by making inquiries in Chersonang, the rival city-state of Hiclantung, only to discover that the whole political situation had changed. A new force had entered this area of the Hostile Territories. From far to the northwest a fresh barbarian horde had swung southward as they had done when the empire of Walfarg in Loh had fallen. From the windy heights past The Stratemsk they had flown astride their impiters and corths and zizils, intent on carving a new land for themselves. They had taken over a country inhabited by Rapas, killing the vulturine people by the thousand, installing themselves as overlords. And here their leader, this Umgar Stro, had suborned and paid the traitor Forpacheng. But now—Umgar Stro had announced his intentions of dominating the entire section of nations centering on his new capital of Plicla, that had once been Rapa, and then of taking over the whole of the Hostile Territories, and the eastern seaboard with its scattering of settlements of nations of the outer ocean, and, so he had said, boldly, he would also march across The Stratemsk and attack whatever lay beyond.

Of course, the inner sea, the Eye of the World, was unknown to these people except in the vaguest of myth and legend.

"And Delia is held in a tower in Plicla. May the veiled Froyvil guard her and keep her from harm!"

"You are sure?" I asked Naghan as Seg's anxious words died.

"I cannot be certain that the girl captured is the princess you seek," said Naghan, omitting all forms of ceremonial or obsequious address. "I never saw her." He was short and strong, with a faded look around his eyes. He had built his face up into a blunt profile with oiled clays, but no one would think him one of Umgar Stro's half-men in any kind of decent light. He had taken his life in his hands to bring me this information, and I was grateful to him. "I can give you all the information of the tower you require; externally, that is. Once inside—" He spread his hands.

Umgar Stro.

The whole area between The Stratemsk and the eastern seaboard had been turned into a place containing a very large number of petty kingdoms. The so-called Hostile Territories were places where a series of nations each followed its own destiny. There were tracts where the original inhabitants remained, there were barbarian nomads, there were cities of half-men and beast-men, there were nations of half-civilized barbarians, there were the cities which had managed to retain much of their Lohvian heritage. The whole was a great quilt of conflicting cultures.

Umgar Stro.

With the legacies left by Walfarg—the long well-constructed and surfaced roads, a common currency, the use of arms, a common law that the barbarians naturally disrupted, a religion based on worship of the female principle in life and

the interesting ramifications following on that—all these ele-
ments of existence held in common had in an ironic way
helped rather than hindered the dissolution and conquest of
the land by factions. A raiding army could move rapidly down the
roads, but they would be exposed to attack at known places by
the flying hosts.

Umgar Stro.

"Once I am inside Umgar Stro's tower," I told Naghan, the
spy, "I shall be satisfied."

He looked at my face, and turned away, and fidgeted with
his sword.

"What is the name of this barbarian nation that flies its
impiters against Hiclantung?"

"They come from Ullardrin, somewhere north of The
Stratemsk and they are called the Ullars."

"We'll need to fly, Dray," said Seg.

"Yes," I said. "I hear the men of Hiclantung do not really
relish flying—the corths are few and far between in the city."
This was true. Corth-flying was in the nature of a sport for the
nobles and the high councillors; the ordinary people and
the soldiers hated all flying beasts, and one could well understand why. Their ancestors had waged ceaseless war against
the aerial barbarians, and it still went on today. They had
developed effective tricks and weapons they could deploy
against impiters and corths and only through Forpacheng's
treachery were they deprived of them on the day of the army
massacre.

We hurried back to the city.

Thelda with tears and protestations tried to stop me from
going. She had seen Delia fall into the tarn and if I went to
this dreadful Umgar Stro's high tower I would surely be
killed.

There was much to be learned about riding a corth and I
put her aside and shouted for Seg. Hwang had insisted on
putting his two best birds at our disposal, and we went along
to fat Nath the Corthman to find out all we could.

Everyone treated us as though we were mad, and everyone
was careful to make full, polite, and emotional Remberee of
us before they let us go.

I told Seg I did not want him to accompany me.

He laughed.

"I'll grant I've never seen a swordsman like you, Dray—no,
and never likely to! But I know that however good you may
be with the longbow, you cannot best me; and bows will be
needed, you will see. Consequently, I shall come with you."
He stared at me and I warmed to the look on his lean, tanned

face, the light of understanding and resolution in his blue eyes, the wild mane of black hair. "And," he said, offhandedly, "I, too, value your Delia Majestrix."

I couldn't speak for a moment, and grasped his hand. I was not fool enough to say what I had been about to say, namely, that I had thought he would welcome the opportunity to stay with Thelda. She had been worrying me, and I wished she would turn to Seg, although I wouldn't have wished her on my comrade for the world—either one—had he not devoutly wished that disaster for himself.

In the confused tangling of politics going on all around me as Queen Lilah sought for strength and allies against the menace of the Ullars, I was conscious only of one objective: I had to reach Umgar Stro's high tower and bring my Delia safely back to me.

I called her "my Delia" and she called me "my Dray" but neither one of us regarded it as selfish possession in thus speaking; rather we recognized we were but halves of a complete whole.

To add to our normal weapons and accouterments we took warm flying furs and silks, extra quivers of arrows, and a couple of heavy flint-headed spears. I packed a complete set of warm clothing for Delia. I had no doubts, now.

That evening I went up to the palace—imposing but, because of the absolute necessity not to allow any perching place for birds or animals, somehow spiritless and without that fantasy of architecture so beloved by the builders of Kregen—to pay my respects to the Queen.

Lilah received me in a small withdrawing room in which the lamps picked out the sumptuous furnishings, the furs and rugs, the weapons on the walls, the leather upholstery and all the crystal wink and glitter, the golden glows and the silver sheen of absolute luxury. The Queen of Pain, men called her, behind their hands. I had heard dark stories about her wayward manner with men; how she used them and tossed them aside. I had met, as I then thought, women of her stamp before. Those fabulous Queens of Loh, notorious, sadistic, cruel, had a devoted disciple in this tall woman with the widow's peak of dark red hair, the upslanting eyebrows, the shaded cheekbones, and the small firm mouth. She welcomed me kindly and we drank purple wine of Hiclantung, and munched palines. She wore a jeweled mesh of clothes so that her white skin gleamed through the interstices. Lovely and desirable she looked; and yet, hard and remote, a true queen with destinies and cares above the mere carnal satisfactions of the flesh. I had the thought that my Delia, however greater an empire she might one day rule, would never take on that hard, polished, ruthless look of despotism.

"You have saved my life, Dray Prescot, and now you rush off to risk that life, precious to me, in the wayward service of another woman."

"Not any woman, Lilah."

"And am I not any woman! I am the Queen—I have told you; my word is law. You flouted my wishes, there in the windlass room of the corthdrome. Many men have died for less."

"Mayhap they have. I do not intend to die for that."

She drew in a breath and the gems about her body winked and flashed in the lamplight. Gracefully she stretched out a white arm and lifted her goblet. The wine stained her lips for an instant, turning them purple and cruel.

"I need a man like you, Dray Prescot. I can give you any thing you desire—as you have seen. Now that the Ullars are forcing themselves on us, I need a fighting-man to lead my regiments. They are well-disciplined, but they do not fight well. The barbarians scorn us."

"Men will fight if they believe in what they fight for."

"I believe in Hiclantung! And I believe in myself!"

I nodded.

"Sit upon my throne alongside me, Dray! I implore you— and there could be a great sweetness between us—more than you can imagine." She was breathing faster now, and her mouth opened with the passions she felt. I—what did I think, then, when every fiber of my being shrieked to be off and away in search of my Delia of the Blue Mountains?

"You honor me, Lilah. Indeed, you are beautiful."

Before I could go on she had thrown herself upon me, her arms were about my neck, and I could feel the gems upon her person pressing into my flesh beneath the white robe I wore. Her mouth, all hot and moist, sought mine. I recoiled.

"Dray!" she moaned. "If I were a true queen I would have had you quartered for what you did! So bold, so reckless, so impious—you defied me, the Queen of Hiclantung. And yet you live and I am prostrate at your feet, imploring you—"

"Please, Lilah!" I managed to disengage, and she slumped to the floor on the gorgeous rugs and stared up lustfully at me. She was breathing in great gasps now, her body convulsed with her own passions. "Please, you are the Queen and a great one. You have wonderful deeds to accomplish for your city, and I will help you—that I swear—!"

"You—?"

"I must go to Umgar Stro's tower, Lilah. If I may not do that then I will not do anything else."

She jumped up, her eyes murderous upon me, and I knew that in an instant I might be struck down on that carpet before her, my head rolling and spouting blood over her pretty jeweled naked feet.

She opened her mouth and a palace slave—a pretty girl with the gray slave breechclout edged in gold lace, and a pair of enormous dark eyes that fairly danced in a goggling kind of amazement at the scene within—put her curly head in at the door and started to say: "The Lady Thelda of Vallia —" when she was pushed aside and Thelda marched in.

The tableau held. It held, I confess, until despite all my lack of laughter I wanted to roar my mirth at these two.

For these two were standing up very straight and erect, bosoms jutting, chins up, hands held quiveringly at their sides, their eyes darting and flashing like rapiers crossing, so charged with emotion were these two ladies—and over a hulking great brute of a man with an ugly face and shoulders wide enough to have encompassed the pair of them—a man, moreover, who wanted nothing so much as to be rid of the pair of them and wing into the night to seek his true love.

So much for the tantrums of beauty!

They did not fight, or spit, or scratch—and, indeed, it would have been an overmatched contest—but the danger signals that flashed between them crackled with eloquent if silent rivalries.

Queen Lilah seemed perfectly to accept Thelda's arrival. I suppose she could, if she wished, have tossed us both into some dank dungeon and had us tortured to death, licking her lips over us the while.

As it was, Lilah simply said with devastating regality: "Does this—woman—mean anything to you, Dray?"

The question differed entirely from that question of like meaning put to me by the Princess Natema on her garden rooftop in the Opal Palace of the Esztercari hold in Zenicce. Then I had lied to save my Delia's life. I did not need to lie now to save Thelda's. And yet—she did mean something to me, although not what either she longed for or Lilah suspected.

"I have the highest respect for the Lady Thelda," I said, with crude formality. The image of the night sky and a rushing wind and the tower of Umgar Stro reared into my mind's eye. I could not wait longer. "I hold her in the same deep and cherished affection as I hold your esteemed and regal person, Lilah. No more—and no less."

"Oh—Dray!" The wail could have come from either woman.

"I must go."

I laid my hand on my sword hilt. An almost instinctive gesture, it brought a flush to Lilah's pallid countenance. Such boorish behavior, clearly, was unknown in her civilized palace. Thelda started across and took my arm. She glared haughtily upon the Queen.

"I am responsible for the safe-keeping of my Lord of Strombor," she said. "Now that his betrothed, the Princess Majestrix of Vallia, is dead."

I would not let her say any more. I turned my wrist and took her hand in my own and crushed it, and smiled at Lilah the Queen, and said firmly but without rancor: "I am eternally in your debt, Lilah, for your goodness to me and my friends. Now I must go to seek out this Umgar Stro and, if necessary, kill him. I believe I am doing you a good favor, Lilah, in doing that, so do not hurt Thelda here or hinder me. I am a good friend—I would not wish you to understand the depth of my enmity."

This was all good fustian stuff, but it had its effect.

As though coming to a decision, the Queen nodded, and the stiffness went out of her poise. Her figure was good, if a trifle on the thin side, but this merely added to the regality of her presence. She put a hand to her breast, over her heart, and pressed it in. Distinctly, I saw a gigantic diamond, scintillant and brilliant in the lamplight, cut into her flesh.

Her gasp forced its way past psychic, mental levels of pain completely unknown to her body.

"Very well, Dray Prescot. Wreak your vengeance on Umgar Stro. I shall not forget. I shall be here when you return. Then we will talk more; for what I have spoken to you I sincerely mean."

"I am sure you do."

"As for you, my Lady Thelda, I would advise a more circumspect tongue. Do you understand?"

Before Thelda, whose blood was up, could answer, I dug my fingers into her hand, so that she winced. Then I dragged her off.

Lilah, tall and resplendent in the jeweled lamplight, called after me: "I wish you well, Dray Prescot. Rembereel"

"Remberee, Lilah!" I called back.

As we got outside, Thelda jerked free and spat out: "The female cramph! I could scratch her eyes out!"

Then, and with some bewilderment, I admit, I chuckled.

Chapter Thirteen

I go swinging at the tower of Umgar Stro

That image of a dark night and a rushing wind I had experienced in the scented withdrawing room of Lilah's palace had come true.

Seg and I had taken off before the twins—the two second moons of Kregen eternally orbiting each other—had appeared above the horizon and with the maiden of many smiles sinking over the western rim of the world. By her dying light we saw the sleeping city beneath us, all its watchtowers spiring into the sky where restless men kept their long vigils, and only the faint lamp-glow falling from their arrow slits to tell of life within.

We passed over the manufacturing quarters where in the enclosed atrium-style houses the work-people lay asleep, and all the long alleyways between the houses lay silent and deserted beneath the stars. Down there the forge fires softly sloughed away into grayness and cold, the hammers stilled, the bellows silent from their slave-driven wheezing. Bronze and copper and iron for implements and weapons of war, silver and gold and nathium for trinkets and objects of art, all lay quietly in their racks awaiting the morrow's labors, for the Queen maintained her industry at a thriving rate against the tide of barbarism.

Farther off lay the tanners' quarters, and the potters' and the glaziers'; great cities do not exist as mere palaces and villas, streets and temples, without visible means of support. As soon as Genodras flooded down in the morning the gates would open and the country folk, ever-fearful of barbarian raids, would trundle in their carts, pulled by asses or calsanys, or trudge stolidly with great burdens swinging over their shoulders at either end of long supple poles of tuffa wood, all seeking to find the best and most advantageous places within the covered markets to display their produce. The city slept; save for its guardians in their spires and along its walls.

On the morrow it would awake to a new day and fresh life, and would thank its pagan female goddesses that it still survived.

I wondered, not without real concern for Seg, if we two would still live to welcome that morrow.

The corths Hwang had provided, not without a deal of cutting sarcasm directed against Nath the Corthman, were docile but sturdy beasts. Their wings beat steadily and we rose and fell in the night air in a strong and soothing rhythm. They were well-trained, as any flying mount for a man must be, and we felt confident that they would do all that we required of them. We rode two and I had attached the long leading rein of the third to my flying saddle. Warmly clad in furs and silks, we lay in a semi-prone position just abaft the birds' heads. We had to be clear of the arc the powerful wings cut in the air. A bird shaped, say, like a falcon or a hawk would be difficult if not impossible to ride; a saddle bird must needs possess a neck of some strength and length if its rider's legs are not to smash catastrophically against its wings.

The sensation of flying thus, of hurtling through the level air, exhilarated me. This was very different from aerial navigation aboard a flier from Havilfar. I began to wonder if we would have stood a better chance of negotiating The Stratemsk astride an aerial monster like the corth, or the impiter which was so much bigger, fiercer, and more powerful.

We winged on our way following the faint glimmer of the road beneath that ran almost straight from Hiclantung. We had been given our instructions—briefed, you would say— and we had no fears of failing to find Plicla, the city of the Rapas that was now the city of Umgar Stro.

Plicla was situated amid a mass of broken hills and dales, good flying country with its updrafts, and yet dangerous with its sudden precipices and vortices of air. The city had been founded by Rapas who had drifted into the area as slaves or mercenaries in the long ago, employed by Loh no less than her foes, and who now had banded together to found their own Rapa nation. Umgar Stro and his Ullars had altered all that.

We saw the high towers, the craggy cliffs supporting the massive walls, with their tops raking for the sky. A suspicious, smelly, unpleasant race, the Rapas, so I thought then, when I was young and new to Kregen and had only unpleasant experience of them to judge them by. Their bird-like faces, their fierce agile ability, made them valued as guards and mercenaries, no less than slaves. I wondered what they would be like as mere citizens of their own city-state.

Natural caution among mercenary-employing nations impelled them to hire mercenaries from many different races. Chuliks, Rapas, Ochs, Fristles—of those I had already met on Kregen—and all the other strange half-men and beast-men I was to encounter, also, when employed by a single government would rest secure in the knowledge that each individual detachment of mercenaries would scarcely ever allow itself to be cozened into a rebellion in association with any other detachment. Mutual suspicion would keep the hired soldiers apart. And no single detachment would of itself be powerful enough to topple the hiring government, when all the others would leap in to combat the first hint of insurrection. In general, then, mercenaries on Kregen can be trusted to earn their hire.

But—there were always the exceptions. And I, Dray Prescot from Earth, took a perverse delight in finding those exceptions and turning them to the general good.

Now Umgar Stro and his Ullars from far Ullardrin with their indigo-dyed hair ruled in Rapa Plicla.

Naghan the spy had given us exact directions.

We could not, of course, converse at the distance apart the wingspread of the corths forced us to fly, and into the teeth of the blustering wind; but at my pointing spear Seg nodded, and we did as we had been taught with the simple reins of the birds and began to glide down.

The tower seemed to grow in size and girth as we floated down to it.

Away to the north we could make out the stone-piled enclosures surrounding the Yerthyr trees to keep out the animals of the city. Seg had reported to me on the quality of the trees of Hiclantung. Wherever we went in our travels it was noticeable how Seg's expert appraising eye dealt with the forestry details. Hiclantung's Yerthyr trees, according to Seg, were excellent and the bows with which we had been furnished brought a smile of delight to Seg's lips.

This first rapid approach was to be a reconnaissance. Our corths, which would never be mistaken for impiter or yuel-shi, could no more make a landing on the tower or its battlemented curtain walls on either hand as could one of the Ullars' mounts land on a roof in Hiclantung. The same rules of elementary tactics applied. My corth—a fine fellow with the boldly delineated eye and pigment streaks running from it that distinguish the Earthly cormorant—wheeled with easy power, swooping past the tower and so away again with a giant rustling of wings off into the concealing darkness. A couple of Kregen's lesser moons were in process of hurtling across the nighted sky, but until the twins rose we had the comforting concealment of semidarkness.

I suppose it is a natural part of nature's progress that more than one species should exist simultaneously—many hundreds insure the survival of at least some—and it would have been extraordinary if Kregen had developed through the years only one kind of flying animal or bird. Think of the enormous multitude of birds on Earth, and given the much greater size of the Kregish fliers, partially due, I imagine, to the slightly lessened gravity, it would be unthinkable for only one kind of giant flying animal to exist on Kregen beneath Antares.

The twins would soon roll above the eastern horizon and flood their pinkish light down over the jagged hills and the gaunt towers of Plicla. Seg knew exactly what he had to do, the doing of which as I had ordered being the only reason I had accepted his insistent offer to come along. I knew he would have come, anyway; I just didn't want to get him killed unnecessarily.

I made a sign to him in the wind-rushing darkness and I saw his wild head nod against the starlight.

Swerving my corth back toward the tower of Umgar Stro I began my final preparations. No normal landing was possible. So the abnormal became necessary.

All my old sailor skills surged up afresh as I knotted the leather thongs. The Hiclantung leather was good, even though I considered it not so fine as that of Sanurkazz. The corth's reins were extended in length. From the flying saddle I unwound the already-prepared thongs and dropped them to swing madly in the rushing wind of our flight. At their ends the trapeze and the loops did not look particularly inviting. I took a breath and then unfastened the flying straps and bands that held me to the saddle and slid over the side. My feet kicked wildly for an instant, then I had control and was able to lower myself down until I sat astride the trapeze, my hands in the loops above me and gripping the ends of the long extended reins that ran over crude blocks on the saddle bow.

An overwhelming nostalgic sweep of memory carried me back to my days in Aphrasöe, the city of the Savanti, and to the swingers. How I had joyed then in swinging in wild free hurtling flight from plant to plant! Now I was swinging again—although this time I clung beneath the hooked talons of a giant flying bird and swung not from pleasure but to save the life of the girl I loved.

The cold struck at me shrewdly, but I took no notice. Umgar Stro's tower seemed to me to swing and sway before my eyes. I fought to make my reeling senses understand that the tower remained still, that it was me, Dray Prescot, swinging so sickeningly. Long practice over the years in straddling out along the topgallant yardarms saved me, then, and I could estimate distance and force my senses to compose themselves.

Seg's corth billowed in from the side, the fingerlike wing-tip feathers altering angles and curvatures as with superb aerial control the great bird matched velocities with my own corth and the led bird. Seg would have to grab the reins of my mount—somehow—and keep it ready for our departure.

The roof of the tower spiked up toward me.

I pulled on the reins gingerly, and the world tilted; then the tower became perpendicular and I could see the fans of cruel iron spikes, the trip wires, the slanting lines of tiling that gave no secure perch anywhere.

I inched forward on the trapeze as the wind bellowed past my head, whipping my hair back, lacerating my eyes and cheeks.

Closer—closer—would the corth never haul up?

At the last moment to the savage jerking of the reins the bird abruptly fluttered his wide vulture-like wingspread. His body reared up into the air exposing his underside, his legs and claws stabbed forward and down. The trapeze hit the tiles with an almighty thump and I pitched off and rolled.

As I rolled and slithered to the sheer drop to the cliffs beneath, the corth, without alighting, fluttered hugely and was airborne. The led corth followed and the two birds wheeled away. I had no time to hope that Seg would catch them.

The lip of the slanted roof was coming up at me with frightening speed. If I went over that there would be nothing anymore—no Delia, no Vallia, no Aphrasöe. . . .

My hand smashed numbingly into an iron fan spike. My fingers curled and gripped without conscious volition. I hung there, spread-eagled on the roof, blatted at by the wind, seeing only the faint star-shot shadows all about me.

After a moment I had breath enough to draw myself up into a posture less exposed. The trapdoor through which inspection parties must come to check the roof defenses opened after I gave it a taste of my long sword. I dropped down, bent-legged, my sword in my fist. Only dust, cobwebs, litter. . . .

From the attic I found the ladder leading below and descended wondering, for the first time, at the silence of this place.

So far the information given me by Naghan, the spy, had proved correct. But he had not penetrated here. From now on I entered unknown dangers. For me, Dray Prescot, that is not an unusual hazard.

It seemed to me that the stone wall and floors of the chamber within the tower still reeked faintly of the distinctive Rapa odor. I padded on, guided from one dim pool of illumination in the palpable darkness to the next where torches guttered low. Desperately I sought to convince myself that my mission had not already proved in vain. But the atmosphere here smelled of abandonment—and then I tensed.

Voices, ahead of me, talking lazily, in half grumbling, half resigned accents brought all my senses alert as I crept stealthily upon the two Ullar guards.

"By the violet offal of the snow-blind feister-feelt! I swear my throat is more parched than the ripe-rotten south lands themselves! Nath! Fetch me a pannikin of that Chremson."

The voices were those of Ullars, fierce, resonant, the voices of men accustomed to shouting across the windy gulfs as their impiters crossed the sky. But—Nath!

"Aye," answered he who was named Nath. "And I'll drink you swallow for swallow, Bargo, and see you carried out heels first."

I crept closer in the gloom. The guardroom had been situated within a circular enclosure jutting out from the main bulk of the tower, and from this aerie the guards could obtain an unimpeded view. My sword did not tremble in my hand. The sound of wine gurgling from a leather wine-bottle reassured me.

"When they left us on guard they did us a mortal mischief, my cloth-headed dom." More drinking sounds. "I've not missed a sack since we left Ullardrin—"

"No more have I, Bargo, no more have I."

A gulping and then a resonant belch. Now I was up to the corner, ready to swoop in through the half open door of lenk. I could just catch a glimpse of them, or one of them, with his indigo-dyed hair flowing from that blunt head, that square mouth pursed to the upended blackjack. The handle of a pannikin showed, moving up and down, up and down, as the other Ullar drank. They were so nearly men, so much more like men than the Rapas they had chased from this tower. They wore leather studded with bronze and copper, and as I moved in, slowly and more slowly to bring them both

KIRK

"As I moved in, I could see how much alike they were, fierce, belligerent, habitual masters of the sky."

into view, I could see how much alike they were, fierce, belligerent, habitual conquerers and masters of the sky. Each had a bundle of leather thongs cunningly draped and knotted about his waist, and, although I knew little of the ins and outs of their mystique then, I knew enough to know this was the clerketer, the meticulously maintained harness with which they fastened themselves to their impiters and on which their lives would depend in the air.

"More wine, Nath, by the ice needles of Ullarkor, more wine!"

I had feathered shafts into men like these and seen them screech and swing out to dangle from that restraining harness, the clerketer.

Each of these—Nath and Bargo—carried himself with a swagger, that was clear enough. On a bench near them lay the leem pelts with which they kept warm in flight. Their long narrow swords were tucked up, thrusting, important, intended to scare and impress by their very angles of attack when seen against the chunky body, the blunt head and those close-set narrow eyes, that luxuriant mane of indigo hair.

I judged the time was ripe.

I entered the room very fast, and struck Nath upon that mane of indigo hair with the hilt of my sword, so that he dropped to the stone and blood burst from his nostrils and mouth. To the one called Bargo I showed the sword point, pushed against the leather over his heart. I leaned on the blade and it punctured leather and skin. Bargo's square harsh mouth clamped down. He glared at me, and there was death in my face, and he read it there, and he scowled back in savage defiance.

"Where is the prisoner, Bargo?" I spoke roughly, yet in a normal voice. I believe that frightened him more.

He gave me back look for look; then he lowered indigo-stained eyelids over his eyes and said: "Below—"

The wild leap of my heart must be quelled, instantly. . . .

There were no other occupants of the guardroom. Leaning against the wall behind the opened door stood two of the bamboo-hafted, gladius-bladed, and single-edge bitted toonons, the personal weapon of the Ullars, favored by them over all others when in the air. Each bamboo haft was twelve feet in length; with a two-handed grip on that, well-spaced, an Ullar could wield a wide swath of destruction about him in the air. The idea of carrying a short sword aloft was incongruous and ludicrous; what the Ullars had done was to mount the short sword upon this extended haft, reinforce it with a single ax-edge, narrow and deeply curved, and thus bring swordplay into a semblance of possibility aboard the back of a bird, albeit they had in reality constructed a kind of halberd.

Bargo's narrow and deeply-set eyes were focused upon my sword as its point thrust against the leathers over his chest. He wore a brave gold-laced sash about his waist. His legs, clad in the bound leather and cloth that gave him protection when in flight, were quivering. I knew that a moment's relaxation of watchfulness with him would be enough; he would be upon me like a plains leem.

"Lead, Bargo." Again I spoke almost normally.

The only precaution I took with him as I shifted the sword so that he could precede me from the guardroom was to relieve him of his sword. The blade was exceptionally long and thin. It was steel, flexible, keen, suited to the kind of blows a man must deliver if he fights from impiter back. I threw it down into a corner. I fancied my Krozair long sword would overmatch these impiter blades. Bargo's torch sputtered redly.

As we walked steadily down the winding stairs noises hitherto unheard became audible at the lower level. The distant sound of laughter, shouting, music from the single-bagpipes and the wilder, melancholy strains wrenched from the triple-bagpipes; I could even hear, I fancied now and then, the chink of bottles and the rattle of the dice cups, the tinkle of money. We went down the stairs in perfect silence. Bargo understood that his life meant nothing to me.

So confident was I of success that I could worry about Seg now, and hope he could keep clear of the impiter patrols the Ullars would have flying about Plicla.

The stones were old with that distinctive Rapa odor upon them still. We entered a corridor where dust lay thickly, marked by a central trail of darker footprints. At each cell door the dust lay undisturbed, at each one—save one!

To this Bargo unhesitatingly led.

"Open it, Bargo."

This he did, in silence, with the keys from his belt; great clumsy wooden keys they were, each a good nine inches in length, cunningly cut from lenk. The door opened, creaking. I looked inside, my emotions held tightly under, and—

An old man rose from his filthy bed of straw, gazing up with weak eyes, blinking, his near-lipless wrinkled mouth working, trying to distinguish us in the torchlit gloom.

"I have told you, and told you," he said in a voice that quavered as much from age as fear. "I cannot do it—you must believe me, Umgar Stro—there are some things forbidden and some things impossible for the Wizards of Loh."

I took Bargo by the front of his leather tunic and I lifted his feet from the floor. My sword point nestled into his throat. He was very near death, then, and he knew it.

"Where is she, you fool? The prisoner, the girl—tell me, quickly!"

He gargled. He managed to spit out words. "This is the prisoner! By the snow-blind feister-feelt, I swear it!"

"There is another, rast! A girl—the fairest girl you have ever seen. Where?

He shook his head weakly, and his blunt snout wrinkled with his fear. His indigo hair hung lankly down his shoulders.

"There is no other!"

I threw him down and my sword struck like a risslaca; but in the instant of striking I turned the blade so that the flat took him across the head and he pitched forward and lay still without uttering a sound.

"You are not of the Ullars, Jikai." The old man stood more firmly now, clutching his rags about him. His eyes in the random light from the fallen torch caught reflections and glowed like spilled winedrops in the wrinkled map of his face. His nose was long and narrow, his lips nonexistent, and the hair that wisped about his temples was still as red as any man of Loh's. It looked blue-black in that half light, but I knew it was red.

"Have you seen another prisoner, old man, a girl, a girl so wondrous—"

He shook that head and I wondered why it did not creak as the cell door had creaked.

"There is only me, Lu-si-Yuong. Have you means to escape from this accursed tower, Jikai?"

"Yes. But I do not go without the girl for whom I came."

"Then you will spend eternity here."

In all the clamor of thoughts echoing in my skull I think I knew, then, that Delia was not here.

"You have been here long, old man?"

"I am Lu-si-Yuong, and you address me as San." *

I nodded. The title of San was ancient and revered, bearing a meaning akin to master, dominie, sage. Clearly, this representative of the Wizards of Loh not only considered himself

---

* Prescot spells out Lu-si-Yuong, and is meticulous about getting the name and pronunciation right. He also elaborates on these famous Wizards, and is careful to use the title San. Jikai, here, clearly is being used in a titular role, and must be assumed to be the general for "warrior."   A.B.A.

an important personage, but was indeed truly so. I do not mind using a title when it is earned.

"Tell me, San, please. Have you any knowledge of the girl captured by Umgar Stro and brought to this tower?"

"I, alone, of the prisoners was spared. The Ullars know of the powers of the Wizards of Loh and they thought to avail themselves of my services. All the other prisoners were slain."

I stood there, I, Dray Prescot, and heard this old sage's thin voice whispering words that meant the end of everything of importance to me in two worlds.

I wanted to leap forward and choke a denial from his narrow mouth, to grip his corded throat in my two hands and wrench words I must hear from him. I think he saw my distress, for he said, again: "I cannot help you in this, Jikai. But I can help in—other—ways if you will rescue me—"

For a moment I could not answer him, could not respond. My Delia—surely, she could not have been so wantonly killed? It did not make sense—who could callously snuff out so much beauty?

San Yuong was whispering again, bending stiffly to pick up Bargo's spluttering torch. "They revel tonight, below. There are many of them, fierce, bold barbarians of the skies. To fight your way through them, Jikai, is a superhuman task—"

"We go up," I said, and I was short with him. All my instincts clashed there, in that cobwebby tower cell of Umgar Stro, torturing me with indecision, with doubt, with a mad and futile rage. She must be here! She must! But everything pointed to the opposite being true. This Wizard—why should he lie? Except, to cozen me into rescuing him!

I faced him. He had recovered his composure now, had drawn himself up so that the torchlight flowed over his gaunt features, over those wine-dark eyes, that long supercilious nose, that near-lipless mouth. He looked at me, clutching his rags, and he was well aware of the horror and superstitious awe in which common folk held the Wizards of Loh.

Indeed, there was power about him in an aura no one could overlook. Many and many a time have the Wizards of Loh performed deeds any normal man would dub impossible, and what their secrets may be are still a mystery to me. They demand and obtain instant obedience from the common folk —of whom, Zair be praised, there are many sturdy souls— and for the lordly of the land they reserve a kind of watching, cynical and amused tolerance, an armed truce of checks and balances of interest. Umgar Stro, for instance, could torture this old man to obtain his services, and his men might murmur but, being barbarians, they would not react in the same way that a man of Walfarg might.

Once having obtained his services, Umgar Stro would have to kill him; for, judging by all the stories I had heard, if he did not then a retribution as horrible as it was inevitable would overtake him as surely as Zim and Genodras rose with each new day.

So it was that this Wizard of Loh, this Lu-si-Yuong, thought he could now safely dictate what was to occur.

He stared at me and I saw the torchlight flicker over his grimed yet pallid face. He took a step backward.

"Listen to me, San. If you speak true, if there is no girl prisoner here, then swear it be so by all you hold sacred of Loh. For, Lu-si-Yuong, if you lie to me then you will die— as surely as anything you know of in your world!"

His tongue rasped those wrinkled sandpaper edges of his mouth.

"It is true. I swear to you by Hlo-Hli herself and by the seven arcades, I am the only prisoner here."

We stood facing each other for what seemed a long time.

I was scarcely aware when I lowered the sword point from his shrunken breast.

"Very well." I could not break out, not now; I could not allow myself to despair and to abandon myself to my grief. Not now, not when faithful Seg orbited outside awaiting me, in mortal danger. "Come, old man. Pray to all your pagan gods you have spoken the truth—and yet, and yet I wish you lied!"

We left the cell and walked on the footprinted way between the dust and so up the spiral stairs, past the guardroom and up to the attic. For me, Dray Prescot, this was a skulking, an undignified way, of tackling my foes.

Thelda had told me Delia had dropped into a tarn and been drowned. San Yuong told me she was not here. Did they both lie?

I told Lu-si-Yuong to wait and went back to the guardroom and took up the two toonons. The bamboo was not a true bamboo but came from the Marshes of Buranaccl. I wondered what Seg would make of the weapon. My mind was beginning to function again.

Seg was mightily joyed to see us. He brought the corths in with supple skill and I bundled up onto the trapeze with the fragile form of the Wizard tucked under my arm. We swung away into the Kregan night and the glow from the twins rolled across the eastern horizon laying pink icing across the towers, battlements, and roofs of Rapa Plicla.

The strong vulturine-shaped wings of the corths beat up and down, up and down, and we rode the sky levels away from the fortress of Umgar Stro until we could alight in a clearing among tuffa trees and so rearrange ourselves for our flight back to Hiclantung.

Seg was very quiet.

He did say, savagely: "I would have welcomed an opposition back there. We need a fight, Dray."

"Aye," I said. And let it lie there.

I did not believe my Delia was dead. Not after all we had been through. Only when I held Umgar Stro's throat in my fists and choked the truth from him would I believe. And, even then, even then, I would go on hoping. . . .

Chapter Fourteen

"It is my Dray!
My Dray Prescot you covet!"

One of the strange and, if the truth be told, weird, aspects of the Wizards of Loh was revealed in that grove of tuffa trees as we rested our corths and rearranged our flight program. Lu-si-Yuong, without a word of explanation to Seg or myself, squatted himself down on the ground in the pinkish light from the twin moons, composed himself and, lifting his veined hands to his eyes, threw his head back and so remained still and silent and unmoving.

Seg whispered: "I think, Dray, he is in lupu."

"Oh?" I really hardly cared.

"Yes. They say the Wizards of Loh can see into the future—"

"A simple story for simple minds. The credulous will believe any mumbo jumbo and it puts a copper into the hands of clever tricksters."

Seg glanced obliquely at me, his mouth open. He shut his mouth, and looked back at Yuong, and did not say what he so clearly thought. I had a mind to speak more kindly toward him, for he was of Loh, but I forbore. Delia! I remembered my anguish when among the tents and the wagons and chunk-rah herds of the Clansmen of Felschraung I had heard my Delia was dead, and I recalled my determination to remain alive and fighting strong so that, if, as I truly believed, she was not dead, I would be able to render her what aid I could. Now, as the Wizard of Loh went through his mumbo jumbo I made the same solemn vow.

Quietly, I said to Seg: "I came away from the tower tonight, Seg, for there were reasons why I should do so. I cannot believe that Delia is truly dead. I shall go on until I find Umgar Stro, wherever he may be. I think he was lucky not to be home tonight, and yet more unfortunate, too."

"How is that, dom?" asked Seg in a neutral voice.

"I would have killed him tonight, stone dead. But if it takes

142

me long to find him then there will be that amount more time in which to store resentment, and to think of ways of making him talk and—pay!"

Seg turned his eyes away from my face.

Lu-si-Yuong began to tremble. His thin shoulders shook and over all his scrawny body beneath the rags he shuddered and then he began slowly to draw his palms from before his eyes. His eyeballs were rolled up, displaying the whites like a bird-befouled marble statue's, and his breathing had practically ceased.

"Lupu," I said. "Is that it?"

"Aye, Dray, that is being in lupu. He is having visions. Who can tell where his mind is wandering now—"

"Get a grip on yourself, Seg!"

All the fey characteristics of his race predominated in Seg Segutorio now, all the dark and hidden lore in his native hills of Erthyrdrin pulsed and answered the weirdness of this old man, this San, this Wizard of Loh.

As the streaming pink moons-light fell upon that gaunt upturned face and turned those blind eyes into cracked yellow pits I looked about the grove of tuffa trees and at the three corths uneasily picking and pecking their feathers, and I, Dray Prescot of Earth, wondered at the faces of Kregen I had not yet seen.

A gargling cry wailed from Yuong. His trembling ceased. Unsteadily, waveringly, he tottered to his feet. He opened his arms wide, the fingers rigid and outspread. Like some blasphemous cross he gyrated, like a cyclone-torn scarecrow, like a whirling dervish in the last stages of exhaustion. Then, as abruptly as he had begun, he sank down, resumed his contemplative position, and so lowered his hands flat to the ground and opened his eyes and looked on us.

"And have you looked into the future, old man?" I said.

"Dray!" Seg's outraged cry affected me not at all.

San Yuong looked at me. I think, even then, he did not know how to size me up or to read me in the context of those people with whom he was accustomed to deal. I do know now, and admit it with only the slightest diffidence, that I must have been in a state of shock still, and hardly recking of what I did or said. In any event Yuong decided to treat me with caution. For this I was later duly grateful; at the time I merely remarked to myself that I must be wearing that old devil's mask of a face again—and joying in it, Zair help me, joying in my pain.

"The future does not concern me at this moment, my friend. I shall thank you properly for rescuing me at a suitable time. What I have been discovering is how I will be received by Queen Lilah—"

"She does not blame you for the defeat of her army in the massacre," I said. "At least, she did not mention you in that context—or at all."

"She would not."

"What have you discovered, San?" asked Seg.

"The Queen will need my guidance and advice in what is to come. But she was cold—distant and cold. There is a woman, another woman, they have fought bitterly—"

"Thelda!" exclaimed Seg. He stared at me in dismay.

I was intrigued. Could this old man in some way have seen what was even now happening in Hiclantung? Impossible! But, remember, then I was young and new to the ways of Kregen and especially to the wiles of the Wizards of Loh.

"The Queen has imprisoned this woman, this Thelda, and she weeps for her lost lover." Yuong canted his head so that his supercilious nose aimed itself over my right shoulder. "Perchance she dreams of you, Jikai?"

"If she does," I said, "she does so without my permission."

"Since when has a maid required permission to long for a man?"

I didn't want to continue this, not with Seg looking and listening, so I went across to my corth and inspected its harness.

"Let us go," I said. "If Queen Lilah has flung Thelda into prison we must get her out again. We owe her that much, at least."

Seg vaulted into his saddle. His fist gripped into his rein knot—and his other hand made sure his great longbow was in position, handy as to bending and loosing, the feather of his arrows protruding from their quiver past his right ear.

I could see the irony in this situation; more than irony, deadly mockery of all I held dear. Here I was setting out to rescue my Delia from the clutches of a malevolent monster and instead was hurrying back to our friends to rescue a tiresome woman.

How all the Clansmen would have roared their appreciation of the joke—until I silenced them with my upraised sword!

We soared aloft with those initial convulsive rippling movements of the corths' wide wings driving us low across the clearing until we had picked up enough speed to rise and bank out past the trees. I scanned three hundred and sixty degrees as I would have done the moment I stepped onto the quarterdeck of *Roscommon* back on Earth—only now I had to sweep again below as well as above the level of our flight height. It was almost with regret that I saw no pursuing impiters, no vengeful corths, no varter-towing yuelshi.

Had I been of the stuff from which the romantic heroes of Kregan legends are constructed—all manliness and pride and stoicism and lofty indifference to personal pain—I would not have felt then as I did, all the agony and the remorse clawing and tearing my spirit. I knew only that I must go on—somehow.

We alighted on the outskirts of Hiclantung.

"If Thelda truly has been imprisoned by Lilah," I said, "then it would be foolish simply to fly back when day dawns."

"Yes," said Seg.

I knew how he felt. His constant cheerfulness with me both heartened and saddened me, for Seg had tried most desperately to interest Thelda in himself and had as desperately failed.

The corths snuffled around, ruffling their feathers, giving clear indication they wished to rest. I looked at Yuong.

"Tell me, San. Can you reach out with your mind and find the woman I seek?"

"Speak more plainly, Jikai. Do you mean Thelda, whom you would rescue from the Queen, or do you mean the woman you love?"

I started violently.

Fool! Why had I not thought of this myself—and before!

I gripped his thin shoulder. He did not wince but stared up at me placidly. I began to speak, but he shook his head.

"Is this woman you love as beautiful as you say?"

"Yes."

"Incredibly lovely?"

"Yes."

He moved my hand away. I let him. "I cannot find her for you, for I have no means of location, as I had with Thelda, who was with the Queen." He started back at my movement. Pink moonshine runneled along his jaws. "But, if she is as beautiful as you say, I believe she still lives. Umgar Stro values beautiful objects."

"Delia of the Blue Mountains is not an object!"

"With Umgar Stro all women are objects."

I turned away from him. Old as he was, cocksure as he was, weird as he was, if I had not turned away I believe I would have struck him down.

"By the veiled Froyvil, Dray! Let us get on!"

San Lu-si-Yuong went through his pantomime again. I call it a pantomime, for that is how I thought then when I was under tremendous strain, tensed up, desperate and weary and vengeful. Yuong did, however, play fair by us.

"She is with the Queen even now, in the Paline Bower—"

"I know it!" said Seg.

"I shall humor you," went on Yuong, "and go into lupu in the morning when the gates are open and we may enter the city."

Seg started violently.

I said: "You do not think Seg and I are men to wait tamely out here for them to open the gates for us, do you?"

He nodded that stringy lipless head with the wine-dark eyes somber and yet full of a spritely malice. "What else will you do, Jikai?"

Seg laughed.

I do not laugh easily, as I have said; I simply stood up and went across to my corth—the one with the trapeze and the thongs—and readied him for flight. Seg followed me.

When the corth was ready I turned to Yuong.

"You had best fly with us—there are leems hereabouts—"

He shook his head.

"Nay, Jikai. If you lend me one of those thick anachronistic flint-headed spears, I will fare well enough."

"As you wish. The spears were unnecessary, after all. They were a failure, like my plans."

"Dray!" said Seg. "All is not yet lost."

"Come!" I said, and I was abrupt with Seg. So we left the Wizard of Loh, San Lu-si-Yuong, there with a flint-headed spear to await the dawnrise of the twin suns of Scorpio and the opening of the gates to Hiclantung.

We rode the same corth for the short journey and by taking turns we both dropped off the swinging trapeze onto the trip-wired and fan-spiked roof of the Queen's palace and let the corth go where he willed. I fancied that sharp eyes peering out in the pink light of the twins would have spotted us from one of the many watchtowers rising in the city. That did not concern me as yet. We padded down stairs carpentered from sturm-wood and opened lenken doors with our swords. We did not kill the guards we encountered, for these were, after all, our hosts.

No incongruity of repetition struck me as we crept silently down past the guards, for this time I carried no high palpitations of hope and fear for my Delia; now we were merely attempting to do the right thing by a comrade—and then I remembered the way Seg felt about the callous and shallow Thelda, and I sighed, and wondered just what I did wish for this baffling comrade of mine.

Truth to tell, I felt a queasy sense of responsibility for Yuong; how could his frailty stand up against the awesome ferocity of a wild leem, flint-headed spear or no?

A young Hiclantung guardsman very smart in the ornate robes of a Queen's spearman with the gold and silver buttons and buckles in place of workmanlike bronze or bone was very pleased to assist us when Seg placed his dagger at the lad's throat. We were led past a doorway into an area of dust and cobwebs. It was a long narrow passage and every now and then thin slits let lamplight fall across the floor, so I knew it to be one of those seemingly essential items to certain palaces—the place of observation hidden behind the walls of the chambers. I have used these observation galleries many times, and no doubt will do so in the future. For some reason the minds of many rulers on the world of Kregen are obsessed with this desire for secrecy and for hidden observers ready to leap out in surprise and deal with the slightest hint of treachery or assassination. I have used these galleries many times—but not for the purpose for which they were built.

Seg tapped the lad lightly on the head when he indicated we had reached the correct loophole and I caught him in my arms and eased him silently to the dusty floor. Then Seg below and I above looked through the slit.

This was a small chamber within the Paline Bower which nestled securely beneath a wing of the palace. The first thing I noticed—before either of the women—was the chased silver dish containing a pile of palines, luscious, full-bodied, juicy, invigorating, and I licked my lips thirstily.

Seg whispered: "The Queen has a dagger in her hand!"

The mellow light from the samphron oil lamps shining through wafer-thin scraped bone shades splintered back in hard-edged reflections from the jewels in the dagger hilt. A star winked and dazzled from the dagger's point. That point hovered over Thelda's breast.

I felt for the edges of the crack that would reveal the doorway. Seg was breathing loudly, almost gasping.

That secret chamber was furnished in casual unostentatious luxury, with ling furs upon the low couches, silks and satins scattered here and there in a riot of colors between the tumbled cushions.

"You forget that I am the Queen!"

"And you forget that I am a Lady of Vallia!"

"Vallia! I spit on your Vallia!"

"What is this miserable dung-heap called Hiclantung? My country is a great nation, united under an all-powerful emperor! The power of Vallia is like a leem compared to the puny rast-city of Hiclantung!"

"By Hlo-Hli! You will pay for this insolence!"

I sighed. The girls were at it again. But poor Seg was taking it all in with a very visible distress.

Lilah wore a long scarlet gown, very tight as to the bodice, slit up the sides to reveal her long legs. Her hair and bosom and arms were smothered with gems. Much of that satanic look about her that came from the widow's peak and her upslanting eyebrows and the shadows beneath her cheekbones was absent now as she argued and wrangled with Thelda. Thelda—poor Thelda—another man than Dray Prescot might have chuckled at her now, knowing what I knew about these two. Thelda was clad in a short and raggedy brown shift that left her thick thighs naked, that hung lopsidedly on her shoulders, sagging, and her wrists were bound behind her back with golden cords. Yet she lifted her head defiantly, and I had to admire her, despite all the ludicrous scenes that had passed between us.

"I know why you're so much of a female cramph!" spat Thelda now, her face flushed, her eyes bright, her breast heaving like the seas of the Eye of the World after a rashoon has passed. "It's my Dray! My Dray Prescot you covet!"

"Your Dray!"

"Yes! You know nothing of what we mean to each other. I love him and, now the Princess Majestrix is gone, he will love me! I know—"

"You know nothing, rast! What can you offer him? I am the Queen, a Queen in all her glory, Queen of a great city and a great nation—"

"Surrounded by enemies waiting to tear your heart out!"

"They may wish to—but they will never succeed. I can offer Dray Prescot everything—you—"

Thelda threw back her dark brown hair and opened those plump lips and laughed. "You!" she spluttered. "A skinny rast-bag like you! Dray Prescot needs a woman, a real woman!"

Lilah's hand trembled and the dagger shot sparks of fire into the corners of the room. "You great fat lump of lard! Dray needs a woman of fire and passion who can meet him, breast to breast, spirit for spirit!"

Seg put his hand on the secret panel. I suffered for my comrade during those minutes.

A sharp rap on the door opposite brought Lilah around, cat-like, the dagger upraised. The knock also halted Seg's pushing hand. The door opened and a little slave wench with golden bands upon her gray slave kirtle skipped in, bending and genuflecting, showing in Councillor Orpus. His powerful bearded face was filled with extreme animation and the many rings on his fingers flashed in the lamplight. He swept his embroidered robes to one side as he inclined deeply. When he straightened up, he said: "Forgive this intrusion, oh Queen! But—great news! We think we have discovered the location of Umgar Stro."

"What do you mean—you think?"

Lilah replaced the dagger in its sheath at her waist. She advanced on Orpus like a leem. She was all queen now, all regality, lofty and cold and demanding, merciless to failure.

"The scouts report—"

"Wait." Lilah beckoned. "Guards! Take this miserable creature to the cells; let her rot there until my pleasure is known. Come, Orpus. We must go to the council chamber—summon the scouts, my generals, and my councillors. We must plan—now!"

As Orpus stood aside to let the Queen sweep past him, her long scarlet gown trailing, her naked legs strong and thrusting before, her guards inclined, their helmets low. They moved into the chamber, and their Deldar prodded Thelda with his spear point. That spear point was steel, as befitted a spearman of the Queen's guard.

"Up, little one. We have need of playthings such as you in the cells!"

They closed upon Thelda and dragged her away and as she went she screamed most piteously.

Seg put his hand to the secret panel, but it was my foot that kicked it open.

Together, Seg and I, we burst into the empty chamber. Our swords were in our fists. Shoulder to shoulder we started for the door.

Chapter Fifteen

Seg, Thelda, and I
stand before Queen Lilah

On the way across to the door I used my left hand to scoop up a great mass of the palines. Juice dribbled through my fingers.

"Here, Seg. Munch on these—"

"No time, Dray! Don't you realize what they're going to do to Thelda?"

I pushed the palines at him.

"Take them, Seg! You need them!"

I stared at him, eye to eye. With a savage curse he pushed past me, scooped up a mass of the palines and stuffed them into his mouth. Then, and only then, I ran for the door.

The guards had just reached the first turn in the corridor. We ran swiftly and silently down toward that corner. I checked at the bend beside an alabaster statue of a risslaca seizing a leem, and the leem in its turn seizing the risslaca, and peered around. Seg hopped with impatience. The guards were moving Thelda along briskly. A few other slaves and functionaries moved along the corridor, which here broadened with a supporting aisle of thick-bodied columns down its center. I had visited the palace enough times to have a vague and general idea of its layout; but unlike most of the palaces I had encountered on Kregen this one, because it had been built in the midst of a city closed up around it within its encircling walls, had not sprawled out in an ever-growing maze of passages and courts and halls.

We marched smartly out and cut along the corridor.

Slaves looked at us, but slaves are slaves, and they took only enough notice of us, two warriors, to keep out of our way. I hate and detest slavery; here was one facet of slavery clearly apparent. The guards hustled Thelda around another bend. When we reached the corner where a vast pot of Pandahem ware—and how old it was I wouldn't care to guess —brought up a few memories, I saw before me a double-corridor I recognized from its decoration. Down that corridor lay the council chamber where Lilah, the Queen, was now meeting the scouts who had brought information of the whereabouts of Umgar Stro.

Without hesitation I started off down the corridor.

"Dray! They went this way. . . ."

I turned. Seg was looking at me, and I could not read the expression on his tanned face. A stray shaft of torchlight caught in his blue eyes and gleamed back lambently.

"Umgar Stro—" I said.

"The guards have taken Thelda down here, into the dungeons!"

At once I came to myself. This was Seg Segutorio, the man who had unhesitatingly followed me to the tower of Umgar Stro in Plicla to rescue Delia. Now I must go with him to rescue Thelda. Of course. How could I have thought otherwise? I would fight my way to Umgar Stro—never fear. So I thought as I ran after Seg down the corridor branching at right angles, through the bronze-bound lenken door at its end, and down bare stone steps into the dungeons of the Queen of Pain.

It was not as easy as I have made it sound. Every cell of my body screamed in agony that I must go to seek my Delia, my Delia of the Blue Mountains. I did not think then, I could not, of what might be happening to her. But the agony I suffered would only increase if I allowed poor Thelda and Seg to be destroyed. I knew my Delia would understand that and approve; and I also knew I used her acquiescence as a mere excuse.

The guards had been joined by men in the traditional uniform of their trade. They wore black aprons and black masks and their brawny arms were bare. Thelda's pitiful brown rag had been stripped from her and she huddled against a stone wall where iron rings fixed into the stone gaped open for her. Two sets along they supported a skeleton clothed in decayed scraps of flesh and skin.

One of the men gripped Thelda and lifted her arm toward the iron ring. Beneath the mask his fleshy face showed a vastly unpleasant sniggering enjoyment.

Seg had sheathed his sword.

Before I could run in with my brand naked in my fist Seg's first arrow punched meatily into the broad black-leather-clad back. The torturer screamed like a de-gutted vosk and toppled away. Then I was in among the guards. I laid about me with the flat of my sword, for in all the desperate anger blazing in me I still retained sense enough to try to mitigate the Queen's rage. One torturer she might overlook; more would cause untold problems for Seg and myself.

"Don't kill them, Seg!" I yelled, as I felled the Deldar and swung back and laid my blade flat into his companion's guts, bringing the hilt down on his head as he doubled.

Seg gasped and swore and stowed that great longbow away and thwacked his long sword down onto the guards. So sudden, so vicious, so fierce was our onslaught that the guards wilted and fell in swathes. Only two managed to bring their steel-tipped spears up and these we slashed through with our brands and then knocked their wielders out, a neat one-two flicker of movement.

"I'll make a swordsman of you yet, Seg!" I said. The brisk action had stirred my sluggish blood.

But Seg Segutorio was cradling Thelda in his arms, holding her naked body to him, crooning unintelligble words over her.

"Oh, Dray!" shrieked Thelda. "I knew you would come! I knew you would save me!"

"Thank Seg," I said with a harshness of tone I had no need to simulate.

"But—Dray—" She struggled free of Seg. She stood there, her arms outspread, her bosom panting, her color very high and flushed. "That Lilah—that Queen—female cramph! I hate her! But you, Dray—you have saved me!"

I did not look at Seg.

He said, in a hard clipped voice: "We must get out of here. Now. Before these sleeping beauties awake."

"Put your dress on, Thelda," I said. "You and Seg must get away at once." I stripped a long, lavishly embroidered cloth from the Deldar, rolling him over and over so that his nose squashed on the filth of the stone floor. "Put this on, too, as a cape. You can make the outside safely; you know the way—"

"Dray! Aren't you coming?"

I did not laugh. "I have a matter to discuss with Lilah."

Thelda started back as though I had struck her.

"You—Dray—you—and the Queen! *No!*"

For all her words a change had come over Thelda, my lady of Vallia. Much of her bounce had gone. I remembered her screams as the guards had dragged her off. She thought then that she was doomed; dark fears of that memory would haunt her for the rest of her days, I expected. She looked more haggard, the plumpness of her sagging; her eyes looked dull.

"Not Lilah and me, Thelda, no—not like that. She has news of Umgar Stro, and I must have news, also."

"If you go to stand before the Queen," said Seg, "then I go with you to stand at your side."

"Seg—"

"And me?" shrieked Thelda. "I dare not go—"

"I do not think, Thelda, the Queen will harm you if Dray intercedes for us all."

Seg's words, so calm, so sure, so filled with all the dark wisdom of his hills of Erthyrdrin, rattled me. Loh was, indeed, a continent of mystery.

"I am frightened—" Thelda looked it, too.

I started to walk out of the chamber, back up the stone stairs. "The Queen will listen to me," I said. "Let us go."

We were not molested on our way to Queen Lilah's council chamber.

It is a strange fact to me now to recall that I have only the dimmest memories of her council chamber. Oh, it was wide and lofty and supported by the massive Hiclantung pillars with their garlands of risslaca and snake, and with pediments fashioned in the form of corths; there was color and torchlight and many people; but I recall only the tall scarlet form of Lilah, with her piled mass of gem-encrusted red hair with its wedge-shape over her forehead, of her deep dark eyes and the unslanting eyebrows, the shadows beneath her cheekbones and that scarlet-painted, small, firm, and yet sensuous mouth.

"So you have come back to me, Dray Prescot."

I remembered her, prostrate before me, groveling, imploring me to take a seat at her side on her throne, offering me everything. Her chin lifted as though she, too, understood my thoughts.

"If you have news of Umgar Stro, oh Queen, then tell me that I may take his throat between my hands and squeeze until he is as lifeless as a rag doll."

"Gently, gently, my Lord of Strombor! It is not sure. The scouts believe; we await confirmation."

"Tell me where and I will confirm—"

"Not so fast." Lilah looked at Thelda. Guards surrounded us, their steel spear-points glinting. Seg held his strung bow in his left hand, and idly held an arrow in his right hand. I knew he could bend the bow and send that shaft clear through the heart of this Queen of Pain long before he was cut down by her spearmen. "Not so fast. What is this—woman—doing with you?"

I stared at Lilah, challengingly, eye to eye. I forced my meaning upon her.

"She is innocent in all this, oh Queen. We found her in circumstances that would displease me mightily if I thought they were of your doing."

She returned my stare. Our eyes locked.

"I see."

"There is a man, a Wizard of Loh, a San, one called Lu-si-Yuong."

She gasped. "What of San Yuong?"

"Seg Segutorio and I rescued him from the tower in Plicla. He was the only prisoner. He will enter Hiclantung when the gates are open at dawn, although I venture he would find it a blessing if you sent guards to let him in now. There are leems."

"Yes." She gestured and a Hikdar moved off at once to carry out her unspoken orders. "The San is precious to me. I grieved at his loss in the massacre. And you have rescued him!"

"Seg Segutorio and I."

"Yes." She seemed somewhat at a loss. It was with a considerable reduction of her powers that she said: "It seems I am in your debt again, Dray Prescot."

"You know what I seek. Umgar Stro. Tell me—"

"As soon as the news of that evil person's whereabouts is brought to me you shall be told. But, my Lord of Strombor, I put a thought to you. We believe he is in Chersonang."

Chersonang was the adjoining country and city in hereditary rivalry with Hiclantung. I could foresee problems.

Lilah leaned forward a little on her throne, her white hand beneath her white chin, brooding on me. "I shall send all my army up against Umgar Stro in Chersonang. I believe we can break both him and them, together. This will be your opportunity, Dray Prescot, to seek and find the woman you desire. I offer you the chance to command my army, with my generals, to go up against Umgar Stro at the head of a host. Come, what do you say?"

At my side Thelda gasped.

The guards pressed more closely about us now.

There was no need to discuss with myself my answer.

"I thank you, Lilah, for your offer. It is generous of you. But I cannot wait. I will leave for Chersonang at once—sleep will have to wait, instead."

"You fool!"

I turned to go and Seg's hand flashed up with the arrow

between his fingers and a spear point tripped him so that he fell sprawling before the throne. My sword was half drawn when something—a spear butt, the flat of a sword—sledged down on my head and I tumbled down that long smooth slope of black oblivion.

Chapter Sixteen

The army of Hiclantung marches out

If you choose to think my actions at this time—and, indeed, for some time past—had been irrational, I could not argue the point with you.

Truly, I now feel that the belief my Delia was dead had deranged me. I know I had acted in ways completely outside my usual fashion, and, yet, too, in ways I have been told are typical of me, as witness that wild moment when I defied the Queen of Pain to rush out from the windlass room in the corthdrome upon the indigo-haired assassins of Umgar Stro. I must have been in a state of shock that allowed me to walk and talk and act and yet held me all the time in a kind of mental stasis.

The ancient Chinese, we are told, had perfected the art of torture by water, the expected drop of liquid crashing onto the victim's forehead like a weight crushing into his brain. A single small drop could not do that; it was the expectation and the mounting terror of the inevitable, alternated with the passive bouts of cringing waiting. First I had thought Delia dead, then I had heard she might be alive, then her death was once more certain, and now again she might be missing and, perhaps, better dead. The sheer vibrationary pressure, the nightmare nutcracker rhythm of it all, had made of me a different animal from the man who had flown over The Stratemsk.

Of only one thing could I be sure. Whether dead or alive, Delia would fiercely insist that I go on with life, that I persevere, that I never give in.

Seg and I recovered quietly in a comfortable room set deep within the palace. The room was as luxuriously furnished as anyone could wish, windowless, lit with samphron oil lamps, and set everywhere with the motionless and watchful figure of guards, spearmen of the Queen's own household in their embroidered robes and gleaming helmets, their steel-tipped spears. We were both naked. We had no weapons.

Seg said: "We could take the spears from these dummies, easily, you and I, Dray!"

I said: "We could. We could fight our way clear if we went together. But—what of Thelda?"

His look distressed me.

"Thelda," he said, and he bowed that mane of black hair to his brawny forearms.

So we pondered our chances of breaking free and taking the plump Lady of Vallia with us.

Wherever we were marched within the Queen's palace we were accompanied by an overwhelming escort, consisting of spearmen and bowmen. These latter, we knew, effectively prevented the sudden dash for freedom. And yet, even then, we knew we were not prisoners in any ordinary sense of that term. We became aware of a sense of heightened purpose within Hiclantung. Soldiers moved everywhere. Preparations were being made and Seg was moved to express a fierce dark satisfaction in the demeanor of the men.

"They have not forgotten what Umgar Stro did to them. Through the treachery of one man, that Forpacheng, their pride was humbled." Seg moved his hands meaningfully. "Well, now they are regrouping, remembering their traditions. They will not suffer the same fate again."

Hwang, the Queen's nephew, came to see us, distressed by what Lilah was forced to do to us—as he said, for our own good.

His young face wore the kind of look one associates with a child's awareness of some mischief, and the desire to brazen it out. He flung his embroidered robes away from his legs, kicking them petulantly, as he sat down. Seg hospitably poured wine—it was a purple beverage of excellent vintage, I recall, full-bodied yet not too sweet, from the western slopes of Mount Storr—and Hwang took the goblet as though prepared to sup and to forget what was on his mind.

"I have just come from the dancing girls at Shling-feraeo," he said. "They bored me."

"Umgar Stro," I said.

Hwang nodded. "Yes, Dray Prescot. You have it aright."

We began a technical discussion concerning the equipment and tactics of the army of Hiclantung, in which Seg pressed hard. I might have felt amusement, with another man, at another time without worries, at the way Seg so passionately concerned himself with the prospects of this lame remnant of the glorious empire of Walfarg. Much of Seg's home country,

that mysterious land of mountains and valleys called Erthyrdrin, I came to know later; but nothing could quench the
burning pride in Seg, a pride echoed in Hwang, that the ancient
virtues of Loh should survive, and that he, as a man of
Erthyrdrin, should participate to the full in their perpetu-
ation. Perhaps I caught a glimpse, there in that silken scented
prison room of the palace of Hiclantung, of the breaking of
barriers of nationality that was so much to affect my life on
Kregen.

Seg was a man of Erthyrdrin, and he had told me how his
people were feared by the other peoples of Loh—there had
been much wild free talk between us—and now, here he was,
dourly determined to smash unknown enemies of the Lohvians.

For the enemies were unknown in the sense that the people
of Chersonang were unknown to Seg and myself, and Umgar
Stro clearly had not flexed all his military muscle and there-
fore was unknown to Hwang and the Lohvian army of Hiclantung.

Presently Hwang said to me, with a smile and a gesture of
the hand holding the wine goblet: "You are a wise man, Dray
Prescot, not to attempt escape. You are a man I think could
escape if you willed it. But you have put both the Queen and
myself into your debt; and we are conscious of that—"

"You are not in my debt."

"For myself, thinking of you as a friend, I am glad you go
up against Umgar Stro with an army, and not alone."

"Huh," said Seg Segutorio.

Hwang inclined his head, squinting along the goblet.
"Assuredly, Seg. By alone I meant with you and without my
army."

"You are in command?" I said.

"In a manner of speaking. Orpus holds joint-command.
There are other generals. We believe you will join us, Dray
Prescot, to give us the wisdom of your advice."

"Seg is perfectly accustomed to commanding men in combat."

Hwang looked with a strange kind of affection upon my
comrade. "Yes. Seg is of Erthyrdrin, and we who remain of
Walfarg know of them well. There was once a time . . .
Well"—he drained the goblet—"no matter."

He stood up to go.

Then, looking down on us, for protocol was not respected
by me so long as I remained a prisoner, Hwang said: "I have
had a messenger from Naghan. You remember Naghan, the
spy?"

"Yes."

"He will return very soon. His report—and it is cautious as befits a spy—says he will have news of Delia—"

Hwang's shoulder was gripped in my fist and my ugly face blazed down into his.

"What?"

He wriggled. I took my hand away, drawing a breath, glowering.

"When Naghan reports I will bring him to speak with you."

"Do that, Hwang. Pray God, Zair, my life—his news is good!"

We had insisted we be allowed exercise and the guard commander would march us to a wide hall where Seg and I jumped and ran and thwacked at each other with quarter staffs until we both slumped sweating and aching and thoroughly worked out. I cannot say we were tired, for this make-believe action merely titillated the muscles of men accustomed to the real hardships of campaigns and battles.

At last Naghan the spy returned.

Queen Lilah, Orpus, and Hwang came to our luxurious prison room with Naghan. With them, also, a grim armored body of the Queen's spearmen indicated clearly she would stand no nonsense from Seg or myself. Also—surprisingly—Thelda walked in with them, dressed in her old brown short-skirted garment and with her hands bound behind her with golden cords. Her color was high. Her bosom jutted. Her head was held erect and arrogantly. She stared around contemptuously, saw Seg and myself, and all her composure crumbled so that, for just an instant, we saw the lonely frightened girl she really was. Then she caught herself, and resumed that haughty patrician air that remained to her the only bastion against insanity.

"Speak, Naghan," commanded Lilah.

The spy did not cringe. He looked at me curiously. His short body was clad in a simple robe with the minimum of embroidery, and his faded eyes sized me up in a way I knew few had done upon Kregen beneath Antares.

He opened his mouth, he started to speak, to say, "I now know for certain that the Princess Delia of Vallia is—" when Lilah stopped him with a single word.

She faced me. Since that dramatic meeting in her private room where we had drunk wine and she had lain at my feet with her garment of gems winking and flashing upon her white body, we had not encountered each other alone. I guessed she had been unsure of herself, unwilling to confront me again without the presence of her courtiers and her generals and her guards imposing an iron restraint upon her conduct.

"Let him speak, Lilah," I said.

"After we have spoken, Dray Prescot."

"Then be brief."

"I desire you to go with my army against Umgar Stro. You will lead them, inspire them. With you at their head they will attack to the victory."

"That is easy enough—it might suffice for vengeance. Is there more than vengeance to be found in Chersonang, Lilah?"

She frowned. Her red widow's peak of hair drew down, it seemed, with the movement of her face, so that she presented a brooding and devilish look. She wore a tunic of green—not the green of Magdag or the green of Esztercari, but green nonetheless—and a short skirt of green over leather-clad legs. Her embroidered robes were put away. Around her narrow waist a golden belt tightened her figure, emphasizing the fact she was a woman, and from it swung a jeweled sword. In her left hand she carried a switch. All the time we spoke and without conscious effort on my part a portion of my attention concentrated on that switch.

"I want you to give me your word, by the sacred name of Hlo-Hli, by whatever pagan goddesses rule you, that you will not leave my army until you have led it to victory."

"And what if the host of Umgar Stro prevails?"

"In that case, the issue will not matter to anyone."

"Nothing is certain in war."

Her whole attitude bespoke extreme uncertainty; she was bandying words with me, and she a queen.

"Give me your word—"

"I will do what I can for your army against Umgar Stro, because that happens to fit into my own desires, Lilah. Beyond that even your Hlo-Hli can do nothing. Now give Naghan leave to speak."

Her small mouth compressed and the switch lifted. But she turned to Naghan calmly enough and told him to report.

"The Princess Delia of Vallia is now known to me for certain as not the name of the female prisoner on whose track I spent a great deal of time—"

I stood there. I could not speak or move. I simply glared at this calm matter-of-fact man called Naghan the spy, and he saw my eyes and he swallowed, that grave courageous man, and went on: "As San Yuong has said, all the prisoners except himself were killed at Plicla. I have been in Chersonang. There is a female prisoner there, who may or may not be the Princess Delia of Vallia. I have discovered only that she is kept penned in a dungeon, miserably. I have had no opportunity to speak with her, but she has female servants and slaves. The talk is that Umgar Stro is too busy to win conquests at this time; when the battle has been won he will deign to try his mettle with her."

Queen Lilah sniffed. "From what I hear of Umgar Stro that fits his contemptible character. He likes his women pliable; drugged, eager for love. He will not waste time fighting a woman; he demands they yield to him with counterfeit joy."

"I know that type of sub-man," said Seg. He would not look at me.

Before anyone could stop her, Thelda burst out: "And is the man who forces a girl any the less of a sub-man, then?"

Orpus stroked his beard, which, as always, lent weight to what he was saying. "No. Passion in either case is unlawful and vile. But—I put it to you that no woman can be raped unless she desires it."

Thelda gasped, looking shocked, and Lilah smiled reflectively. I remembered the stories of her cast-off lovers, the abandoned detritus of the Queen of Pain.

I said: "When do we leave?"

"On the morrow." Orpus nodded, and he seemed pleased. "The plans are perfectly laid. You will ride at the apex of the host, Dray Prescot. The Queen's generals have planned everything with meticulous attention—"

Seg Segutorio, highly incensed, cut into Orpus' words.

"What of Delia?"

Naghan remained silent. Lilah moved her switch, but she, too, did not say anything.

"Delia may be the woman," Seg said. "We do not know—"

"We will ride at the head of the host, Seg, you and I," I said. "We will fight. If the army of Hiclantung can follow me, then it may. But I shall fight through to Umgar Stro, I think, or I will be cut down."

Orpus nodded briskly. "Excellent. Our plans call for a great charge that will reduce the cramphs of Chersonang to slime beneath our feet. They are but Harfnars—"

"Harfnars, yes," said Naghan in his quiet voice. "But they fight exceedingly well. And Umgar Stro with his Ullars has drilled and strengthened them. Half-men they may be, but they will fight."

Orpus boomed a great basso laugh.

"There will be no treachery in our ranks, this time, when the Ullars fly down upon us. We have learned how to defend ourselves against impiters and corths. When the accursed harfnars see their new allies retreating, bloodied and torn, they will not fight as they have done in the past."

Clearly the sense of historic conflict sounded in Orpus' words. For many years the hatred and rivalry between Hiclantung and Chersonang had festered. Now a new element in the Ullars had been added. There was sense in what Orpus said—sense, and a deadly danger these Lohvians would not see.

So we sallied forth on the morrow, a proud and eager company. Queen Lilah was with the host. Wearing her green tunic and with a glittering gilded breastplate, she led out for a space. With Seg and myself, mounted upon nactrixes, rode Hwang's regiment of cavalry. Heavy horsemen, with long lances and armor, and with a breathtaking panoply of embroidery and silken banners, they rode arogantly, confident in their own prowess.

The infantry marched in their regimented formations. Varters rumbled in the intervals. There were also many strange contrivances mounted on carriages whose purpose I was to come to understand passing well in later years. At this time I saw them in action but the once, and was impressed.

Thelda rode with Seg and me. Lilah wanted to keep her under her eye. Seg and I wore half-armor, bronze breastplates and shoulder-pieces, beautifully made. There comes a time in a people when armor is so splendidly made that its very beauty cancels out much of its function. The empire of Walfarg had fallen to interior problems as much as by barbarian invasions, and a symptom of that ancient disease showed in the conspicuous artistry of the armor, its incredible standard of workmanship, its comfortable fit, its padding, its cunning fastenings—and in the ominous clefts between piece and piece, the gaps at neck and shoulder.

I did not care.

I felt a lightening of my spirits. I had been imprisoned in a silken bower unable to break free; and now I once more rode beneath the twin suns of Scorpio and advanced into Kregan warfare. I did not know if Delia lived. I would find out. Of that I was certain.

The whole glittering procession marched firmly toward Chersonang and following us tailed a massive baggage train. No comforts would be missed on a Lohvian campaign. We would, in any case, spend only a few days on the march before we crossed the border and approached Chersonang city.

"You do realize, Dray, that that she-leem only wants you to lead her army? She wants you to rush in first and break a way for the rest of her lackeys. You've had no say in the strategy, have you?"

"Yes, Thelda, and no, Thelda," I said. "I have more or less promised. You must understand why I agreed."

"But there's no need!" She bit her lip while Seg shot a quick glance at her as she rode between us. She wore a proper riding habit, and once more looked a great lady, her switch in her gloved hand.

"Oh?"

Her nactrix jostled closer to mine; she reached out her hand to me and her face showed a strange look, of compassion, baffled desire, remorse—self-doubt, even. Thelda had never been one to exhibit the slightest self-doubt; even the business of the vilmy and fallimy flowers had not fazed her for long.

About to pay attention to what was festering in her, I was caught by the long shrilling sounds of Hiclantung trumpets, those fabled silver trumpets of Loh. Intense activity boiled up.

"Look!"

Low over the horizon, skimming the ground and rising and falling over groves of trees, a myriad black shapes darted down on us. A swarm of midges they appeared at first; and in seconds the narrowing distance converted them into fanged and wide-winged impiters, metal-jangling, with fearsome Ullars perched on their backs waving their spears in ferocious glee at the onslaught.

Between the scattered clumps of trees the ground undulated gently in waves of rippling grasses, a motionless sea endlessly in motion. The Ullars flew their mounts directly down on us, disdaining any attempt to stalk us from the sun. Instantly the compact formations of the Hiclantung infantry shook out into fresh patterns and I saw the forest of upraised left arms, the longbows bent, the sunlight glinting from the jagged arrow barbs.

"They will not catch us again!" yelled Seg.

He lifted in his stirrups, dragging out his long sword, his whole body animate with a dreadful yearning.

The strange contrivances of Hiclantung now revealed their purposes. As the impiter host struck so rose the arrow storm to drive feathered shafts deep into breast and wing and belly. And, with that rustling arrow storm rose spiraling, tumbling, spreading, spinning nets, and chains, and bolas, and starred-blades. Great was the execution that day, as the army of Hiclantung repaid their score, as they showed the fliers of Umgar Stro how they treated any impetuous airborne assault.

A warrior flying a great bird, even a creature so fierce and powerful as an impiter, must necessarily be at a disadvantage against a warrior on his own two legs armed with a projectile weapon. It is difficult to shoot an accurate shaft from horseback—or zorcaback or sectrixback—and even more difficult from the wind-gyrating back of a corth or an impiter. It can be done by expert marksmen; and such marksmen were these indigo-haired half-men of Ullardrin. But the longbowmen of Hiclantung outshot them with ease. Aerial beast and man, one after another, more and more, fell helplessly from the sky.

I saw two impiters entangled in the same net, their wings striving to beat and break the strands, saw them twist and fall and smash terminally into the ground. All around us the flying host was falling. Occasionally men of Hiclantung staggered back with an arrow shafted into them, or a spear gouging its way down past the soft skin between neck and collarbone. But the winged attackers had met their match. Discipline, training, knowledge of weapons, and no taint of treachery brought the victory.

Watching those half-men up there as they wheeled aimlessly about above us, screeching their hatred and their defiance, shaking their weapons, trying to loose shafts down upon us, I was vividly reminded of the useless French cavalry charges I had witnessed on the field of Waterloo—and I began to build together ideas on how one should use this aerial cavalry, the proper function of airborne infantry.

In all the blaze of action I had not loosed a single shaft. Despite his exultant energy, Seg, too, had not shot. We both sat our nactrixes with full quivers strapped to our backs.

Queen Lilah rode across, her peak of hair giving her narrow face that demon-haunted look, her mouth open and shouting. She indicated by her carriage, the brightness of her eyes, the abandon of her gestures, how great the victory was. Everywhere over those undulating hills the sprawled corpses of impiter and Ullar showed how sorely the half-men had paid, how bloody had been the vengeance of the men of Hiclantung.

"You see, Dray Prescot!" Lilah screamed across at us.

"I see, Lilah."

"Nothing can stand against us now!"

I pointed.

Over the crest of the hill appeared a long dark line. I could see the wink of suns-light on spear and sword, on bronze helmet and breastplate. Regiment after regiment, already deployed, broke into a jog-trot down the slope of the hill.

And then, around the flanks broke a spray of cavalry, squadron on squadron of nactrixes. Their riders whooped in the saddle, lifting, their weapons glittering bright.

Lilah's face twisted into itself. Her switch came down with a thwack into her nactrix's flank. Before she bounded away she screamed at me: "There is your enemy, Dray Prescot! There are the Harfnar of Chersonang! Charge! Destroy them all!"

But, already, it was too late.

Whoever had organized this affair, be it Orpus or Hwang or Lilah herself, had miscalculated. After the formations adopted by the Hiclantung army which had so successfully defeated the flying troops of Umgar Stro, they were in no position to resist the punishing and sudden attack from the army of Chersonang. In an instant the leading echelons were upon us. Even as the men of Hiclantung broke and ran I was surrounded by viciously-striking half-men. Queen Lilah's army was converted in an instant into a running, shrieking, panic-striken mob. And Seg, Thelda, and I were marooned in a savage and destructive sea of hostile blades.

Chapter Seventeen

Of downfall and of bondage

I fought.

Oh yes, I fought. To have once more a tangible foeman before me, to feel the bite of his steel on my blade, to swing and feel that psychic shock as my brand bit back into his skull or body or limb, to feel the electric energy of it tingling up my arm, to do and feel all these things came to me with a great and dark joy. I confess it now; I joyed, then, in that battle as I seldom joy in mere fighting and killing. It seemed to me that every foeman who came up against me might be Umgar Stro, although common sense told me he would be directing the battle from some safe spot in the rear. I felt a personal animosity against every one of these Ullars and these harfnars. For, between them, had they not taken my Delia of Delphond from me?

The Harfnars were a strange-looking people, and yet close to men as men are known on this Earth, and in nowise as weird or uncanny as the Rapas or Ochs or Fristles with whom I was familiar.

Hereditary foemen of Hiclantung, they were, whose animosity stretched back to the day when the Harfnars had taken over the city of Chersonang after the withdrawal of Walfarg's forces. They were strong, cunning, devilish, with flat noses as wide across their faces as their lips, with brilliant lemur-like eyes set above, which gave their countenances a curious boxlike construction, forcibly abetted by the squared-off chin and forehead. They were brightly clad in checkered garments of flowing silk and satin and humespack, trimmed with fur, with the dull gleam of bronze corselet and pauldrons shining through ominously.

So we fought, Seg and I, seeking to protect Thelda and reach a solid knot of Hiclantung cavalry isolated on the crest of one of the small hills. This was the remnant of Hwang's regiment.

Arrows darkened the air about us. The turf stank sodden with the tang of newly-spilled blood. The hooves of our nactrixes pounded out erratically as we jerked the reins, this way and that. Seg's longbow sang and sang again. Every shaft found its mark. He shot rearward, turning with supple ease in the saddle, shooting with contemptuous ease. Anyone who came within reach of my long sword died.

With Thelda crouched low in the saddle in the lead we thundered toward Hwang's remnant.

They opened ranks for us, then closed. Each man there knew he must die. I could see the knowledge stark on their faces, deep within their eyes, but they stood and they fought and they died.

We skidded to a halt and dismounted. Hwang greeted us with a grim and brooding humor whose genesis I recognized with a pang; his imperturbable mien outraged Thelda.

"The army ran away!" she said. She sank down to the ground, sobbing with fury.

Seg tried to comfort her and—to my joy and amazement —she welcomed his attention. I saw her put her hand in his. He did not look back at me, but I saw the way his back straightened and the way his head went to one side. They talked together as the battle outside eddied past. There would be plenty of time for Seg to loose the remainder of his shafts.

"Is all really lost, Dray?" asked Hwang.

"We are not dead yet."

"The Queen? Have you seen her? Is she safe?"

"I do not know."

I looked over the ranks of troopers who shot with precision and care, breaking up attack after attack. There was nothing wrong with the soldiers of Hiclantung; first treachery and then bungling had undone them. The army of Chersonang swirled into the pursuit, and the Hiclantung rout vanished over the hills. There was still time. . . .

"If you break for it now, Hwang, a regiment like yours can break out, can carve a way through."

"Perhaps."

What had happened to Hwang had happened many times to many men in an abruptly lost battle.

"Do not joy in sacrifice," I said. "Rather, rage at death. This is no worthwhile sacrifice. If your regiment can be saved, then it is your duty to save them. It is not arguable."

"Perhaps."

"If you are to do it, it must be done before the Ullars rally and return. Isolated as you are and without your varters, you will not repel them as easily as—"

An arrow thunked into the turf at our feet.

The wounded had been collected in a huddle to one side of the nactrix lines. The uneasy beasts chomped and snorted, but they kept under good control. I did not know the full extent of the field supply situation, but I figured that the army, being a sophisticated part of a civilization descended from a great empire, would have ample regulations. The arrow supply would hold out yet; men were continually running from the supply carts with great sheaves up to the shooting lines. Hwang's officers kept a tight rein on their men. Order, efficiency, going by the book—all these undoubted benefits were amply demonstrated—but . . .

"You've got to break out, Hwang, before you are all cut to pieces!"

He started again to say, "Perhaps," when Seg approached followed by Thelda. She looked dreadful, the tearstains shining on her cheeks. Seg looked mean.

"You can't stay here," he began at once. "We'll all be chopped. Mount and ride! The longbows of Loh can ride through granite walls!"

Hwang looked from Seg to me, and back. He took a grip on himself, and I could fully sympathize with his position. As for myself, I was perfectly content with what I must do. Then Thelda took my arm as Seg and Hwang, arguing hotly, moved off to confer with Hwang's staff officers.

"Dray—"

I found a scrap of cloth and wiped her face.

"You'll get out all right, Thelda. Seg will see to that."

"Dear Seg—"

"He is the finest man you're likely to meet, in Vallia or elsewhere, Thelda."

"I know. And I've treated him so badly. But, Dray, I had to! Surely you see that? I had to!"

"I don't see it."

Above the bending ranks of bows and the nodding plumes of Hwang's men sudden onslaughts of the Harfnars boiled up to the lines and then the long lances thrust in drilled precision, the slender swords disemboweled, and the onrush turned once more into a retreat. But every mur that passed thinned the ranks of the soliders of Hiclantung. Unless Hwang broke out soon the end was very near.

Thelda gulped, and her hands gripped and twisted together. She looked as though she had reached the last of her strength.

"But I had to! I was ordered to—"

"Ordered?"

"Yes, Dray. You know how the proposed marriage between

yourself, a mere Lord of the Clansmen, and the Princess Majestrix is viewed in Vallia? Even the Presidio could not agree on a complete approval. Each member has his own rapier to sharpen."

I did not smile at her—we would say "ax to grind"—but I had already guessed what she would say. Indeed, only a credulous idiot like Dray Prescot would have missed the unmistakable signs before. "Go on, Thelda, my Lady of Vallia."

"Oh, Dray! Say you don't hate me, please!"

"I don't hate you, Thelda."

She regarded me with a wary misery through her tears.

"When Delia insisted on flying out herself I, as her hand-lady, also would go. The Ractor party gave me my instructions and they are very strong, Dray, terribly powerful!"

I nodded.

"They have their own candidates for the princess' hand. They are determined you shall never marry her—"

"So you were told to deflect my interest from Delia—to yourself."

Poor Thelda! How could she imagine that any woman in two worlds could prevent me from thinking of Delia for a single instant? Even Mayfwy, dear, loyal, wonderful Mayfwy, had not deflected me.

The battle could not go on for very much longer. The lines of wounded stretched now past the uneasy nactrixes. I fancied Hwang would not abandon his casualties and he would need every man in the ranks who could wield a sword. I reached down a hand to Thelda, to touch her shoulder and reassure her, but she gripped my hand and pressed it to her face and I could feel the tears, hot and sticky.

"I had my instructions, and I tried to follow them. And, in truth, Dray, I did fall in love with you. I believe any woman would. But Seg—he is—"

"For your own sake, Thelda, forget me. Care for Seg Segutorio. He will afford you all the love and shelter any woman could desire."

She lifted her eyes to me, and the tears brimmed there, silver and shining.

"But, Dray—I have been foolish, for I have been brought up to obey. The Ractors demand instant and total obedience in their schemes. But, Dray—"

She was trying to tell me something extra, a fact she had to force out. Seg shouted and I turned. He waved an arm. In all the uproar of shouting and screams, of the shrieks of wounded men and beasts, the incessant clang of steel on steel and steel on bronze, I just caught the tag end of his words.

". . . now and not a moment to lose!"

Hwang's men were going through their drill with the precision of English Guards. Now the missiles were flint-tipped arrows. But they could strike through the bronze we wore, they could slice into the heart through the interstices in our armor, gaudy and beautiful as it was.

"We're leaving, Thelda. Up you come. And mind you stick close to Seg!"

She came up softly into my arms, limp and trembling. "But, Dray—I must tell you! I must!"

I held her as the roaring battle smashed and boomed about us.

"Dray—Delia did not fall into the tarn. I did not see that. I said that to make you forget her—"

The roaring was in my head now. This story, this falsehood of Delia tumbling into the tarn had been the single dominant fear, bringing on all the rest; if she had not died then, she would still be alive now. I knew it. I felt it with every fiber of my being. No cynicism could deter me, now. Delia lived—I believed that. Delia lived!

The Lohvian soldiery of Hiclantung ran smartly to their nactrix lines, mounted. Detachments maintained a covering shower of arrows. With an access of energy like the release of icy water in the spring thaws of the north, I flung Thelda up into her saddle. I straddled my own mount. Seg was with us.

Hwang shouted. The emptied supply cars were loaded with wounded. A wedge formed. I thrust my way to the apex—thinking ironically that this was the spot Queen Lilah had wished me to occupy, a spot in which my own foolhardy valor would spur on and encourage her army. Now I obeyed her wishes in order to save a paltry remnant of the Lohvians of Hiclantung.

Like some bursting summer storm cloud we broke away down the grassy slope. The nactrix hooves pounded. Arrows crisscrossed. Men and beasts shrieked and reared and fell away. We went bounding on, bouncing in our saddles, and yet maintaining that incredible accuracy of shooting that is the pride of the Lohvian.

Seg spurred up with me, his bow bending and releasing with a smooth inflexible rhythm. He controlled his mount with his knees, as did most of the men of Erthyrdrin, although some cavalrymen of Hiclantung tended to gather up their reins in the hands that grasped their longbows. I had followed the example of Seg, although my training stemmed from those far-off days riding with Hap Loder and my Clansmen across the Great Plains of Segesthes. Had I a phalanx of voves at my back now—we would smash like a roller of the gods across the Harfnars of Chersonang!

Seg turned his tanned flushed face toward me. Every thing about him was instinct with the passion of battle. I saw his face change; the expression of absolute horror and then of fanatical determination that crossed his features told me, without the need of personal verification, what had happened.

With a tremendous shout Seg swirled about. He thrust his great longbow away as he spurred cruelly back.

Back there Thelda's nactrix had taken an arrow in the belly.

She was sprawled across the grass to one side of the following wedge of cavalry. Arrows nicked the air. Arrows feathered into men and beasts. The carts rolled and bucked as they bounced after the cavalry wedge, their wounded occupants shrieking in time to the jouncing. Dust spurted. In all the crazed uproar I knew Seg could see only Thelda.

As he reached her a flying wing of Chersonang cavalry swept over them. I saw his long sword shining red; then he was down.

Somewhere in that melee of spurring beast-men and trampling nactrixes, of cutting steel and thrusting lances, lay Seg and Thelda.

I thought of Queen Lilah, and of my place at the apex of the wedge—but we were in retreat, we were not charging to victory. I brought the nactrix around with as much cruelty as Seg had shown, dug in my spurs, sent the half mad beast crashing back.

Harfnars with their flashing weapons reared before me.

Arrows cut the plumes from my helmet. Arrows clanged away flintily from the armor. One sank deeply into the neck of the nactrix. It went on and over in a somersault. I flew from its back, turning over, still grasping my long sword. I did not see Seg and Thelda again in that maelstrom of barbaric savagery.

Then, for a space, I did not see anything at all save a red-flaming blackness.

During this period of misted movement and dulled perception I was aware of a voice speaking in the common language of Kregen, so I knew it would be an indigo-haired Ullar talking to a Harfnar of Chersonang.

"Bring him. He will furnish sport for a while."

There followed movement and the sensation of flying and

the thrashing sounds of great wings beating the air. The ache in my head diminished to proportions just short of bearable and I came back to my senses chained and bound and strapped up to a granite wall in a dark dungeon.

Dungeons are dungeons, as I have remarked before, and some are worse than others. This particular specimen contained all the unpleasant features a human-operated dungeon would have, plus a few the Harfnars had thought up out of their own culture of bestiality.

A groaning and moaning sound told me there were others of the men of Hiclantung with me, reserved for sport. There was no need to elaborate on what was in store for us. Cultures approximate, given the original dark impulse that began the gene trail.

By the time the first set of jailers flung open the lenken door and descended the greasy steps toward us I had freed my left wrist and partially broken away the links chaining my right. Under the impression that it was now or never I exerted all my force. My shoulders are not only wide, they are blessed with roping muscles that can surprise even me. The last link parted with a ringing ping.

In the fresh dazzlement of light I blinked and caught two of the Harfnar jailers about their throats and squeezed and flung them into their companions. All the time a low bestial growling rumbled and raged in the dungeon. The Harfnars hoisted themselves up, yelling, and their swords flicked out. They approached me warily. I was still securely fastened by my legs, so that between fending off the beast-men with swung chains I bent and tried feverishly to unfasten my legs, only having to straighten up and lash out again to make them keep their distance.

"Put down your chains, you Hiclantung cramph!"

"I'll slit your belly up to your throat, rast!"

At first I did not deign to answer them as they yelled at me and I worked on my bonds and swung the chains and all the time that sullen bestial roaring boomed and thundered in the dungeon.

"Keep them occupied!" shouted a Hiclantung cavalryman. The other captives were attempting to break their bonds, but they could not succeed. I still do not recall the exact strengths I exerted to snap those chains.

"Smash him over the head!" screeched the guard commander.

They danced in, one went down with his face ripped off, then they had entangled the chains, were bringing up spears to strike at me.

"Come on, rasts, and by the Black Chunkrah, come to your deaths!"

As I shouted the words, that bestial roaring stopped in the dungeon. Only then was the realization borne in on me that it was I, Dray Prescot, who had been roaring and thundering in so savage a fashion.

The shock sobered me.

In that instant the dungeon door was blocked off by the entry of a bulky half-man and the guards finally lost their patience with me and one thrust hard and in deadly earnest. His spear point darted for my breast.

I smashed it away and took him by the throat with my left hand, held him squirming and kicking in the air as I snap-reversed the spear and de-gutted the next guard. Then I hurled the one I held into their midst and swung the spear down again in low port.

"What are you waiting for, offal and dung feeders?"

They hesitated. They were splashed with the blood of their comrades. They could see the dead bodies sprawled on the dungeon floor, dreadfully mutilated. And all this from a man chained up by his legs!

The newcomer shouted, harshly, loudly, angrily, beside himself with fury.

"Dunderheaded dolts! By Hlo-Hli the Debased! I'll flog every man of you! Take him! *Take him now!*"

Goaded by twin fears, the Harfnars flung themselves upon me in a body. They entangled my left arm in flung ropes and dragged me down cruelly. I gasped and forced myself upright. A spear blade slogged down on my temple and I only half broke its force. But I slashed through the ropes—the flint-headed spear was sharper than any cheap steel—and reared back, blood obscuring my vision, my legs clamped as though trapped by a chank of the inner sea.

The man giving the orders moved closer. he peered at me in the light streaming down the dungeon steps. He put both hands on his hips and jutted his head forward, so that his indigo-stained beard shot forward like the ram of a swifter.

"You must be the one they call Dray Prescot, Lord of Strombor."

"And if I am, much good it will do you!" I shouted and hurled the spear full into his stomach. He gobbled and fell back, his hands clawing himself, seeking to stem the dark rush of blood welling past the neat flint-knapped semicircles of the blade.

His opened mouth sought to shriek, but only blood poured forth.

He fell.

And then I, Dray Prescot, laughed.

It did not last long after that.

The other captives were taken out one by one and when it was my turn I was tightly wrapped around in chains and ropes and carried up the dungeon steps. I saw clearly on the square boxlike faces of my captors a gloating kind of good humor. They knew what lay in store for me and they joyed in their dark fashion for the horrors I must endure. Indigohaired Ullars met the cortege—an apt word, I remember thinking, wryly—at the entrance of arched brick where the brilliant hues of the suns of Scorpio flooded down in topaz and opal and incandescent light.

We entered an open area rather in the fashion of a theater or arena. The anti-flier defense had been rolled away, and hung in nets at the sides, rather after the style of a Roman velarium not paid for by the gladiatorial promoter presently putting his show on and awaiting the next one, who had.

The amphitheater-like atmosphere continued in the storied series of seating terraces, all jam-packed with spectators. Dark blood lay seeping into the sand. Ullars moved about officiously. I looked for Umgar Stro. He must, I considered, be the chief man among the lolling group of dignitaries and nobles gawking down from an awning-draped box over the arena steps.

In the air and cutting through the familiar reeks of spilled blood and dust and sand and sweat a new and strangely disturbing odor laid a nasty taste in my mouth.

At the far end of the stretch of sand a monstrous erection of red brick reared. It was barred down the front. Beyond I caught the vaguest of glimpses of writhing motion, a flicker of evil eyes, the sway of tentacles.

And then—and then!

A wooden stake reared from the sand, surmounted by a triangle of logs, all bound together with thongs.

Naked she was.

All naked and white in the suns-light.

Thick and heavy ropes bound her to the triangle of logs, their rough bark harsh upon her soft skin. All white, her body glowed in the suns-light, bound by the constricting ropes that crossed over her spread-eagled legs, cutting into her thighs, her stomach, her arms, her throat.

Openly displayed, she hung there naked before the taunting gaze of the Ullars and the Harfnars, hung there by express order of Umgar Stro, baffled of a willing conquest, victim of his lusts for sadistic pleasure as much as the sweeter pleasure of voluptuous surrender. White and virginal and hanging, Delia, my Delia of Delphond, hung there awaiting the doom that writhed beyond the iron bars. And I stood stupidly before her, bound head and foot, helpless.

Chapter Eighteen

On my own two feet, then

Some little Ullar with his silly blue-dyed hair was prancing and yammering on the sand before me, but I could not pay much attention to him, even when he jabbed a spear into my stomach, because I was looking and looking at Delia. She hung there in her bonds, roped to that blasphemous triangle of rough-bark wood. Her head was raised in defiance, her chin high, and her glorious brown hair shone radiantly with those outrageous auburn tints beneath the suns of Scorpio.

She saw me.

She did not scream out.

We looked at each other, Delia and I, we looked, and between us passed the knowledge that if we were to die now, at least, we died together.

The Ullar was shouting and his flint-headed spear was becoming decidedly uncomfortable.

I managed to fall sideways against my chains and the Ullar on my right side, and as his arms automatically constricted about me to support me I lifted myself against him. Like a jackknife I doubled up in the chains and my feet shot out and crashed into the Ullar's face. He yowled and went over and I heard the answering roar from the massed spectators.

Yes, we were a spectacle, staked out for the enjoyment of the half-men peoples of Chersonang. Well-divided they were, I noticed, Ullars to my right and Harfnars to my left. The ornately canopied box of Umgar Stro frowned over the assemblage. The Ullar picked himself up, clasping his nose from which the blood poured. He would have done for me with his spear then, but a shout arrested him and he swung away under orders from Umgar Stro.

All around the walls of the stadium perched giant impiters. Their coal-black plumage cut stark arabesques against the bright sky. The heat stifled down, intense and sweaty. I went on working with the chains, testing, seeking, straining.

Was that a link, thinner than the rest? Malleable? Subject to a straining twist? Surreptitiously I pulled and levered, feeling the thinner link distorting its shape.

We prisoners to be offered up as sacrifices had been fed some nauseating swill so as to keep our strength up to prevent us from fainting and so cheating the populace of their spectacle. If ever I had needed strength in my life, I needed it then.

Now the noise from the rows of seats began to settle into a rhythm and recognizable words beat out in a roar of sound.

"The Ullgishoa! The Ullgishoa!"

As if in response to some blashphcmous call the thing in the iron-barred cage stirred and rippled its tentacles.

Whatever the thing was, the Ullars had cvidently brought it with them from far Ullardrin. As I watched and worked on the chain everyone's attention centered on the cage and the thing within.

"The Ullgishoa!"

Half-men with their indigo hair streaming ran joyfully across the blook-soaked sand. Approaching the cage, they moved with a sureness of purpose that contrasted oddly with their sudden and completely unfeigned caution. Quickly the iron bars were flung back. Like a scatter of leaves before a gust of wind the Ullars scampered back to the side walls. The cage gaped open.

Movement. Slithering, sly, obscene movement. The Ullgishoa sprawled forward out of the cage, spilling over the iron lip onto the suns-warmed sand. I took a single look and then went at my chains with the crazed fury of a madman.

Huge, the thing was, squamous, slimy, its scales extending only over the upper portion of its hemispherical back, its lower portions a writhing mass of tentacles. But those tentacles! Each undulated and squirmed and writhed like a beckoning finger. Each began at the thing's body with a thickness of a man's calf, but as the tentacle thickness neared the tip it lessened until it was perhaps as large as a man's thumb, finished with a protruding lump that glistened scarlet and black, ichor dripping.

Inch by inch the Ullgishoa crept over the sand. Set in the center just below the squamous back a single eye stared lidlessly, yellow and red, focused unerringly upon the white, bound form of Delia. I knew what that thing would do once its tentacles were within reach of my Delia's body.

I struggled as the devils of Dante's Hell must struggle. If Hell exists, then it took this scene as its template.

I felt the link weakening. I felt it bending, slightly, and now the very technology of Kregen came to my assistance. I have mentioned how of necessity culture varied over the surface of Kregen, and as a corollary, technology and science varied also. It is manifestly unrealistic to imagine a world with every part at exactly the same level of advancement, unless that world be one under a central government, or a world of the far future wherein our Utopians love to direct their thoughts. So the long thin swords of the Ullars and the men of Hiclantung had to be forged from iron of a good quality. I knew because Hwang had often complained that the iron deposits around his city in nowise matched in quality the ores of ancient Loh; most of the swords had been handed down, from father to son, treasured heirlooms of a misty and grandiose past.

But for the iron of their commoner weapons and tools the men of the Hostile Territories had to employ local ores, and their weakness came now as a great blessing to me. I felt the link move, bending as I strained. All the time the people in the terraces howled and the stink of the Ullgishoa befouled my mouth, and I tried to think of iron technology and not of what those obscenely-seeking tentacles of the creeping monster would do to my Delia.

And, too, this lack of high-quality ore locally came as a surprising, but not unexpected, boon to me, as you shall hear.

The thing was almost upon Delia now.

She hung there, defiant, her head up, her face composed.

I risked a more obvious movement as I struggled. I braced my arms and stretched; those wide shoulders of mine gave me a leverage and my muscles jumped and roped and bunched and—snap!

The link parted.

Now I must move with extraordinary swiftness.

The chains stripped from me with a clanking lost in the frenzied din of shouting from the thousands ranked on the terraces. Twin shadows from the suns of Scorpio paced me as I ran. Ullars must have attempted to stop me. I swung my bunched chains. I had become expert with swinging chains; I had had experience. I left a trail of blood and brains and shattered skulls strewing the sand.

The scarlet haze enveloping my sight concentrated vision only onto the Ullgishoa and Delia.

Its tentacles were looping and coiling and reaching out for Delia. Each bloated head of scarlet and black dripped a foul ichor. They thrust and withdrew, thrust and withdrew, in congested anticipation. I ran.

Delia watched me.

As I reached the Ullgishoa her eyes widened.

"Jikai, Dray Prescot!"

I swung the chains. I swung the chains high and I put all my strength into that vicious and barbaric blow. Gone were the polite trappings of civilization. Gone the veneers of gentle conduct. Now I was a simple barbarian, filled with hate and loathing for this thing that sought so obscenely to destroy the woman I loved.

All that primordial savagery nerving me added cunning as well as bestial strength to my arms. The chains sliced cuttingly down upon that single lidless eye where mucus ran in a continuous dust-cleansing stream. The eye pulped and exploded into a scattered mass of scarlet and yellow. The stench sickened me—and yet nothing could sicken me now—not when Delia of the Blue Mountains watched as I fought for her life!

The Ullgishoa was not finished.

It emitted a high whickering shrill and its tentacles lashed back to envelop me. I skipped agilely aside and an arrow slashed past me. Again I moved, constantly maneuvering myself as more arrows sliced the bright air. Many of those shafts feathered into the bulk of the Ullgishoa—and I laughed!

I took the thick coarse ropes that bound Delia into my fists and I pulled and the rope snapped in a fray of threads.

She fell forward into my arms, her body against my chest, my face enveloped in her hair.

There was time for neither greeting nor the taking of a breath now.

The whole amphitheater was in turmoil. Ullars and Harfnars gesticulated and screamed, arrows scythed toward us, warriors ran fleetly over the sand, their swords and spears bright in the streaming mingled light of the suns of Antares.

"Umgar Stro!" I looked up at the ornate box.

I put Delia aside and met the first of the Ullars. I broke his neck, took his sword, slashed the face from the next, disemboweled the third. Delia had snatched a sword and fallen into place at my left side. I felt a terrible pang of fear for her safety there, but she urged me on: "Jikai!"

We ran in a jinking zigzag path. The sword broke and I took another from the first Ullar foolish enough to cross my path.

A flint-headed arrow scored a bloody line across my back. Another nicked a chunk of skin from my calf. I ran on.

Delia's hair streamed behind her head as she paced me.
Straight toward that awning-draped box we ran, and the
bedlam increased and surged into a continuous shattering
wash of sound.

Umgar Stro stood up and gripped the gilded rail before his
royal box. Large he was, bulkier than me, with his indigo-
dyed hair contorted into a fantastic prancing shape above his
head. His blunt features and those narrow close-set eyes
brooded on his warriors as they sought to stop my advance.
He wore a fancy gilded armor, risslaca and leem designs
hammered onto the breastplate. His thick neck rose above,
ridged with corded muscle and congested veins.

"Stop him, you fools!" he roared. "Cut him down!"

But I had seen what I wanted.

Strapped to Umgar Stro's side hung a great long sword
that made the long thin swords of these people mere tooth-
picks in comparison. That sword was a Krozair long sword. It
was the weapon given me by Pur Zenkiren in Pattelonia,
before we set off to fly The Stratemsk and the Hostile Territories. I could well understand how a man like Umgar Stro
would value such a brand.

An arrow hissed into the sand before my feet and I jumped
and jinked and the following volley split air.

Delia paced me, running very quick, her circulation
coming back and yet not impeding her movements. I knew
what she was suffering and if it were possible my heart har-
dened even more against Umgar Stro and his Ullars and these
Harfnars of Chersonang.

Only this man had prevented us from continuing our
journey. He it was who had caused Seg and Thelda to go down
before his allied cavalry. He owed me much, this half-man,
this beast, this Umgar Stro. I ran toward him and I did not
shout and he saw me coming. He drew that great brand that
was my own and he threw himself into a posture of defense,
cursing those about him.

Arrogant and conceited, puffed with pride like many
Earthly Politicians, was Umgar Stro, but he did not lack
courage.

His massive frame dangled and clanged with golden ornaments, barbaric dyed leem pelts flaunting weird colors. He
towered there, glowering in the light from the Suns of Scorpio,
his indigo-dyed hair waving with the violence of his movements, his arms bulging with muscle.

"If these cramphs of mine will not kill you, then, by the
violet offal of the snow-blind feister-feelt, I will send you to
hell myself!"

He vaulted the gilt rail and landed very nimbly, swinging at once into that trained posture of defense. He was a swordsman. I made no attempt to cross swords with him. I was only too well aware of the quality of the Krozair long sword he brandished; as to the blade I had snatched up, it was as like to break at the first blow for all I knew.

A sudden and tense silence descended. All eyes fixed on the drama being enacted before the royal box. Into that silence came the screech and hacksaw rasp of the impiters from their perches around the amphitheater. There was one, a giant of the air, fluffing its feathers immediately over the awning.

There was no time for fancy swordsmanship, for feint and riposte, for lunge and parry. There was space for swordplay —of the brutal cut and thrust variety I knew so well and that had brought me thus far alive—space but no time. Umgar Stro's coarse and bloated features broke into a crude guffaw as he brandished that splendid sword before my eyes.

"Die, little man! Die and spit your guts on the ice needles of Ullarkor!"

Beyond him as he stood so confidently his companions in the royal box guffawed in lackey-like approval. There were scented and painted women, females of the Harfnars and the Ullars, jeweled courtiers and soldiers, impiter-masters, sword-masters. And there was one man, with the red hair of Loh, who sat unsmiling and tense, clad all in dark blue and unhappy. This, I guessed, must be Forpacheng. I marked him, too, for through his machinations my Delia had been snatched when he plotted the downfall of the Lohvian army of Hiclantung.

My great Krozair long sword slashed down—aimed at my head!

I dodged easily enough but I did not reply. Delia stood a little to one side, her toothpick sword lifted, her breast heaving; but her face showed the same strong resolution I had come to know so well through all adversity.

Umgar Stro shouted, and stamped his foot, and thrust. I risked the clang of blades as I parried and dodged—and the sword I wielded snapped clean at the hilt.

The gush of laughter from Umgar Stro was like an oil well breaking surface in the desert, dark and spouting and greasy.

"Dray!" shrieked Delia, then—and she lifted her weapon to fling it to me hilt first.

"Hold, my Delia!" I shouted. I jinked left, then right, took a spring and before Umgar Stro could orient himself I had

vaulted clean over him. I landed and twisted like a leem. My
left hand raked across and took his right arm biceps in my
fingers. My right hand went around his neck and jerked his
head back. I squeezed.

He tried to gargle something.

I exerted pressure with the fingers of my left hand and his
right hand slowly opened so that the Krozair long sword fell
to the sand. He sagged and then thrust with desperate
strength. I hauled back. Without remorse, without pity and,
now his time had come, without hatred, I pulled back until,
loud and sharp, his backbone snapped.

I cast him from me.

I bent to retrieve my long sword and the arrows sang past
me and, in that instant, the suns-light was choked off as a
wide-winged shape plummeted from the walls.

Umgar Stro's own impiter! Come to avenge his death!

He was a monster, coal-black, wide of wing and ferocious
of talon, with gape-jaws distended so that the rows of serrated teeth gleamed dull gold. His tail lashed wickedly at me
so that I had to leap back. I shouted.

"Delia! This is our mount—be ready, my heart—"

"I am with you, always, dear heart!"

I intended to stand no nonsense from this savage beast. I
leaped. I took the reins close up to the fanged jaw and I
wrenched. I brought the flat of the sword around and laid
it shrewdly alongside that narrow and vicious head.

"Let that teach you who is to be master here!"

I drew the impiter's head down, twistingly, dragged that
beast low, hit him again, forced him to bend. Delia mounted
with a supreme confidence that brought the breath clogging
into my throat. As she wrapped the flying thongs about herself and adjusted the clerketer for me, I vaulted up and
dragged the reins upward. The impiter's head rose. He was
in a vile temper. An arrow whistled off the black sheen of
his feathers and he rasped a hacksaw whine and struck three
massive blows with his wings. He ran forward and then, with
a massive fluttering and a great roaring of down-driven air,
he was aloft. I had to strike but three more arrows away before we were well airborne and sailing above the anti-flier
defense and away into the bright air of Kregen.

Below us in the amphitheater we left an incredible scene
of confusion as Ullars whistled for their impiters, as Harfnars
ran uselessly, shooting upward, only to see their shafts fall
short. Strongly we beat across the sky. Umgar Stro—who
was now dead—had trained his mount well. Crazed and savage and bewildered it might be; the impiter understood well

enough what the point of my sword thrust into his side meant.
His wings beat metronomically. The wind blasted back
through our hair. Naked, we shivered in the slipstream. But
up and up we flew, faster and faster, winging away from
Chersonang and all the barbarity festering there.

For some time I fancied I could detect the foul taint from
the deliquescing corpse of the Ullgishoa.

From the city of Chersonang behind us rose the black
swarm of impiter-mounted warriors. Like a column of smoke
they rose and leveled off and, wind-driven, soared after us.
I jabbed the tip of my sword into the impiter and forced him
to beat a faster stroke.

The twin suns of Scorpio cast their mingled light down
upon us, and the land beneath spread out with its cultivated
fields giving way to heath and wasteland cut through by the
magnificent stone roads of the old empire. The host of impiters on our trail must have been visible for dwaburs in
every direction. Our own beast flogged the air, driving us on,
putting an increasing space between us and our pursuers. As
befitted the power and glory, as well as the bulk, of Umgar
Stro his impiter was a king among fliers. But the double
burden would tell in the long flight, and eventually the flying
nemesis would catch us.

If such a thing as Fate exists, it has sometimes come to
my aid as well as dealing me many shrewd blows. Unaccus-
tomed to such things, I confess it was Delia who first spotted
the distant dot, and who cried out in joy—and then alarm as
other reasons for the presence of an airboat here, over the
Hostile Territories, occurred to her.

But there was nothing else for it. The distant flier changed
course and bore through the upper levels straight toward
us.

We strained our eyes. I made out a lean petal-shape, high
as to stern, a much larger craft than the one in which we
had flown The Stratemsk, larger, even, than those airboats
of the Savanti in unknown Aphrasöe. Flags fluttered from the
upperworks. Delia screwed her eyes up. I felt her body close
and warm against me, and my arms tightened in instinctive
protection.

"I think, my darling, I think—" she said. And: "Yes! It is!
She is from Vallia!"

"Thank Zair for his mercies," I said.

She must have spotted the massed fliers from a long distance off, for I knew the Vallians possessed telescopes. I knew
without doubt why the Vallian airboat was here, why it
turned at once, sensing the answer to her quest lay with

that flying host of impiters. The airboat swung alongside. I hauled the impiter up and looked down.

The craft was compact and trim. I was reminded of the order and discipline of a King's ship or of those swifters I had commanded on the Eye of the World. The sights of varters of design strange to me then snouted upward at us. At the first sign of treachery or the first false move we would be blasted from the sky. A group of men on the high stern looked up, and I saw the familiar Vallian costume mingled with a smart dark blue uniform I took to be that of the air service of Vallia.

"Jump down, Princess!" shouted one of the men, a barrel-bodied individual in dark blue, with wide shoulder wings, and a flaring orange cloak. At his side swung a rapier, matched by the main-gauche on the other. He wore a curly-brimmed hat with a blazing device of gold on the front band, and an orange tuft of feathers. His face was seamed and wind-lined, the crow's-feet at the corners of his eyes testimony to his days in the air scanning distant horizons.

Carefully I edged the impiter lower so that the ratings below ducked against the beat of wings. Delia went over first and I followed to be caught instantly in strong hands. Umgar Stro's impiter, relieved, spun away into the bright sky.

"Princess Majestrix!" said the burly man, A Chuktar, an exalted rank in any man's army or navy or, as I encountered for the first time, air force.

"My Lord Farris!" said Delia. She was wrapped in a swathing orange cloak, and her face showed high and proud and yet mightily relieved. "You are most welcome."

The Lord Farris, the Chuktar in command of this airboat, the name of which was *Lorenztone,* bowed deeply. He did not incline, a depraved custom, and this pleased me. "And this—?" He gestured toward me in a way that was most polite.

Delia smiled. "This is Dray Prescot, Lord of Strombor, Kov of Delphond, and betrothed of the Princess Majestrix."

Farris bent his head in a stiff but exquisitely formal little bow. He turned back to Delia. "The Emperor, your father, learned that you had taken a flier and—" He hesitated and I could guess the scenes that had followed on that discovery. "There have been many airboats seeking you, Princess, and I am overjoyed that it was to me and *Lorenztone,* that the honor of finding you has been given."

"I am pleased, also, Farris. But—"

A lookout sang out from forward.

Everyone turned. The sky seemed filled with impiters.

Farris looked pleased. He smiled and rubbed his hands. "Now these debased descendants of a decadent empire will see what a new nation can do!" His orders were given in a calm and matter-of-fact tone of voice that heartened me.

During that fight as the winged hordes of Umgar Stro fell on us I was mightily impressed by the way the air service men of Vallia handled themselves. Their swivel-mounted varters coughed a steady stream of projectiles. Impiters fell fluttering from the sky. Archers using smaller bows than those of Loh, it is true, took a toll. Any Ullar venturesome and lucky enough to gain a footing on the deck was instantly cut down. The Vallians, in this kind of aerial fighting, did not deign to disregard the effective uses of a boarding pike. With my long sword, which they looked at with a kind of amused awe, I joined in. The battle, in a sense, came to me as an anticlimax. Delia was safe, now, and before us lay the flight to Vallia and then the meeting with her father, that imperious, relentless, awe-inspiring man, the emperor of all Vallia.

At last the impiters and their Ullar warriors gave up.

We forged on across the landscape of the Hostile Territories as gradually the twin suns, Zim and Genodras, sank to the horizon. I took stock of this Vallian airboat, this *Lorenztone*. She was all of fifty feet long and her widest beam, which came some two-fifths of her length aft, was twenty feet. Her leanness of appearance came from the sheer of her bows and the sweep of her stern where the sterncastle raised. Varters lined the bulwarks much after the fashion of the broadside guns of the ships of Earth with which I was familiar. Somewhere below her deck in a safe place would be that mysterious mechanism—mysterious to me then— by which this bulk was upheld in thin air.

The designs on the many flags she bore surprised me with their functional formality; but some were so embroidered that leems and risslaca, graints and zhantils as well as chank and sectrix, figured in that fluttering panoply.

An obliging crewman found me a length of cloth. He handed it to me expecting me to wrap my nakedness in it. It was green. I merely wiped the bloodied blade of my long sword upon it, carefully, mindful of the way that young tearaway of a Vallian, Vomanus, had so carelessly wiped his ornate rapier, and handed it back. From a great pile of flying silks I selected a length of blazing scarlet. This, with as always a pang of memory, I wrapped around my waist, drew up between my legs, and tucked the end in. Delia came up with a broad leather belt, of a leather I did not then recognize, soft and pliable, with a massive silver buckle. With this I kept the breechclout in place.

"There will be no scabbard for your great sword, Dray; not until we can have one stitched up for you."

"No matter. It can hang at my side naked, with a fold of cloth to keep me from being cut—"

After the action the reaction—we were both just making noises. The airboat rushed on through the sky levels. Delia looked at me, her head a little to one side, her face grave.

"Seg? And—Thelda?"

I shook my head.

She gave a little gasp, immediately choked off, and lowered that mane of glorious brown hair, shining in the dying light, and put her dear head into my shoulder. So for a space we stood there on the deck of the airboat as the twin suns sank and the strange and yet familiar constellations crept into the night sky with three of the lesser moons of Kregen hurtling low over the horizon.

Presently we were called away for food and we sat to a fine aerial feast in the aft cabin. The Chuktar, the Lord Farris of Vomansoir, introduced his officers and other high dignitaries who had been assigned the craft searching for the emperor's daughter. I caught at some of the conversations, guessing at hidden meanings, trying to sort out the people who would not object to Delia marrying me from those who took a violent exception. I did not think I would meet any Vallian who would actively wish me to marry Delia—not even Vomanus, if I cared to dwell on it.

I noticed one young man, with a mane of blond hair and a frank and open face, with that high beaked nose of the Vallians—a characteristic in noses that I myself shared—and took particular notice of him after he had said, with a light laugh: "I have never seen so large a sword wielded so expertly, my Lord of Strombor. I venture to think that a regiment of cavalrymen well-versed in its use would rattle even the best infantry line."

His name was Tele Karkis, and he did not appear to be the lord of anywhere, which was refreshing. He was a Hikdar. If I paint him in flat and stereotyped colors, it is because that was how he appeared to be then, when I first met him. I leaned over the table to help myself to a handful of palines, and before I popped the first luscious morsel into my mouth, I said: "And on what steed would you mount these hypothetical cavalrymen of yours, Hikdar Karkis?"

He laughed, not easily, but without unease. "I have heard

of the voves your Clansmen ride on the Great Plains of
Segesthes, my Lord of Strombor."

I nodded. "I hope," I said with the politeness habitual to
the cultured Vallian, "that you will have the opportunity one
day to pay us a visit and be our guest."

Then *Lorenztone* shuddered and lurched and Chuktar
Farris spilled his wine and reared away from the table.

"By Vox!" he said. "I'd like to teach those rasts of
Havilfar how to build like honest men!"

A man with a face I had taken no notice of at first
sight, and thereby should have been warned, let out a string
of oaths that were mere fancy verbiage, and quite fit for the
ears of a lady, even for a princess. He was one Naghan Vanki,
the lord of domains on one of the outlying islands of
Vallia. He wore, unlike the air service men and the soldiers
and court dignitaries, a simple silver and black outfit in the
Vallian style. There was more about him than his name to
remind me of Naghan, the Hiclantung spy.

We all went on deck.

The airboat was sinking and nothing the crew could do
would bring her up. In the event we camped for the
night among thorn-ivy bushes by a stream and were not too
uncomfortable. Delia and I were quartered well away from
each other, as was proper. As we prepared for sleep we al
talked in a low-key kind of grumbling way about the prof
iteers of Havilfar. The name of Pandahem also figured in the
conversation, usually with a round Vox-like oath or two.

A fire was built and we sat around it for a last cup of
warmed wine. Naghan Vanki kept on making casually sar-
castic remarks about barbarians, and uncouth individuals,
and praising the civilization of Vallia. Delia shifted uncom-
fortably as he spoke. I saw well enough he was digging at
me, but I did not care. Was I not with my Delia of Delphond
once again, on the way to Vallia, if temporarily halted until
repairs could be effected, and was not the future rosy with
prospect?

"The Emperor raised heaven and earth to seek you,
Princess," said Farris, smiling now the mission was successful.
"You mean a very great deal to him and to all the people of
Vallia."

"I am grateful, Farris. I am also aware that I mean a very
great deal to my Lord of Strombor, as he to me. Remember
that."

"Still," said young Tele Karkis, unthinkingly, "it is going
to be an ordeal, standing up to the Emperor." He spread his
hands. "I would not relish crossing him—"

"Hikdar!" said Farris, and at his Chuktar's words young Karkis colored up and fell mute.

But the seed had no need to be sown; everyone there knew the ordeal I faced, and I guessed many of them secretly wondered if I had the nerve to go through with it.

Truly, all I had heard of Vallia warned me off the place. The warmed wine we drank was a good vintage. I remember that. It came from the province of Gremivoh, so I was told, and was much favored in the air service. It held a sweet and yet bitter savor unfamiliar to me.

Delia leaned close just before we parted for sleep.

"You do not truly wish to go to Vallia, dearest?"

"Can you ask!" I took her hand in the firelight. "I shall go to Vallia and face your father, never fear."

"But—" she began. And then: "Yes, dear heart, I know you will."

Perhaps, I thought then, being back with her own people had shaken her belief in me; perhaps she had been shocked by my own uncouth ways into seeing me in a new light. I tried to shrug that feeling off, but it persisted.

I crawled into my blankets and silks and yawned. I felt sleepy—not surprisingly, perhaps, but—ah, if we could foretell the future, then—!

I awoke in the morning as the twin suns of Scorpio sent down daggers of fire through my eyes into my brain to find myself rolled into a hole beneath a thorn bush.

I staggered out, cursing the pricks, and looked about.

The airboat was gone.

Alone, I stood among the thorn-ivy bushes on that endless plain of the Hostile Territories, and as I stood I heard a screech from above and I looked up and there, floating in wide hunting circles above, the gorgeous golden and scarlet raptor of the Star Lords surveyed me with a bright and implacable eye.

I shook my fist at the Gdoinye.

A moment later the white dove of the Savanti flew into sight, but, this time, the birds ignored each other. They surveyed me for a few moments and then turned and flew away. Whatever my plight it did not interest either the Star Lords or the Savanti, then.

My position was perilous in the extreme. I had the mother and father of headaches, and a stomachache, to boot, and I realized—dolt that I was—that something in the food or the wine of the previous evening had poisoned me. Whether or not the intention had been to poison me to death I did not know. I stood up, feeling grim, and looked about.

Some way off a blazing spot of scarlet caught my eye. The remains of the campfire and discarded rubbish showed where we had camped. The marks the airboat had made were still fresh; evidently the technicians among the crew had repaired the craft working overnight. I walked across to the scarlet patch.

It was a length of scarlet silk wrapped about my own long sword, a rapier and main-gauche, a bow and a quiver of arrows and, tucked in at the end, a water bottle and a satchel of provisions.

I was not fool enough to believe these had been left for my good.

Whoever had drugged me and had me dumped here had also taken the trouble to leave these items, typical of those a man would need if he must survive in a hostile territory, so as to color the impression that I had left voluntarily and surreptitiously. The plot had worked. The people aboard *Lorenztone* must believe I had run away because I was unable to face meeting their emperor.

And the people aboard included Delia—my Delia of Delphond!

Did she believe I had left her? Could she believe?

I did not think so—but . . . But so much pointed to a desire on my part to evade going home with her. However much I tried to tell myself my fears were groundless, that she would keep faith in me, the more I doubted. I was in low spirits. My guts hurt, my head throbbed like the freshly cut-out heart of a graint, my limbs trembled, and my vision blurred.

I snatched up the Krozair long sword.

This I believed in—I had been cruelly wronged. My beloved had been snatched from me, and I could not blame her if she believed the worst of me. I could imagine how the situation would look, and the pressures that would be brought to bear on her to renounce her love for me.

Well, the Star Lords clearly had had no hand in this. The Savanti, too, were not implicated. They had merely assured themselves that I still lived, ready, no doubt, to seize me and toss me once more into the turmoil of their plans when the occasion demanded. Until then, I had men for enemies, men of Vallia who sought to take my Delia from me. Well, then, I would go to Vallia, I would march all the way to the eastern seaboard of Turismond and take ship, and march all the way into the great palace of this dread emperor of Vallia, this father of Delia's, and confront them all to prove my love for Delia.

I picked up the gear and strapped it about myself. I took a great breath. I looked at the distant eastern horizon of hills.

Then, with my long sword in my fist, I took the first step onward.

Above me the suns of Scorpio blazed down and about me the land of Kregen opened out with the promise of danger and terror, of beauty and passion. I could not fail. Not with the vision of my Delia before me.

Steadily, I tramped on eastward to whatever destiny held in store.

PROTECTOR
LARRY NIVEN

Phssthpok the Pak had been travelling for most of his 32,000 years – his mission, to save, develop and protect the group of Pak breeders sent out into space some 2½ million years before . . .

Brennan was a Belter, the product of a fiercely independent, somewhat anarchic society living in, on, and around an outer asteroid belt. The Belters were rebels one and all, and Brennan was a smuggler. The Belt worlds had been tracking the Pak ship for days – Brennan figured to meet that ship first . . .

He was never seen again – at least not in the form of homo sapiens.

Larry Niven is the author of **Ringworld** which won both the Hugo and Nebula awards for the best s.f. novel of the year.

JANDAR OF CALLISTO
Lin Carter

Lost in the jungles of Cambodia, among the ruins of a vanished city. Transported to the mysterious land of Thanator on Callisto, moon of Jupiter. Jandar, the alien from Earth, finds himself in a world of black and crimson jungles where the hand of every man is lifted in eternal enmity against every other.

A savage, hostile world in which he is first held prisoner by the fearsome insect-men, only to be freed for a more binding slavery in the deadly clutches of the Sky Pirates, and in the service of the Princess Darloona, the most beautiful woman in two worlds, who demands love almost beyond the limits of his mortal soul.